SECRETS OF THE MAFIA KING

MAFIA KINGS
BOOK FOUR

BELLA MOONDRAGON

For George

CONTENTS

_1_

BAD NEWS

Tony

The cold glass touches my lips as I sip from my whiskey, my eyes watching Estella over the rim. She's dancing in front of a group of fucking loud guys who came here for a bachelor party. I'm in my usual booth at Aphrodite's Lounge, and even though she's a hell of a dancer, I can't seem to keep my focus on her for more than a few seconds tonight.

This is a clear sign that I'm losing interest in her, no matter how hot and good in bed she is. In all honesty, I'm getting bored of her.

And it's not like I should feel guilty about it since I know she only likes my money anyway—like all of them do. But as much as I like to have women keep me company every once in a while—especially when I need to blow off some steam—Estella isn't managing to entertain me any longer.

I rub my temples, trying to make this fucking headache that's been gnawing at me for the past three days go away. Estella's gaze finds mine from across the club, and I fight the urge to look away. I have no intention of indulging her tonight, but I don't want to be rude either.

A couple of patrons walk past my booth and wave at me, drinks in hand as they head to the VIP section at the far end of the room. I greet them by raising my glass, recognizing them from a few nights ago, but not bothering to give them a hint of a smile.

Estella's dance is coming to an end. I can tell that by the way those fucking losers are waving their dollar bills at her, one of them attempting to slide one under the strap of her thong. She smiles seductively at them, practically counting the money she'll be taking home.

If I want to escape her tonight, I need to get out of here before the song ends. I won't be able to tell her no if she approaches this booth and sits on my lap, no matter how bored I am of her.

I pour the remnants of my drink down my throat, feeling the liquid burning my windpipe, and stand up, heading toward the back door without turning around. I pop open the button on my suit jacket, feeling it too tight and uncomfortable all of a sudden.

My black SUV is in the club's private parking lot, and thankfully, I don't bump into anyone on my way out. I ponder heading home, but there's still work to be done tonight that can't be postponed anymore. For the past four years, it has felt like my days are endless and filled with countless shit to handle. It's a fucking rollercoaster with no end in sight.

Whenever I come close to having a glimpse of peace, something happens to start a war all over again.

Another problem to be solved; another business deal to close….

It never ends.

So, with that in mind, I go back to Lou's Deli instead.

I haven't gotten out of that hole yet. In fact, as much as I hated it when I took over from Dante as the new head of the Saints, the space kind of grew on me with time. I don't even gag at the smell of cold cuts anymore. I don't even notice it, to be fair, my nose already used to it by now.

It is spacious after all, and after looking over the entire city for a better place, nothing seemed to convince me to move our headquarters from here, so we simply stayed. It's been serving us just fine so far.

The street is dark and empty as I step out of the car and walk inside. It's so damn late, I shouldn't be expecting the place to be fully functional. It feels odd to find this place completely empty, without a single soul around.

As soon as I get to the deli's basement, I notice there's no one here either.

It's better this way anyway. I work better on my own with just utter silence keeping me company–and the voices in my head reminding me of darker times and nightmares from the past. Seb's voice is one of them, still visiting me when I least expect it. My visions of him are not as frequent as they used to be, but I still see him.

I walk over to my office and round my desk, finding it covered with stacks of paperwork. I shuffle through them, searching for what I need to work on tonight. The inventory being shipped out tomorrow has to be checked and approved before heading off to the port, so I need to handle this before going home.

It's lost on me why I procrastinated so long to do this, but it's no one else's fault but my own. This file has been on my desk for at least a week now, so I can't put the blame on anyone else.

When I finally find the document I need, I plop down in my chair, urging my brain to function properly so I don't make any mistakes. I fucking hate the detailed and thorough part of this job. But as much as I'd love to have one of the guys do it for me, there are things that require my eyes only. No one else's.

So, I lose myself in the endless list of numbers and names, papers in one hand and a pen in the other.

Footsteps echoing on porcelain tiles a few minutes later–or has it been hours?–make me snap my head up and crease my brows in confusion. I glance at my watch, which reads 3:00 A.M.

Who the fuck is here at this hour?

"I figured I'd find you here." Armando's voice reaches me before I can even see him. My second steps through the doorway, his face hooded by shadows since I only have one lamp illuminating my desk. I can tell he's tired by the way the dark circles under his eyes are evident even from this distance, but he's looking sleek as always in his black suit.

"Aren't you supposed to be at home with your wife and kids?" I ask with a frown, leaning back in my chair, watching as he walks inside the room. His footsteps are heavy and loud, especially since I've been hearing nothing but the ticking of the clock and the shuffling of papers for the past two hours.

"I'm afraid I have some bad news that couldn't wait until tomorrow, Boss," he tells me, sitting in the chair across from me.

"Couldn't you have called?"

Armando shakes his head, his jaw clenched slightly. "It's delicate news, so I thought you'd prefer that I delivered it personally."

He's right. Armando is extremely attentive to how I like things to be done, not to mention overly cautious, which is a good quality to have in this type of business.

"All right, just fucking tell me then. What happened?" I press, getting impatient with all his rambling and unnecessary suspense.

"I just got a call from Nicky Bertolucci," he starts gloomily. "Apparently, Carlo had a heart attack this afternoon and died at his house in Miami."

I stare blankly at him, taking in the news. Not that I cared too much about Carlo because I damn well know he didn't like me. When I took over the Saints, he didn't agree with me being the new boss. So, faster than lightning, he retired and moved to Miami with his wife and daughter.

He worked with Dante's father for longer than I've been alive. He had good networking and good insight on how things were done, so it was a great loss to our businesses.

But if he didn't trust me, he was better off elsewhere. I couldn't risk having someone with me who might stab me in the back at any moment.

But I do feel sorry for his wife and daughter.

Nicky and Chloe Bertolucci.

Pale skin, cornflower blue eyes—Chloe.

Chloe—who I haven't seen since we met on a ferry going into the city and drunkenly ended up having sex with—Chloe.

"The Bertolucci family has a plot in the local cemetery, and the mob wives are getting together in the morning to start planning the funeral," Armando continues, pulling me back from my trip down memory lane. "Nicky is having his body shipped back for the burial. I wasn't sure if you knew about it or not yet. That's why I came here to tell you."

Again, he did the right thing. It never hurts to be too careful.

It's not like our lives are a fucking fairy tale.

One missed step, and we're as good as dead.

I rub my neck, trying to think of what to do.

"Tell them I'll pay for the funeral," I say bluntly, not wanting to go further into details. I don't want to know about any of it now. I don't want to know about how Chloe is. It's been two fucking years since I heard from her, and it is better this way. "In fact, I'll charter a private jet for the Bertolucci women and Carlo's body."

I still find myself daydreaming about her, against my will, and I don't know if it's a good thing or not that I can barely remember the night we spent together. I still find myself wanting to remember the details of her lying naked in my bed, the soft feel of her skin under mine, the way her smooth hair felt on my fingers, the way she moaned my name over and over until she was out of breath and wasted beneath me.

I haven't been able to stop thinking about her since, wondering how she is and if she ever thinks about me the same way. I feel like a fucking teenager fantasizing about having her again and again. Night after night.

No matter how many dancers I have in my bed, none of them make me forget her. Her sweet, floral scent. That's one thing that I could never forget.

It hurt my ego to not have her reach out to me and come looking for me after that night, but I can't blame her for not wanting to have anything to do with this life anymore.

Moving away from this city—and from me—was the best thing she could have done.

Armando is looking at me with an enigmatic face, but he knows better than to ask me about whatever it is he's thinking.

"See that they have everything they need." I carry on, ignoring the way my stomach twists when I imagine Chloe's blue eyes filled with tears as she mourns her father. "And let me know when it's happening so I can be there to offer my condolences."

"You're going to be there?" Armando asks, his tone serious but wary. "Do you think that's wise? Who knows who might show up, Boss?"

It's not like I can miss the funeral of a former member of the Saints. Not as their new boss.

I nod. "Carlo used to work for the Saints. I need to pay my respects. It's the right thing to do."

I don't tell him that I'm also secretly eager to see Chloe again, even if I have to watch her crying from afar, not able to do anything to comfort her.

2

———

COMING BACK HOME

Chloe

MEMORIES OF THE PAST COUPLE OF YEARS PASS BEFORE MY EYES AS I stare into my now empty bedroom in our family home in Miami. When Dad decided to move away from New York and come here, I was upset to leave my old life behind, but the idea of starting anew, of getting away from all that craziness, was somewhat exciting.

So much has happened since that I still can't decide if this was indeed a good idea or not.

So much has changed.

And now, Dad is no longer here to protect us. To tell us what to do. To comfort me with words of wisdom and experience whenever I need to hear them.

He's gone. In the blink of an eye.

One moment he was here, and the next... *pfft*, gone.

All that was left are the memories we created together.

And some of them will remain behind as soon as we walk out the door and move back to New York.

"Chloe, sweetheart?" Mom's sweet voice calls me from the door. I look over my shoulders, my eyes blurry with unshed tears. "Come on, baby. The car is waiting outside," she tells me kindly.

I nod, turning back to look at the spacious room, feeling nostalgic. "I'll meet you downstairs in a second, Mom."

She doesn't say anything else before I hear her footsteps fading down the hallway. I glance around once more, taking in my old bedroom for the last time before leaving.

And then I realize I'm actually thankful we won't live here any longer. This place doesn't feel safe anymore. It doesn't feel like *home*. Without my dad here, I don't feel like we belong in Miami.

So, determined and ready for a new beginning, I take a deep breath and walk out the door, meeting my mom in the hallway.

In her arms she holds my most precious treasure—Ellie. Her dark hair is tied up in two tiny ponytails on top of her head, and her big, round blue eyes–exactly like mine–are looking up at me as I finish descending the stairs.

She lets out a high-pitched squeak as she sees me, saying, "Mama," and I smile at her, taking her from my mom's arms and gently rocking her back and forth.

"Hey, baby," I whisper to her. "Ready to go? We're going to mommy's old house in New York. Are you excited?"

She mumbles a "Yes," something she learned a month ago, as if she understands my question, and I look at my mom, unspoken words being conceived in the form of an understanding glance.

For a moment, Nicky Bertolucci doesn't resemble the woman I know. The strong leader of the mob wives. For a brief second, she allows me to see her vulnerability. She looks exhausted, the black Chanel suit she's wearing representing the darkness in our hearts. Her thin form looks like she carries the weight of the world on her shoulders, but her chin is raised in determination, and the fire in her eyes tells me that she is not giving up.

My mother is one of the strongest women I know, and if there's anyone who can reassure me that everything will be fine, it's her.

Just as quick as it comes, her vulnerability disappears as if it had been just a glimpse from my imagination. She gives me a sharp nod and gestures for us to go.

We get settled into the car, Ellie in her car seat and Mom by my side as the driver takes us to the airport. I get lost in my own thoughts all the way, watching the beach pass by us in a blur outside the window.

"It will be nice to be home, don't you think?" my mother asks me. I turn to look at her, and even though her words are meant to convey relief, she seems nervous.

I know *I'm* nervous. But probably not for the same reasons as her.

Last night, she told me that Tony would be sending a private jet to pick us up and take us to New York. I don't know how I feel about that. Everything involving him makes me nervous.

"Yeah, I guess so," I finally answer, not sure what else I should say. I'm still trying to comprehend my own feelings. I can't offer her any reassurance or comfort right now.

We remain silent for the rest of the ride, except from occasional yelling and mumbling of random words from Ellie.

As soon as the driver rolls up to the hangar, I see Tony's private jet already waiting for us. The driver and some of the airport staff help us with the luggage, and Mom takes Ellie, who's now sleeping, from my arms. It's a good thing she's out because I'm not sure how she'll behave on the flight since this is the first time I've traveled with her by plane, and I'm not in the right state of mind to deal with her crying for the next three hours.

We're about to get on the plane when I spot a black SUV pulling up behind our car. I instantly tense up. I glance at my mom, my fists tightened beside me.

"Take Ellie inside, Mom. I'll be right there with you," I urge her as soon as I see Eduardo stepping out of the car.

My mother's eyes dart to him and back at me. "Hurry up," she warns me, and then she climbs the stairs to the plane with my daughter safely in her arms.

I'm instantly relieved, but we're not out of harm's way yet.
Will we ever be?

"Ms. Bertolucci," Eduardo greets me in his serious tone as he approaches me. "I must tell you my boss is not happy about you leaving without saying goodbye."

"Mateo has no right to be happy or angry about anything concerning me any longer," I tell him bitterly.

Eduardo sneers, the sound causing shivers to run down my spine. "Right," he mumbles. "Well, I hope you enjoy your *short* vacation in New York, Ms. Bertolucci." He tilts his head toward the plane and grins at me.

I hate the way it makes me feel–vulnerable, insecure, as if there is no place in this world where I can escape from Mateo's claws.

"He expects you to be back in Miami within a few days," he adds, his hands instantly darting to his belt where his gun is holstered. He's obviously trying to scare me, but I won't let him.

"Mateo already knows I'm not coming back," I reply with my chin up, not willing to show him how easily he can affect me.

Eduardo stares at me expressionlessly. "My boss takes care of his own. If you think you can take his daughter away from him, or yourself, for that matter, you're sorely mistaken."

I gulp, unsure of what to say to that. In fact, I shouldn't say anything. Mateo and I already went through this conversation. Sure, he didn't agree to it, but there's no way he's telling me what to do any longer. I'm tired of it. I'm tired of letting other people control my every move, my decisions, my life.

Especially Mateo.

So, instead of coming up with a witty remark, I simply turn my back on Eduardo, leaving him standing on the tarmac as I board the plane. I try to ignore the way my legs are shaking as if they have turned into jelly. My heart rate is so fast right now that I fear it might burst out of my chest at any minute.

But I need to remain strong.

For Ellie. For Mom. For myself.

I can't give in. I can't let Mateo win.

"I'll see you soon, Ms. Bertolucci!" Eduardo yells from behind me, and I briefly close my eyes, taking a deep breath and trying to steady myself.

My mom is already in her seat, her seatbelt fastened, by the time I step inside. Ellie is still peacefully sleeping in her arms.

"Is everything okay?" Mom asks me with a concerned expression on her face.

I sit across from her, settling down in my seat so the plane can depart.

I don't trust my voice yet, so I simply nod at her in response. I know she can tell I'm not okay, but thankfully, she doesn't insist.

"Miss, please tell the pilot we're ready to leave," my mother tells the young flight attendant who nods at her and goes into the cabin.

I look out the window and find Eduardo in the same spot I left him. He's Mateo's right hand, the guy who does all his dirty work with no guilt in his conscience. He's just as scary as Mateo, and that's saying a lot.

I watch as he reaches for his phone, sliding his finger on the screen to answer an incoming call. I don't need to see it to know who's calling him. Eduardo's eyes find mine from across the distance, and as much as I want to look away, I still don't want him to see how scared I am.

This move has been a bold one on my part. I never thought I'd have the courage to move away from Mateo, to leave him behind, but after my father died, it was our best chance of surviving.

Eduardo waves at me, wiggling his fingers in a mocking way. I fight the urge to vomit. I close my eyes again, inhaling sharply through my nose and letting it out through my mouth.

"We're safe now, sweetheart," Mom reassures me in a soft voice, her eyes studying me. "No one can touch us when we're back in New York and under the protection of the Saints. They'll look after us."

Her words are soothing, but why don't I feel safe? Why can't I believe her?

I look down at my arms, spotting the bruises on my wrists and the tiny scars on the skin of my forearms. My throat tightens.

It's been less than a month since I told my mother the truth. For too long, I was mad at her for not seeing what was so evident, happening right under her nose. Why couldn't she save me from the nightmare I was living in? But it isn't fair of me to put this on her.

It isn't anyone's fault but my own.

And Mateo's

However, once I told her everything, she proved to be a safe harbor for both Ellie and me.

I can't imagine doing this without her. I could never step away from Mateo without her encouragement.

"I really hope you're right," I answer.

In the back of my mind, I still wonder if moving back home is the right choice. What if we're just delaying the inevitable?

Mateo is not the type of man to be messed with. He doesn't like to share. And he certainly doesn't like his "toys" making a run for it.

He's incredibly possessive over me and Ellie.

It scares the shit out of me just imagining what he's capable of doing to get us both back under his wing.

I don't know how long I stay awake, looking out the window, feeling the peace the clouds and the orange sky offer me. Eventually I nod off into a dreamless sleep. Before long, I'm waking up to see the Manhattan skyline before me.

And an instant feeling of belonging washes over me.

He will protect us. I know it.

3

FUNERAL

Tony

IT'S A VERY CLOUDY DAY IN NEW YORK, SUITABLE FOR A FUNERAL. IT'S as if God knows people are mourning the loss of a beloved member of their family. I'm not necessarily grieving, but I can't help but feel sad. I know the reason behind it, but I choose to think my emotions have everything to do with the fact that Carlo was one of us—and are not because of his daughter.

I park my car in front of the church and brace myself for what's to come. It's been a few days since I heard about his death, so it's understandable why there are so many people here. Everyone's had enough time to make it to New York, even the ones who live far away.

The church is surrounded by a crowd in black, chattering and waiting for the service to start. I take a deep breath and step out of my SUV, heading inside the church. I blend into a sea of black suits and crying women, greeting everyone I know on my way.

I'm not surprised to see Carlo had a lot of friends who have come to say goodbye. Dante told me once that his father trusted Carlo like his own flesh and blood. I've learned in my time as boss that that means more than having a trusted capo at your side. Having a brother, even one birthed by the streets instead of by blood, is often the difference between life and death when things go south.

Most of the Saints are also here—except the ones I have out in the field, doing their rounds and keeping us safe.

I have to give it to Armando, handling everything and helping the wives to prepare the funeral service—which included shipping the old man's body to New York so he could be buried in his hometown. That was the least I could do for Chloe and Nicky. It's my job to take care of them now, after all.

The church looks nice and peaceful, with the colorful stained glass windows casting a rainbow of beams on the wooden floor, making it look almost ethereal. I notice a table filled with flowers in the corner, many expressing the condolences of those who couldn't attend. I glance over the signed cards and a familiar name catches my attention.

Dante and Eleni sent their condolences in the form of a huge bouquet of yellow tulips, apparently Carlo's favorite. Dante told me he wouldn't be able to be here since Eleni is due to have their third child any day now. That's a lot of kids to take care of. I have no idea how Dante does it, but he seems to have adjusted to his new life just fine.

Sounds kind of boring if you ask me, but who am I to judge?

I lift my head to take in the familiar—and not so familiar—faces around me. There're a lot of people here I've only seen once or twice, who I can't even remember the names of. And others that I see every fucking day.

One in particular has me grinning and walking away from the table. The boss of the Irish Kings in New York, Cal, waves at me, his dark red hair slicked back with gel, his light brown eyes widening slightly.

"Didn't think you'd be here today," he says in his Irish accent as a way of greeting when I approach him and pats me on the shoulder with more strength than necessary. I bite my lip so as not to curse him in church.

Cal and I have become close friends during the time I've been running the Saints and even closer allies. He's proven to be a reliable businessman more times than I can count and an even better company during evenings when I need a fucking drink.

"It comes with the job," I muse in response, shrugging.

Cal grunts in agreement. "Brought a few o' me men to pay their respects, too," he tells me, looking around. "Is the daughter of the old man the same one you brought to the club that night a couple o' years ago? The pretty lass?" he emphasizes, reminding me of that same day I can't seem to get out of my mind, no matter what I do.

"What are you talking about?" I feign ignorance, even though I know exactly what he's talking about.

He sneers, the freckles on his face crinkling across his nose.

Why is this fucking service taking so long to start?

"Don't mess with me, lad. I recognize a pretty face when I see one."

I roll my eyes, but then Cal points at someone behind my back, and when I turn on my heel to see what this is about, I can no longer play dumb.

Because there, in the middle of the crowd of wives, stands the most beautiful woman I've ever seen.

"The pretty lass," he repeats close to my ear as if I'm deaf. I can hear the note of sarcasm in his voice, and I fight the urge to punch him in the face, even if we're inside a church.

As my eyes roam over Chloe, it feels as though the entire world around me fades away and time stands still. It's been two years since the last time I saw her, and somehow, she looks even more stunning than before. Her smooth light brown hair cascades over her shoulders and down her back, her alabaster skin glowing against her black dress. Even though there's nothing remarkable about her gown, it hugs her in the right places while maintaining the decency required for such a respectful event.

I can't tell if she's wearing any makeup, but again, she's so effortlessly beautiful that I wouldn't be surprised if she weren't. Her lips are a bit pale though, and her intoxicating blue eyes are swollen and red from crying.

As if summoned by my staring, Chloe's gaze meets mine, and it's like I'm being pulled into a whirlpool. How come she still holds this much power over me? It's fucking ridiculous. I'm not one to be controlled...by anyone.

But she seems to hold this *force* over me that I can't escape from.

I notice that her lips tremble a bit, and unexplainably, I think it has something to do with me. But why would it? Of course, she's just sad because her father died.

Get your shit together, Tony.

I think about offering her a comforting smile from afar, but before I know it, my legs are working on their own accord.

"Excuse me," I say to Cal. He mumbles some shit to me that sounds like *"I knew it,"* but I ignore him. My focus is solely on Chloe as I wade through the crowd to get to her.

But as if fate is laughing at me, the organ starts playing this lugubrious song, and we're all requested to take a seat so the service can start.

Great timing.

I take a detour from where I was heading and find a spot at the back of the church. I'm not very fond of funerals. I don't think anyone is, actually, but in any case, I prefer to stay off the radar.

The service doesn't take long. Neither does the graveside service outside in the cemetery, and soon, we're gathering in a reception hall a few blocks away. Drinks are served and there's this huge table with all sorts of food, but I'm not in the mood for either. I wish I could go home, but I don't want to be disrespectful.

I check my surroundings, looking for that one particular person I so desperately want to talk to. And when I spot her, heading toward the exit, I simply follow.

Before I can get close to the door, though, someone walks in my way, halting me in my steps.

It's another beautiful woman, but not the one I'm looking for. It's her older version.

"Nicky," I say, pursing my lips and pretending I'm annoyed to be interrupted. Again. "I'm really sorry for your loss."

The woman smiles at me briefly. "Thank you. And thank you so much for this beautiful service, Tony," she replies. "It means a lot to me and Chloe."

I nod. "Of course. It was the least I could do."

"You know, we lived a very good life in Miami after Carlo retired," Nicky carries on, and I glance over to the door and realize I've lost Chloe. I take a deep breath, hopeful that I'll have the opportunity to talk to her before I leave. "He gave us all an extravagant life, but I must confess I'm happy to finally be home. I never wanted to move in the first place." She chuckles, lowering her voice as if she's telling me a secret.

My eyebrows furrow in confusion. What does she mean? Is she implying she's moved back to the city for good? "You're staying in New York?" I finally ask, trying not to show my surprise through my voice or expression.

"Yes. Carlo and I never sold our old house. This was actually something I wanted to discuss with you, in a more… proper setting, but I decided to take advantage of the opportunity," she tells me, gripping my arm so I give her all my attention.

"What is it?" I press.

Nicky clears her throat, her eyes filled with determination. "Would you allow Chloe and I back into the circles of women? We can help out with the families of the Saints or whatever you need."

"Of course, Nicky. What made you think I would be against that? The Saints will always take care of their own, so you have nothing to worry about," I reassure her.

She widens her smile at me, and even though I've known Nicky for being this self-assured, confident, and empowered woman, she looks relieved that I gave her my word.

"Thank you, Tony. You have no idea how much this means to all of us. It will be great for Ellie, too, to grow up in a safe environment."

"Who's Ellie?" I counter bluntly.

"Ah, she's Chloe's daughter." She dismisses it with a wave of her hands, as if she didn't just drop an enormous bomb on me.

I'm at a loss for words, unable to form a coherent sentence. Before she can give me more information, Val calls her, and she excuses herself, apparently unaware of how stricken and confused I am.

Chloe has a daughter? Since when?

Does that mean she's also married?

I look at the door I saw her walking through a few minutes ago and debate with myself whether I should follow her and sort this out.

But maybe I shouldn't. She *is* better off without me. What good would it do if I followed her? What if she tells me she is married? So what?

Nothing will change, and there's a reason why we didn't contact each other back then after we slept together.

It's better this way. Or at least, that's what I'm trying to convince myself of.

So, in the end, I give up going after her, making a sharp turn and returning to the reception.

4

SURPRISE VISIT

Chloe

I THOUGHT I'D BE STRONG ENOUGH TO ENDURE THE FUNERAL UNTIL THE
end, but I was wrong. I feel emotionally drained, physically
exhausted, and also so damn confused after seeing Tony, even from
afar. For a moment, I thought he was coming to greet me, to talk to
me, but he never did.

Which was a good thing. I don't know if I'm ready to face him yet.
I don't know if I'll ever be.

Talking to everyone I haven't seen in a long time was also a bit
stressful, with them offering their condolences, asking me how I've
been, and trying to keep me updated on their lives.

Halfway through it, I couldn't take it anymore, so I simply left to
get some fresh air and ended up walking home without even
meaning to.

My childhood home, a big brick house in a residential neighborhood in Staten Island, comes into view as I turn the corner, my heels
echoing on the pavement. It looks the same as I remember it being
when I used to live here, always neat and well kept. My mother

always had high standards when it comes to where we live. She always says people will notice and talk, and she doesn't like giving them a reason to be negative by having her house less than perfect.

I've always wanted to tell her that people will talk no matter what, but I choose to keep my mouth shut every time because I know there are things and habits you can't change. My mother is a big example of that.

It's still the middle of the afternoon, but I walk inside trying not to make too much noise, afraid that Ellie might be taking her nap. I hope she's not. Otherwise, she won't go to sleep early tonight, but I also don't want to wake her up if she is.

Lorenna is watching her today, so Mom and I could attend the funeral. I didn't want to take Ellie with me because I figured it'd be too much for someone so little. Val's twenty-year-old daughter is a great babysitter and someone I can trust, so I decided to leave Ellie at home under her watch.

As soon as I get to the living room, I spot her playing with my daughter; some toys spread on the floor. Lorenna's head snaps up as she hears me approaching, and she offers me a kind smile.

"How did it go?" she asks, her voice soft. Her brown hair is tied up in braids on each side of their head, her expectant eyes staring at me as I head to the couch and kick off my shoes.

"Mama!" Ellie shouts as I enter the room.

"Hi baby!'" I smile at my daughter who giggles before returning my attention to Lorenna. "As good as a funeral can be?" I squat down to kiss Ellie. "It was nice seeing everyone again, though. It's been so long since I've been in New York."

I scold myself for instantly remembering the last time I was here, when I bumped into Tony. One thing led to another, and well… I ended up in his bed.

I clear my throat, shaking my head slightly so I can focus on Lorenna and Ellie, who's mumbling something I can't understand, waving her little hand at me while holding a toy that Mom bought on her first birthday.

Lorenna nods, turning her attention back to Ellie.

"You can go now. It's getting late, and I know you have homework to do, right?" I tell her, and she rolls her eyes at me.

"Ugh, don't even remind me about that. I really hate college, you know?" she grumbles, standing.

"I know." I chuckle. "Been there, too. It will get worse, don't worry."

"Thank you for the encouragement."

I reach for my purse, handing her some cash to pay for her time before I lead her out and thank her for being so helpful today. As soon as I close the door behind me, my phone vibrates. I pull it out of my purse and see it's a message from my mother.

'I'll be home late tonight. Going out with the wives and catching up. Call me if you need anything.'

I'm still getting used to this new phone, so I struggle a little to reply to her text. After my huge fight with Mateo where I ended things between us, I decided to change my number and my phone, in case he had the last one chipped or something.

'Have fun, Mom. God knows you need it. I'll get Ellie to bed and crash myself. I'm exhausted.'

It feels like I haven't slept a full night since Dad died. I'm constantly caught up in my own intrusive thoughts, and whenever I manage to close my eyes and relax for a moment, nightmares of Mateo getting to me and Ellie jolt me awake, making my heart beat so fast that it takes me hours to get it back to normal.

I put my phone down and squat to grab Ellie from the floor.

"Come on, baby. Time to go to upstairs."

I take my time giving her a bath, reading her a story, and getting her a cup of milk before we head to her new nursery. Ellie takes longer than usual to fall asleep, but when she finally does, I ponder just crashing on the floor beside her. But I haven't changed out of my funeral dress yet, and I'm in desperate need of a shower, so I head out of her bedroom and go to the living room to grab my phone so I can listen to some music while I'm in the bathroom.

My phone rings as soon as I grab it, as if sensing my presence. I swallow hard, a sinking feeling in my stomach as I see it's a private number. My hands start shaking as I stare blankly at the screen, convincing myself this isn't anything to worry about. There's no way Mateo, or any of his men, found this number.

The device vibrates in my hand for almost a minute and then it goes to voicemail. Whoever was calling doesn't leave a message but also doesn't try again. I can't relax, though, my entire body tense and shivering with fear.

A knock at the front door scares the shit out of me, and I almost drop my phone on the floor.

Who the fuck could it be? Mom isn't supposed to be home until late tonight.

Maybe Lorenna forgot something?

I'm probably just being paranoid, I tell myself.

Shaking my head, I inhale sharply, steadying myself before opening the door. I glance at my arms and pull my sleeves down, hiding the healing bruises Mateo left me with when he found out I was coming to New York. Whoever is outside doesn't need to see them.

Praying that the person on the other side hasn't come here to harm me, I pull the door open. My jaw nearly drops to the floor as I find icy blue eyes staring back at me.

"Tony?" My voice comes out in a hoarse, sharp whisper.

Being so close to him like this does things to my body that I was definitely not expecting. It's been so long, but it feels like every fiber of my being remembers Tony so well, the magnetism between us is almost palpable.

"Sorry to show up unannounced," he says apologetically, offering me a side grin. *Ah, that voice... I missed it so much.* "I didn't have the chance to offer my condolences at the funeral, but when I searched for you, I found out you had already left."

I'm aware that I'm still staring at him, but for some reason, my body is not cooperating.

"Ah, thank you," I finally mumble in response. "And yes, I just needed to get out of there, you know?"

"I know. I'm really sorry for your loss," he adds sincerely.

"Thank you. Do you want to come inside?" I offer but regret the words that come out of my mouth immediately.

No, Chloe. This is a terrible idea. Why would you invite Tony inside? Besides, Ellie's upstairs. What are you thinking?

"Sure, if I'm not intruding," he agrees, and all I can do is step aside so he can come in.

As soon as he crosses the threshold, his musky, cedar wood scent hits my nostrils, and I'm momentarily taken back to the night we spent together two years ago.

Get yourself together, Chloe.

Why am I feeling like this?

I close the door and head toward the living room so Tony and I can talk comfortably, and hopefully, with a safe distance between us. I gesture at the couch while taking a seat in the armchair across from it.

I can't help but notice that he seems tense and a bit out of place. I don't blame him. It's a bit awkward meeting like this after so long, especially in such a situation.

Our eyes lock again, and I can feel my heart shattering into tiny little pieces.

Tony clears his throat and asks, "How have you been? I mean, before all of this… happened."

I lean back in the chair, considering his question. I can't tell him the truth. I can't tell him my life has been a nightmare ever since I started dating Mateo. The only good thing I have is Ellie, but I also don't want to bring that up now. Not to him anyway.

"All right, I guess." I shrug. That's when I notice his gaze lowering to my left hand, as if searching for something. Is he… checking if I have a ring?

No, that can't be it. Why would he care?

That's just wishful thinking on my part.

"Uhm… do you want something to drink?" I offer, hoping to break the ice and ease the uncomfortable silence that has settled between us.

"Actually, I have some things to do this evening, so I can't stay long. I just wanted to… see you."

His hesitation catches me off guard. Am I wrong to read too much into this?

He said he wanted to see me. Why? Just because he wanted to offer his condolences, or did he... miss me?

Tony stands suddenly, surprising me. My eyes widen slightly, and I jump to my feet as well. I didn't think he was in that much of a hurry.

"Oh, okay. Sure, you are a busy man, after all. Thank you for stopping by."

"Of course," he muses.

I guide him back to the door and open it for him, watching as he walks outside and turns to look at me.

"Before I go, I guess congratulations are also in order," he says.

"What for?" I frown, confused.

"For becoming a mother."

I feel like I've been punched in the gut. My chest tightens, and I have to remind myself to breathe.

I don't need to think hard to figure out how he heard about it. My mom probably let it slip after the funeral.

No wonder he was looking at my ring finger. He must have thought I got married.

It'd be expected, and it had been my plan to go down the traditional road before I found out I was pregnant with Ellie. Having a baby out of wedlock might be seen as a huge stain on my family, and therefore, the Saints, since they all pretend to be super conventional.

If only he knew.

My lack of response seems to make him uneasy, and he opens his mouth to say something else, but decides against it. And just like that, he walks away, leaving me staring at his back as he climbs into his car and disappears.

5

FRAGMENTED TRUTHS

Chloe

THE DAYS THAT FOLLOW ARE BUSY BUT UNEVENTFUL. AFTER SETTLING IN and getting the house organized, most of my time is spent with Ellie while Mom does God knows what with all the old friends she's been missing. She promises me she's been catching up with the mob wives and finding out how we can be helpful, but with taking care of the house and Ellie, I can't find it in me to worry about that.

Honestly, I don't know if I want to get involved.

I know I have to if I want to be protected and considered part of the Saints. Just because Dad used to be one of them that doesn't mean they have to take care of us forever. Even if their moral code says so.

I have my old bedroom to myself and had Mom's old office turned into Ellie's bedroom, since it is the closest to mine. The house looks the same as when we left it, but I told Mom I wanted to make some changes so we can feel less nostalgic and more at home. With Dad no longer here with us and many things reminding us of him, I thought it might be nice to make a few changes to the place.

Whenever Ellie is napping, or I get to finally take a break from the house chores, I feel trapped inside… and bored. For the first few days, I struggled to go outside, too afraid to that Mateo might leap out of the bushes. But one day, Ellie was being a handful and I had to be creative and entertain her. Otherwise, I'd snap. So, I put her in the stroller and walked with her to the corner and came back.

It wasn't as bad as I thought it'd be, so I've been going for a walk with her during the afternoon for her to take her nap. Today, I decide to take her down a different route, going a couple of streets beyond the limit I set for myself. I still keep ourselves within a few blocks of home, afraid to go out of the neighborhood.

The weather is great today, no clouds covering the sky, the sun warm and comforting above our heads. I missed Staten Island. People are outside, some jogging, others rushing to get to appointments, a few taking their dogs for a walk. It's relaxing.

I spot a park a few miles away and consider taking Ellie there. But when I peek inside the stroller, I find her already asleep.

That's when my phone rings in my pocket. I reach for it, and my head snaps from side to side as soon as I notice the private number is calling me again.

Since the day of the funeral, I haven't received any other calls from whoever this is.

Is someone watching me?

I spin around in a full circle, scanning my surroundings for anything suspicious. There's no one around me. No cars with tinted windows nearby. Not a mysterious man peeking through a window.

My finger hits the red button, and I swivel the stroller around, ready to return home. I'm so nervous I can barely think straight. I really hope no one is following me.

I consider calling my mom, but before I get the chance to dial her number, I bump into someone.

"Chloe, honey!" a gentle voice squeaks, and it takes me a second to adjust my vision and make sense of the woman standing in front of me.

"Val!" I breathe in relief, the sight of my mom's best friend and one of the mob wives reassuring me instantly. "What are you doing here?" I ask, hoping she doesn't notice how keyed up I am.

"I live nearby, remember? I was just heading to meet your mom actually," she tells me, but then I notice her brow creasing at me. "Is everything okay? You look a bit pale."

I nod eagerly, not wanting her to delve into it. "Yeah, um… are you sure Mom's at home? She wasn't there when I left."

"She called me and said she was on her way. We're going to get our nails done," she starts rambling in her cheerful tone. "I figured your mom could use some time to herself after everything she went through. You went through," she corrects, her eyes finally landing on the stroller in front of me. Her face lightens up as soon as she spots Ellie. "Oh, if this isn't the sweetest little thing on Earth. She is so cute."

I smile at her proudly. "Thank you."

"Well, since we're heading the same way, we could walk together?" she offers casually, straightening up and adjusting the strap of her Gucci purse on her shoulder. "Unless you're going somewhere?"

I shake my head, relieved to see a familiar and reliable face. My heart is only now starting to calm down, but I still don't feel safe out in the open because of the phone call.

"I was already going home since Ellie fell asleep," I reply, pushing the stroller and starting to walk beside her.

Val murmurs to herself, looking ahead. I wonder why she's going to my house by foot instead of in her Audi, but I rather keep my curiosity to myself. I don't want to indulge her and keep her talking all the way back. As much as I love her, I'm not in the mood to chat.

But she doesn't seem to acknowledge that since she continues talking anyway.

"It must be really hard to do this by yourself. Nicky told me about your lame, irresponsible husband. Or should I say ex-husband?" She looks at me sideways, prying.

Lame and irresponsible would never be the words I'd use to describe Mateo. Funny Mom told them we were married when we never were.

"Handsome and wealthy, but with no interest in making things right when you got pregnant?" she carries on. "Leaving you by yourself? This is unacceptable! Mateo should be helping you with the little one."

Handsome and wealthy? Maybe. Those could be words to describe him, but they don't even scratch the surface of who Mateo really is.

A beast? A cruel, heartless man? Evil incarnated? That's more like it.

I can't believe my mom went on to talk about my personal life and told Val what I've been through. I hope she hasn't told my secrets, too. Val doesn't seem to know everything, but still, it leaves me upset to know my mother couldn't keep her mouth shut. I understand she might be going through a lot and needs to blow off some steam, but gushing about my life isn't right. I trusted her with a huge burden, and I don't want everyone knowing about it.

Sure, to be fair, her telling Tony about Ellie wasn't that big of a deal. As if he wouldn't know I'm carrying a baby around town, especially since he has eyes everywhere, and I am one of the Saints' women.

I have so many things I want to say in response to Val, but I keep them to myself. The less she knows, the better.

She keeps the one-sided conversation going until we get to the house, with me eventually murmuring a word or two so as not to leave her talking to herself completely. I don't like being rude, and I don't want her to think I'm not enjoying her company.

Which I am. I just have too much on my mind right now to be fully present.

I'm fumbling to get my keys from my purse when Mom heads out the door. "Oh, Chloe! Val! You're already here," she gushes, looking from me to her friend.

"Yes, I bumped into Chloe by the park, and we walked here together. Are you ready to go?" Val asks with excitement.

"Sure," my mom says, adjusting her expensive sunglasses on her face and bowing down to kiss Ellie.

"Actually, Mom, do you mind having a word for just a minute? I won't take long, I promise," I interject in a low voice. If I sound too suspicious, I'm certain Val will ask what this was about as soon as I'm out of reach.

My mother looks at me with a concerned face and nods, telling Val she won't take long. She helps me inside with the stroller, but we don't go far from the foyer.

"Is something wrong?" she asks bluntly.

I take a deep breath, not wanting to accuse her of anything and risk being unfair. "Mom, you can't go around mentioning Mateo's name."

"I didn't go around mentioning his name. I told *Val* about it. She's my best friend. You know she won't say anything to anyone," Mom counters.

"I know, but still. It is dangerous. Not only for us, but for her, too."

"Don't you think you're exaggerating? It's Val we're talking about," she insists.

"Exaggerating? Mom, are you being serious right now? I've been getting calls from a private number ever since we arrived in the city. Eduardo basically threatened me when we left on that plane. Do I need to remind you how serious this is?" I hiss, lowering my voice in case Val is close to the door, eavesdropping. She means no harm, but she loves a little gossip.

My outburst seems to pull my mother back to reality. To *our* reality. She gulps, shifting on her feet uncomfortably.

"You know who Mateo is and the power he holds. So, please, please be careful," I carry on, feeling my energy drain from my body.

Mom takes a step forward, reaching for my shoulders as she steadies me and forces me to look at her. "We are safe here, darling," she reassures me kindly. But no matter how many times she tells me that, I still can't believe her. "We're with the Saints now. You have nothing to worry about."

"How can you be sure?" I whisper back.

"Because I know. Tony guaranteed he'd watch over us, and all the other Saints, too. Try and relax a little. You're still so young. You shouldn't be carrying the weight of the world by yourself." My mother leans forward and kisses me on the cheek before heading to the door. "Call me if you need anything."

The door slams behind her, and I sigh. Why can't she understand the gravity of our situation? Why can't she see how bad this is for us?

Maybe it's partially my fault. I told her the truth, but not *all* of it.

I left some of it out.

Mateo is violent; a man who doesn't care about anyone or anything but himself.

A cartel god, in every sense of the word. Drugs, weapons, skin trade... I'm afraid to guess what else.

And he is coming for me. It's just a matter of time. There's no way he's going to let me go so easily. And what kills me is that I can't do anything about it. I can't protect myself. I can't protect Ellie.

I could never live in a world where he takes her from me. Just the thought of it makes me want to vomit.

But I know someone with as much power as him. Someone who might be able to help me.

Someone who will do everything in his power to protect me and my family.

With renewed determination, I swallow my pride and decide to go after Tony.

6

ASKING FOR HELP

Tony

I don't know what came over me to go to Chloe's house when I had decided she was better off without me. But when I found out she had left the funeral, I got worried. I needed to check on her, to make sure she was all right. I could still use the 'I'm the Saints' boss' card, and no one would suspect I had ulterior motives to see her.

More than that, I needed to confirm if she was married. Sure, I wanted to know if she was feeling okay, or if she needed help, not to mention to offer my sincere condolences for her loss. However, every fiber of my being was screaming at me to go and see for myself.

Nicky had just dropped a bomb on me about Chloe having a daughter. I'd assumed she had a husband to protect her. Someone who looks like that, with such a kind spirit—why wouldn't she?

But then, why would she need the Saints? Why didn't they stay in Miami where they probably had a more comfortable life?

Unless her husband was a nobody with no particular power.

It made me wonder why Nicky was so worried about giving her granddaughter a *safe environment* to grow up in. Was that just an ordinary thought for a concerned family member, caring for the safety of their loved ones, or was there something else?

Judging from the lifestyle Carlo used to have–even though he was retired before he died–I'd assume it was the latter.

Seeing her looking distraught but also surprised to see me did things to me that I wasn't prepared for. Yes, I had seen her at the funeral, but from afar. In front of her door, inches away from her, was a completely different story.

Her kind blue eyes widening at the sight of me, her soft, glowing skin, her flushed cheeks, her sweet scent... it was overwhelming. I could barely restrain myself.

Then she invited me inside, and I pondered politely refusing. It was a stupid idea; anyone could tell that. But I couldn't say no. If I could have a few minutes of her time just for myself, I'd gladly take it.

And that's when my eyes fell on her left hand.

There was no fucking ring there. Not even a fresh tan line from one being there recently. Could that mean what I think it does? Why do I feel such joy at the mere idea of her not being married?

"Boss?" Armando's voice pulls me from my thoughts. His dark eyebrows are creased as if he has been observing me for a while.

"Yes?" I grumble, a bit annoyed he's interrupted my thoughts. I realize I've been daydreaming for God knows how long, all my work stagnated around me on my desk. No light reaches us from outside since the basement has no windows, so I have no clue what time it is.

Armando looks slightly suspicious and disoriented when he tells me, "Nicky's girl is here and asking to see you."

Chloe is here? Why? What could she possibly want from me?

"Let her come down," I tell him, feeling confused as fuck.

It doesn't take him more than one minute to bring her, and I'm left speechless–not to mention surprised–when I see her showing up with a baby in her arms. It doesn't take a genius to know who that is since I already know Chloe has a daughter. However, the little girl– what's her name? Elena, Ellie... Ellie!–has her mother's eyes. So, anyone would be able to tell she's Chloe's daughter, maybe even people who haven't heard the news.

Or am I the only one observing her closely enough to tell that?

Armando is still behind them, and by the way his eyes are locked on me, I know he's been thinking the same.

It shocks me a little to see her daughter is this big. I was expecting a newborn, but definitely not this.

"Can I talk to you for a moment, Tony?" The sound of my name coming out of her mouth is like music to my ears, and for the second time in less than ten minutes, my thoughts are interrupted.

This time, though, I'm not annoyed by it. I lean back in my chair, taking in the scene before me. "Sure," I say nonchalantly. "Although, if you came here to tell me that's my kid, I must tell you I'm not interested in being a dad, but I'll definitely give you money if that's what you need."

It was meant to be a joke, but I regret it the moment the words fall from my lips, and Chloe winces, her cheeks turning to crimson.

It makes her look even prettier than usual, but I can tell I made her feel bad by my poor taste in jokes. I shouldn't attempt to be funny. I clearly fucking suck at it.

"I was just joking, I'm sorry," I say right away, throwing my hands up, trying to clear any misunderstanding. The last thing I need right now is Chloe hating my guts. "Sit down, please." I gesture to the armchair in front of my desk.

I watch as Chloe walks toward me and sits down, pulling the little girl closer on her lap. I look up at Armando and nod, letting him know he can leave us alone.

"So, what can I do for you?" I ask, fixing my gaze on Chloe. Her daughter is distracted by some toy she has in her hands, and surprisingly, utterly quiet—something I was not expecting from someone her age, however old she is.

She must be what, one? Maybe two? I don't know much about babies.

Chloe shifts in her seat, clearly uncomfortable. I wish I could do something to ease her mind or at least make her feel safe around me. I know I'm not the one making her uncomfortable, but still, it gnaws at me to see her like this, as if she needs to walk on eggshells all the time.

"I feel like I need to give you an explanation first," she begins, locking eyes with me. "Mom and I decided to come home because we didn't want to go to Miami in the first place. It was Dad's idea, and at the time, it seemed to be the best choice for us."

I nod. "I figured as much. It's good to have you back, if you're worried about—"

"That's not the reason why I came," she cuts me off softly, dismissing me with a shake of her head. Her expression is deadly serious, her jaw so tense I can almost hear her grinding her teeth.

Why the fuck does she look so worked up?

Then, with a swift move, she takes her phone from her pants pocket and puts it on my desk between us. I frown at the device, wondering what she could possibly want.

"Is it possible for someone to track me through a private number?" she asks bluntly.

She's in fucking trouble.

I can tell just by analyzing her—the dark circles under her eyes, her pale lips, her tense shoulders, the constant glances she throws over them to see if someone is behind her, the way she holds onto her little girl as if she could escape from her fingers at any minute...

Now it all makes sense.

That's when my eyes travel down her arms, and I see red.

There are fading bruises on her wrists, and even though she has sleeves covering most of her arm, I can see a few almost invisible scars when she moves slightly to adjust Ellie on her lap.

It takes me a moment to compose myself. All I want to do is fucking kill the bastard who did this to her. To smash his face with my fist until he can no longer feel anything. To cut off his balls and feed them to sharks. To send him down the ocean with a fucking anchor tied to his ankles.

But I don't want to scare her. She looks spooked enough already, so I need to tread lightly here.

"What's his name?" I hiss through clenched teeth.

Chloe shakes her head eagerly, refusing to answer my questions. She swallows hard and looks away from me. "I just need protection,

Tony. I'm worried he might come for Ellie. I can handle myself. I've been doing this for so long, but Ellie…." She trails off, her voice breaking.

My feelings are all over the place at hearing this. I want to comfort her, to hold her in my arms and assure her she is safe with me, and nothing will happen to her–or her daughter. It breaks my heart to know she's been going through all of this when I could've kept her safe.

But I'm also fucking pissed and wanting to murder the mother-fucker who caused this.

"I'll get you a new phone and have this one destroyed, or thrown in the Hudson, whatever you prefer," I assure her. "One of my men will also check in on your house every night to make sure no one is watching you or your family."

Chloe just nods, looking exhausted and drained. I don't press her for an answer or urge her to talk to me. Instead, I focus on the little girl on her lap who is now staring at me.

It's my time to shift uncomfortably in my chair. It's like the baby knows all the bad thoughts I have rolling inside my head. I feel judged.

But then, she grins at me, as if she's telling me she approves of everything I want to do to protect them.

The corner of my lip curls up on its own accord. Ellie is really cute. For a moment, when she smiles at me, and her little dimples make an appearance, something inside me snaps. It's like I'm seeing my brother in front of me–the young version of him, at least. But that is obviously a figment of my imagination. I have so much in my head lately that I'm starting to see and imagine things again.

I shake my head to dismiss that stupid idea and focus on Chloe again. "Is there anything else I can do for you?" I ask. "I can fucking kill the bastard for laying his hands on you."

Chloe snaps her head at me, her eyes narrowed as if analyzing me.

"Sorry for the language," I attempt to joke again, nodding at Ellie, and hoping I can break the ice a little.

An almost nonexistent smile appears on Chloe's face, and my

stomach churns. "There's no need for that, but thank you, Tony. Really."

She gets to her feet, preparing to leave.

"You can come to me whenever you need, Chloe. Anytime," I tell her before she turns her back to me. She holds her daughter tighter and nods, her eyes firm on me.

God, I wish things could have gone differently between us all those years ago. If I had been honest about how I felt, if I hadn't been stuck up, afraid to face my feelings, things could have gone differently for her. She would never have a fucking bastard laying his hands on her because I'd make sure to chop them off before he had a chance to lay a finger on her.

But then, I'd be the one married to her. The baby in her arms would be mine. I'd be leading a life the same way Dante and Eleni are leading now. And I promised myself I wouldn't go down that path.

It isn't for me, and I've made peace with it.

When Chloe leaves, I turn my attention to her phone that's still in the same place she left it. I unlock it, glad she doesn't have a password on it. I get to her recent calls, frowning when I see the last couple of calls have been from the private number she mentioned.

I try calling it back, but an automated message tells me the line is no longer in service. It's a stupid attempt, but I wouldn't forgive myself if I didn't try it anyway.

Reaching for my own phone, I dial the number of one of my most reliable men who I'm certain can help me with advanced security measures.

"Dice," I say when I hear him answer.

"Yes, Boss?" he replies with a firm voice.

"Do you have time to do some hunting today?"

7

STALKED

Chloe

ON FRIDAY MORNING, MY MOM CONVINCED ME TO GO TO LUNCH WITH the mob wives so we could all catch up since I haven't gone to the last two meetings. I wasn't in the mood–especially after my father's funeral–and I am still not. However, I have no choice since I'm officially part of their "family" now. It's not like I can enjoy the privileges of the life and not be actively involved.

So, after she lectured me for almost fifteen minutes, I decided to indulge her and accept the invitation. Otherwise, she wouldn't leave me alone. I know she's been trying to distract herself, but it's starting to be too much, even for her.

I used to participate in these meetings and gatherings before we moved to Miami, and true, I used to enjoy them. The girls are actually fun. However, ever since my life drastically changed after I met Mateo and had Ellie, my perspective on life simply changed, too.

Also, it's not the same to be at a restaurant, listening to twenty women chattering and laughing around me while holding my baby and trying to distract her. It's past the time for Ellie's nap, and by the way she's been throwing her doll on the floor and whining at whatever I try to do to keep her entertained, it's clear she needs to to to sleep.

I feel like I'm ruining everyone's lunch. No one is saying anything, or even throwing side glances at Ellie, but I just know I'm being a nuisance. I'm the only one with a baby here, after all.

I tried asking Lorenna to watch Ellie again, but she told me she had exams this afternoon, so she couldn't help me.

One more thing bothering me is my mom. She's been acting as if everything is okay since we came back to Staten Island. I don't know why it annoys me so much, but it does. I should be happy that she's getting back on her feet. I feared she wouldn't be herself again when I saw how distraught she was when Dad died.

However, pretending like our life is simply a fairy tale is insane. Maybe I'm just jealous that I can't turn a blind eye to my past like she seems to be doing. That I can't stop looking over my shoulder whenever I'm outside. That even though I've gotten another cell phone, I still shiver whenever it rings, thinking the person with the private number somehow found me again.

It's been a few days since I went to Tony to ask him for help. And I still wonder if I did the right thing. I wasn't planning on telling him much, but of course, he was observant and insightful enough to put two and two together. When his eyes spotted the bruises and scars on my arms, my entire body froze.

I saw the way his eyes darkened and his jaw clenched at the sight of them. I didn't mean for him to see that. Sure, I had to share *some* information to get him to help me with my phone, but I was planning on being as cryptic as possible, not revealing too much.

The way he looked at me and offered to take down Mateo made my heart jump for several different reasons. But most of all, I was afraid *for* him. I should not have involved Tony, or the Saints, for that matter.

Mateo is dangerous, and even though I know the Saints can take care of themselves, and that Tony is very powerful as well, just the thought of him being hurt because of me... it's too much for me to handle.

"Honestly, Chloe, Ellie is just one of the prettiest babies I have ever seen," Amanda gushes by my side, waving her hands in front of Ellie in a playful manner.

She was a good friend of mine when I lived here, and we managed to keep in touch while I was in Miami, although not as frequently as I'd like. Amanda is sweet, nice, and thoughtful. She's also the main reason why I accepted Mom's invitation to come today, since we're helping her plan her wedding with Tony's soldier, Kian. I didn't want her to feel like I don't care about her or her wedding.

I smile at her. "Thank you."

"Have you ever thought of getting her into modeling? I can totally see her being famous in the future," Amanda asks, still playing around with Ellie. "She has so much potential."

"Yeah, that is indeed a good idea," Val chimes in from across the table. A few other wives nod in agreement.

My mom looks at Ellie with eyes filled with pride. She straightens her shoulders and flips her hair over them. "Oh, that'd be interesting. I could be her manager. Or maybe her '*grandmager*.'" She laughs at her own joke, a chorus of chuckles following after hers.

I shake my head, turning my attention back to Amanda. "I guess I don't want Ellie to be thrown into a career she might not want to follow in the future, you know? She's also too young to start working. Life is already hard enough, I don't need to place that burden on her so soon." I tell her softly, hoping the others won't hear me.

Knowing them, I can almost hear them calling me uptight and unambitious. They care a lot about money, so I can't see them wanting to pass up a revenue stream at any cost.

"Yeah, I can understand that," Amanda replies, nodding. "I think about that a lot, too. Now that I'm getting married, I wonder what it'll be like to build a family in the underworld. You should know that better than me."

As if on cue, Ellie starts crying so loud that half the customers in the restaurant turn their heads to look at us. I feel my cheeks burn with embarrassment, and I immediately rock her in my arms, shushing her and trying to calm her down. But it doesn't matter what I do, Ellie simply cries harder and harder.

I get to my feet, feeling like I might be thrown out of this establishment if I don't leave willingly.

"I'm so sorry, ladies. But I guess I'll just go home. She really needs to take her nap. I'm really sorry," I repeat, gathering my purse and Ellie's baby bag and throwing them over my shoulder.

"Do you need me to go with you?" Mom offers, but I can tell by her tone that she's just saying it to be polite. She doesn't want to go, and I don't want to be a party-pooper, so I tell her I'll be fine.

I wave goodbye to everyone and head outside with Ellie, directing hushed apologies at the tables I pass by on my way out.

Since the restaurant is just a short walk from home, I don't see the need to call a cab or an Uber. Instead, I hold Ellie in my arms and walk down the familiar streets, looking at shop windows and taking in the warm weather of this sunny day.

Soon enough, Ellie falls asleep. I think about turning around and returning to the luncheon, but honestly, I'm closer to home than the restaurant now. And Ellie could wake up with all the noise around, and then things would just be worse than before.

That's when I notice a black car slowly following me. At first, I think I'm imagining things. But when I turn three corners and it is still on my tail, I start freaking out. Its tinted windows are so dark that I can't see a thing inside, but my gut tells me all I need to know. With my heart pounding in my chest, and blood pumping in my ears, I cut back toward the restaurant, even though I'm closer to home.

If I am being followed, I don't want to take my stalkers to my house. Especially since I'll be alone with Ellie there. No, it's better to stay out in the open where I can scream for help if needed.

I ponder calling my mother, but she won't hear her phone inside her purse. When I left, they were talking so loudly that I feared they would be the ones to get kicked out.

The car comes closer, turning onto the same street as me again. There's no one around, so I can't ask for help. Just when I need a kind soul to cross my path, I find the streets empty, even though it's still the middle of the afternoon on a Friday.

I decide to turn right into an alleyway, which, fortunately, is a one-way street in the opposite direction, so the car can't follow me here. At first, I don't recognize the man leaning against an iron gate, calmly smoking a cigarette. My brain takes in his dark hair, his large body, and his stoic expression. And then it comes to me.

This is Armando, Tony's second hand.

That's when I realize I'm in the back of Lou's Deli, the Saints headquarters.

I'm still panting when Armando's eyes narrow in on me, his forehead creasing in confusion.

"Ms. Bertolucci?" he asks, confused. "Are you all right?" He pulls away from the gate, slowly approaching me.

I'm definitely not okay. But I can't find the right words to answer him. I fear I might be hyperventilating. I take deep breaths, just focusing on getting my heartbeat back to normal. Thankfully, Ellie is still asleep in my arms.

Noticing something is wrong, Armando doesn't press on with his questions. Instead, he guides me inside, gesturing for me to lead the way. I notice he doesn't touch me, which I'm eternally grateful for even though he has no idea why.

We walk through some dark hallways until he leads me to the front of the restaurant. There aren't any customers other than a couple eating at a table in the corner, and they don't even seem to have noticed our arrival.

A guy who appears to be in his late fifties looks at us from behind the counter, a ragged towel in his hand.

"The lady needs a sandwich and a drink, Lou," Armando says from beside me. Then he turns to me. "Come and sit at one of the tables while you wait, Ms. Bertolucci."

I look at where he's pointing, and a shiver runs down my spine.

"Could I please sit away from the window?" I ask, pleading at him with my eyes.

Armando and Lou, who I now realize is the owner, exchange glances.

"Sure, follow me downstairs," Armando offers, and I instantly feel relief coursing through my veins. I've been to Tony's office, and it surely felt safer than staying out here.

I follow along, being as careful as possible not to wake Ellie. I'm still scared and slightly embarrassed to be making such a scene in front of Tony's second and the owner of the establishment that covers his headquarters, but what else can I do?

I nod at Lou as a way of thanking him without saying the actual words and follow Armando down the stairs. I feel relieved to notice Tony isn't here. However, there is no way on this Earth that he won't hear about all of this.

8

ALARM BELLS

Tony

WHENEVER I'M IN MANHATTAN, I FEEL UNEASY. I DON'T LIKE TO FEEL out of control. Staten Island is my territory. That's where I feel most comfortable. However, I had to come personally because of an important matter, so I couldn't send anyone on my behalf.

As I stroll into the bar Cal uses as his office, I take in my surroundings, noting it looks different from the last time I was here. Now I can't tell if it is a casino, a bar, or a strip club. Or maybe all of those things combined. It looks fancy though, and there's a lot of patrons already even though it's still early afternoon.

Some Irish Kings members nod at me as I make my way through the club and head toward the back door where I know Cal's office is. One of his bodyguards opens the door for me and steps aside so I can pass. I go through another door before reaching the hallway. Cal's office is the last door on my right. I knock and turn the doorknob as soon as I hear him call me inside.

"Ah, if it isn't the man himself," he says as a way of greeting me, standing behind his desk and approaching me. He gestures for me to

43

sit on a black leather chair then takes a seat on a similar chair across from me. "I thought you'd send someone."

I shake my head, sitting down and tossing the manila paper folder I'm carrying onto the table between us.

"This is a private matter, so I decided to come myself," I tell him, nodding at the folder so he can grab it and check the reports I brought. "I just got these from one of my men. I've been tracing a few calls and wanted to check if you know this guy, Eduardo Martinez? Ring a bell?" I ask, studying his face.

Cal leans forward and grabs the folder from the table, crossing one leg over his knee and leaning back on the couch as he studies the reports. Dice didn't find too much on the private number bothering Chloe, but a name and a location is already something.

"Apparently, he's a ghost online, but he has ties to Miami," I add.

Which makes sense, since that's where Chloe lived, and probably whoever is after her lives there, too. My mind flashes back to the moment I saw the bruises on her skin, and I clench my fists, fighting the urge to punch someone.

"I don't think I've ever heard of him, lad," Cal finally tells me, closing the folder, his gaze finding mine. I can see a glimpse of a smirk starting to form on his lips, but I give him a deadly look so he knows better than to attempt to joke about this. "Mind if I ask if this has anything to do with the girl?"

I tense my jaw, determined not to give him the satisfaction of knowing he's right.

"Yah, thought so. Never seen you go to these lengths for any of the dancers at Aphrodite's," Cal points out, his tone amused.

"She has someone after her," I offer as an explanation.

Cal simply shrugs. "Some of the dancers you've fucked have boyfriends who beat them up every night like the nine o'clock news."

He has a point, but I won't indulge him. "This is just business," I dismiss, my tone unyielding. "She's under the protection of the Saints, so it's not like I can turn a blind eye to it. It's my duty as the boss. I'm sure you'd do the same if you were in my shoes," I add, hoping he'll drop the prying and give me something useful.

The trip here is a bust. I was hoping Cal would be able to help me, but I'm back to square one. I'll have to do more digging to find out who this Eduardo is and why he's fucking calling Chloe and scaring her like that.

I stand up abruptly, surprising Cal who's lighting up a cigarette. "Leaving already, lad?" he asks.

"Can you let me know if you hear anything about the guy?" I press.

Cal nods, puffing smoke into the air. "Sure thing. I've got you covered."

As soon as I shut the door of Cal's office behind me, my phone vibrates in my suit jacket, and I reach to grab it, seeing Armando's name on the screen.

"Yes?"

"Boss, we have a situation at Lou's," he informs me promptly.

His voice doesn't sound like it is a 'we're being attacked' kind of situation, but it still gets me anxious. I tell him I'll be right there and rush to my car, starting the engine and speeding toward the expressway. It's usually a forty-five-minute drive back to Staten Island, but I manage to do it in less than thirty minutes. I'll probably need to have an officer on my payroll to handle the fines I've likely gotten from those damn cameras.

Armando is nowhere in sight when I get to the deli. I rush to my office, and the scene I'm met with is bewildering, to say the least. Chloe is sitting on my couch, looking as pale as if she has just seen a ghost. There's an untouched sandwich and orange juice on the coffee table in front of her. Her daughter is toddling across the carpeted floor, carefully balancing on her tiny feet and playing with a little sailboat I had sitting on one of my shelves.

Armando is leaning against the opposite wall, eyes on Chloe and Ellie as if he fears someone might show up at any time to take them away before I arrived.

What the fuck is going on here?

When he called me, a lot of ideas popped into my head as to what might be considered '*a situation.*' But this wasn't one of them.

Crossing my arms, I nod to Armando, gesturing for him to come to meet me at the door.

"What the fuck is going on here?" I ask in a hiss as soon as he comes out into the hallway. I don't want Chloe to overhear, but I also don't want to go in there without knowing anything.

"I found her scared as hell out back. After she calmed down, I tried to ask what happened, and all she told me was that she thought she was being followed," he explains. "She hasn't said anything else since."

I nod, already aware of her situation. Then I enter my office and head toward my desk, circling it and sitting in my leather chair.

"Take the kid upstairs, and get her an ice cream or something," I order Armando.

Chloe looks up at me with wide eyes and seems about to protest, but I dismiss her with a shake of my head. "Armando has four kids. He knows how to handle a baby." I don't mean to sound rude, but by the way she winces, it certainly seems like I must sound that way to her. I inwardly curse myself. I just want to hear what she has to say and see the whole picture. I hate being left in the dark.

Armando nods and carefully approaches Ellie, who giggles at him. "I certainly do," he agrees, looking at Chloe. "Come on, little one. Let's go see what we can find upstairs," he adds in a cheerful tone, smiling at her.

He takes Ellie in his arms, assuring Chloe that everything will be okay and that he will be right upstairs with Lou's wife, who also loves kids, so she has nothing to worry about.

As soon as he is out of sight, and the door is closed behind him, I turn my attention to Chloe. She still looks pale and small, as if she wants to disappear into the couch. I notice how she's pulling on the fabric of her floral dress above her knees, her knuckles turning white from the lack of blood circulation.

"Do you want to tell me what happened?" I offer softly, gesturing for her to start, and folding my arms across my chest while I wait.

Chloe nods slightly, her beautiful eyes lowering to her lap.

God, how I wish I could walk over to her and take her in my arms. Fuck, my entire body is tense, and for the first time in years, I don't know what to do. I need to fucking help her, and I promised her I would, but I don't know from what or who.

"I wasn't transparent with you the last time I came here asking for your help," she begins, sounding sorrowful. "And that wasn't fair. I just… my ex has people working for him, and he wasn't happy that I left Miami. And *him*, for that matter."

I rejoice at hearing she has an '*ex*.' But this shouldn't be a moment to feel joy. *Get a fucking grip, Tony!*

"Okay… and do you think he is here now? To get you back?" I attempt.

Chloe shakes her head. "No, he's not. At least not that I know of. Last time I heard, he was in Columbia."

Alarm bells go off in my head.

Columbia? That doesn't sound good.

"He has guys who can get to me, though," she continues. "Maybe to scare me. I don't think they would kidnap me or anything, but still… I don't know what to do. What if they take my baby from me?" She starts getting worked up, and I get to my feet, walking toward the couch. I don't get too close to her, in case she might feel like I'm invading her personal space, but I'm still close enough in case she has a panic attack or something.

"My mom thinks everything is okay now, but she's wrong. We're not safe. I don't think we'll ever be safe," she cries, a sob coming out of her throat.

My stomach twists at the sight of her so distraught and vulnerable. It kills me not to be able to kiss her worries away, to reassure her that no one will ever touch her again.

Sure, I made that promise, but what if I can't keep it? I have no idea what we're dealing with here, and that scares the shit out of me.

"I don't think you'll tell me his name if I ask, right?" I guess.

She looks up at me, her blue eyes glimmering with tears. "I don't want to get the Saints even more involved. I'm sorry I came here, actually. I just bumped into Armando by accident, it wasn't my intention to bring you more trouble…." She stands and turns toward the door, signaling her intention to leave, but I grab her arm before she manages to escape from my reach.

"You're not bringing me any trouble, Chloe. I told you I'd protect you," I attempt to assure her, or at least I hope to. "No one is going to hurt you, and if they try, they will have to go through me first. But you need to let me in on the details."

Every fiber of my being is on fire. My fingers touching her skin are tickling, and my body is thrumming with excitement from being this close to her after so long. But I have to shove these feelings and thoughts away. Chloe needs my help, and I can't do that while being distracted.

Her eyes fall to where our bodies are connected, and I drop my hand from her arm as if I've been burned. I don't mean to scare her. I shouldn't have grabbed her like that, but I can't just let her walk away either.

"Armando will take you both home and stay near your house for a while," I continue, clearing my throat and changing the subject since I know she won't tell me anything else today. Maybe I can try another day when she is less agitated and on edge. Pressing her to tell me more won't get me anywhere.

As soon as she leaves with her daughter and Armando, I rush back to my desk and call Dice.

"Any news?" I ask as soon as he answers the phone.

"Yeah, Boss. I finally got a working number," Dice tells me. "I was just about to text it to you. Hang on. There you go."

I pull my phone from my ear, and sure enough, there is a text message from him with a phone number. I murmur a thank you and hang up on him, dialing the number right away.

After the fourth ring, a man picks it up.

"Eduardo," he answers bluntly.

Fuck. It really is the motherfucker who was calling Chloe.

Eduardo fucking Martinez.

Without even realizing what I'm doing, my mouth acting on its own accord, I snarl into the phone, "If you don't fucking leave my girl alone, you will have to answer to the Saints, and I'm sure you know how that ends."

But of course, Eduardo only laughs at my threat.

"Ah, my boss will certainly love this new development. He's been dying for some action," he replies, his tone disgusting as he mocks my attempt to scare him away. If he were in front of me, I'd punch that stupid laugh down his throat.

"Tell your boss to call me," I order, realizing the alarms in my head were right from the moment I heard the word Columbia coming out of Chloe's mouth.

She messed with the wrong people. The worst kind, to be more precise.

"Sure, Morales will be thrilled to have a word with the man who stole his girl," Eduardo says before hanging up on me.

Fuck! Fuck, fuck, fuck.

Chloe is involved with a fucking cartel. This is way more serious than I had expected.

9

BOLD PLAN

Chloe

It astonishes me how a human being so small and who can barely stand can make such a mess in my house. For the last twenty minutes, I've been putting away all of Ellie's toys that she spread across the floor, her crayons and drawings, and the cushions from the couch she threw around the living room.

Today was supposed to be a cleaning day for me, but I'm not really in the mood for it. Maybe I should accept Mom's offer to hire someone to do it for me, but even though I hate it, I need to do something with my free time. Otherwise, I'll go insane. My brain needs to be kept busy so I don't think about all the awful things that could happen to us twenty-four/seven.

I didn't tell my mother about what happened at Lou's Deli the other day with Tony. I didn't want to worry her. Although, maybe I should since she's acting like nothing is happening. But I still don't know if it was all paranoia on my part. Even though I want her to take things more seriously, I don't want to alarm her unnecessarily either.

A car screeching to a halt in my driveway puts me on high alert immediately. I drop the stuffed elephant I'm holding, my breathing becoming erratic, and my eyes going wide. I don't have the time to panic before someone pounds heavily on my door.

Shit.

I consider calling the police. Ellie is upstairs with my mom. Whoever is outside will have to go through me first to get to them. But if I don't open the door right now, they could break it down and barge in. I don't have the time to wait for the police to come here.

In a flash of clarity, I remember I have a gun hidden on the top shelf of the coat closet. I rush to it, reaching for it under a few pieces of clothing I used to cover it, and cock it before heading for the door.

Taking a deep breath, I use my free hand to grab the doorknob and twist it, pulling the door open and pointing my gun straight into...Tony's chest.

I gasp as I take him in. He looks... furious, his icy blue eyes darkening. Maybe it's because I'm pointing a gun at him, or maybe it's something else, judging by the way he parked his car in my driveway and banged loudly on my door as if his life depended on it.

"Holy shit, Tony," I hiss, dropping the gun to my side.

"What's going on?" my mom asks from behind me as she rushes down the stairs.

I'm asking myself the same question, so I turn to look at Tony again, finding him still staring at my hand holding the gun.

"Go upstairs, Nicky," he orders in a low, but firm, voice. Then he steps forward, grips my arm and pulls me inside, kicking the door closed behind him.

My mother looks from him to me then back at Tony, and realizing he's not joking, she nods and turns on her heel to go upstairs again. Hopefully, Ellie is still sleeping. I don't hear her crying, so that's a good sign.

That's when I notice Tony is still holding my arm. His grip is firm but not violent. However, it still brings back memories I wish to forget. I wince, pulling myself away from his grasp, my eyes still on my arm.

When I look up to ask him what the hell does he think he's doing, his gaze is also on my arm where he held me. He seems upset for acting the way he did, but he doesn't apologize. Instead, he rushes inside, heading for the kitchen.

I follow him, my brain scrambling to find a potential explanations for why he's here. Did something happen? Did he find out anything on my cell phone about the private number that was calling me?

I set my gun on the kitchen counter, making sure I put the safety on. Tony is pacing from side to side, his fingers running nervously through his curly, dark hair. It was beautifully styled when he arrived, and even though he's ruined it completely now, he still looks effortlessly handsome.

"Tony, wh–"

"Why the hell didn't you tell me that your ex is Mateo Morales?" he snaps, his icy blue eyes darting at me in a deadly gaze. "The head of the De La Cruz cartel?" he hisses, lowering his voice so the neighbors don't hear him.

I'm so shocked–although I don't know why; it was a matter of time until he figured this out–that I'm speechless as I stare at him.

"Didn't you consider this to be important information to share when you came to me?" Tony carries on angrily. "Fuck, Chloe!"

"I didn't know at first," I try to make an excuse. It would be better if I had stayed quiet. This is a lame explanation, even I know that.

Tony sneers, turning his back to me and resuming his pacing all over my kitchen.

"He was just this rich guy I met in Miami. He showered me with gifts and attention, and I fell for it. When I realized who he was, it was already too late," I carry on, hoping I can make him see and understand my side of the story.

"How could you not have known? Someone like him must have given you a hint. And even so, why did you continue seeing him after learning the truth?" he asks, his voice dripping with accusation.

I swallow down the bile threatening to find its way up my throat. I feel sick. I don't need Tony to remind me of the mistakes I made in the past. He has no idea what I've been through. What I'm *going* through. I know he's trying to help me, but he has no right to point fingers at me right now.

"I tried breaking up with him, but you probably know that he isn't someone who takes no for an answer. Let alone a rejection," I reply, looking away from his accusatory stare.

Tony is silent for a moment, and I plop myself down on one of the kitchen stools, suddenly feeling weak, as if my legs have turned into mush.

"Is Ellie his kid?" he finally asks after what feels like hours in utter silence.

I'm glad I'm not looking at him. Otherwise, I'd have given myself away with my shocked expression. I was not expecting this kind of question. I don't know what to tell him. I feel cornered, like a prey animal face to face with its predator.

I can feel Tony's eyes on me, but I don't dare look at him. Instead, I just nod, not trusting my own voice.

He remains silent, so I don't know if he interpreted my nodding the right way. So, I look up, finding him studying me.

I need to say something.

"He never showed any interest in Ellie, though. Not until I made it clear that we were leaving him," I explain. "He's always been possessive of me, and when he realized I'd do anything for Ellie, he started to control me through her."

Tony's jaw clenches, his muscles rippling under his cheeks.

"He's threatened to take me back to Columbia to live at his compound, but I'd rather die than go anywhere near him again," I continue, my voice breaking a little at the thought of living with Mateo again. "I don't want to be his next victim."

"What do you mean?" Tony asks, his forehead creasing with confusion.

"I'm not convinced my dad died of a heart attack."

The tears I've been struggling to hold back overflow as I remember the moment I found my father dead in our house. I remember holding him in my arms, his skin still warm as if he had just been sleeping.

The first thought that crossed my mind at that moment was Mateo had done it.

A sob escapes my throat, and I cover my mouth with my hand, not wanting to make a scene in front of Tony or risk my mom hearing it from upstairs and scaring her.

"Mateo was threatening my father," I continue, my voice shaking. "I don't know why, but there was something going on between them. My father didn't trust him. Mateo could have poisoned my dad or something. I don't know…." I trail off, too worked up to say more.

Tony stops pacing and leans forward on the kitchen counter across from me, both hands steadying him, leaning forward. His chest is moving up and down so fast that it scares me.

But I don't say anything, afraid to worsen the situation.

He inhales sharply, looking at me. The intensity in his eyes is so much that I can't think straight anymore.

"You're not safe," he tells me bluntly. As if I didn't know that already. "Mateo is the worst of the worst when it comes to crime bosses. You probably know that better than I do. Even if I shipped you both off to Greece to live with Dante and Eleni, I'm sure he'd still find a way to get to you."

I nod, swallowing hard. My mouth and throat are dry as if I gulped down a handful of sand. He isn't wrong. Mateo would go to hell and back to have what he wants.

"I just want to protect Ellie. That's the only thing I care about," I murmur.

Tony's eyes instantly soften as he takes me in. I must look so weak and vulnerable. I hate that he has to see me like this, but what else can I do? I'm lost, unable to take a single step without fearing for my life or my daughter's. Feeling incapable and out of control is the worst feeling someone could ever have.

"I know." He breathes, his tone calmer and softer this time. "I'm afraid I might have fucked things up even more now."

"Why do you say that?" I frown. *What did he do?*

"Because now Mateo thinks I claimed you as my woman."

I must confess I wished I could have heard these words in another, better circumstance. I'm sure it would do things to my core that I'm not be prepared to deal with. But right now, all it does is scare the shit out of me.

Because I realize I put Tony in danger, too.

"Why would he think that? What did you do?" I ask, needing clarification. I don't want to overthink this, so it's better to be sure first.

Tony shakes his head, straightening up. "You know what? It might have been for the best. You're safe with the Saints, but you'll be safer with me. By my side. It's a good thing he thinks you're mine now."

I clench my teeth hard so as not to let my mouth drop open. What the hell is he saying? What does he mean *by his side*? Does he mean figuratively or literally?

"So, you're saying… that I'm yours, like…." I raise my eyebrows, encouraging him to complete the sentence.

"We have to make it real so he knows I wasn't joking," Tony clarifies, but I don't feel any clearer at all.

"What are you saying? We'll fake date now? Is that what you want us to do?" I ask, exasperated.

Tony shrugs as if this isn't a serious matter. "Why stop there? We'll get married."

What. The. Actual. Hell?

10

CONVINCING

Tony

CHLOE BLINKS AT ME, TOO ASTONISHED TO SAY ANYTHING.

What the hell just came over me? Did I just propose to her? Was this really the best plan I could put together?

A sneer escapes her lips, and I narrow my eyes at her.

"Did you hit your head on your way over here or what? Of course we're not getting married," she counters, her voice not sounding very convincing. It seems like she is trying to convince herself other than me.

"Yes, we are," I affirm. "Think about it…. It's the best way to keep Mateo away. As my wife, you'll not only have the protection of the Saints but of my allies as well," I reiterate, hoping to sound more persuasive.

"I don't need to be your wife for that. We can just pretend we're dating," Chloe retorts, crossing her arms across her chest, her eyebrows rising in defiance.

I offer her a smile. "As sweet as it may sound, girlfriends don't carry that much weight to men like us," I explain. "None of the guys from the Irish Kings or the Triads in Chinatown, for example, would give a shit about my *girlfriend* if there's no ring on her finger. It's a statement, Chloe, and well, girlfriends don't scream that in our world. Some of us have plenty, if you know what I mean."

I bite the side of my cheek so as not to smile at the way she grimaces at what I implied. It's cute, actually. If I didn't know her any better, I'd think that was a glimpse of jealousy.

But she dismisses it with a scoff. "Seems to me you gave this a lot of thought."

I ponder telling her that this idea just crossed my mind, but I don't want to feed her information about how unprepared I was when I came here.

So, instead, I smirk at her, the side of my lips curling up slightly as I realize I've been moving toward her this whole time. There's barely any distance between us now. She's even turned on the stool a little to face me. My eyes roam over her face, and instinctively, my hand reaches to move a strand of her smooth, beautiful hair out of her face, brushing it over her shoulder.

It doesn't go unnoticed the way goosebumps spread across her skin when my finger grazes her shoulder.

"We don't have another choice," I answer, my voice barely above a whisper. "This is your only option."

Chloe gulps, her eyes fixed on mine as she considers my words. I need to control every muscle in my body that wants to reach out to her, to close the distance between us, to make sure she feels how much I still want her, even after all this time.

But I can't do that.

We're only doing this to keep her and her family safe. I have no right to her.

"Do you really think that's gonna work?" she asks in a quiet voice.

Maybe this is all in my head, but Chloe seems to be just as affected as I am with our proximity. For a single moment, I wish she could be the one to close the space between us, throwing her arms around me and pulling me to her.

Is this too much wishful thinking on my part? I feel stupid to be thinking like that. What am I, five?

Fucking focus, Tony! I scold myself.

I nod, answering her, "If Mateo is coming for you and Ellie, you'll need all the help you can get, all of the New York underground forces on your side," I tell her calmly, but firmly. "What better way to have that than being the Saints' queen?"

Only when Chloe's hand pushes against my chest, shoving me away, do I realize just how much closer I've gotten to her. It's like my body gravitates toward her, even without me realizing it. As if there's a magnetic force bringing us together whenever we're in the same room.

She blushes aggressively, and the sight of that makes my cock twitch in my pants.

Fuck, that's annoying.

A chuckle rips from my throat, and I shove my hands in my pants pockets, straightening up and lifting my chin. "I guess I will see you in the morning," I say, unbothered.

Chloe widens her eyes, standing from her stool in a blink of an eye.

"Wait, no! We're not seeing each other in the morning. We need to discuss this," she presses, a little worked up with all the information I just dumped on her.

"What else is there to say, Chloe? Unless you have another suggestion, I think this is the only choice we have now." I look at her, waiting to see if she'll suggest something different.

I don't think she will because, otherwise, she wouldn't have come to me for help in the first place, but still, I don't want to impose myself on her. Although that's exactly what I'm doing. But we don't have a choice. There's no ulterior motive behind any of this on my part. I just want to keep her safe. And I have no clue about how to do that other than keeping her as close to me as possible.

Chloe shifts on her feet, uncomfortable under my intense gaze, but I remain quiet, waiting to see if she offers anything else.

"I don't have another idea," she answers shyly. "But we need to discuss this. It's not that simple..."

"It is, actually. You get your stuff and Ellie's packed by tomorrow, and I'll have someone coming to pick it up," I tell her with a shrug. "You'll be living in my house."

"Why?" She sounds shocked.

I frown. "What do you mean *why*? If we're getting married, it's only logical that my wife would live in the same house as me, isn't it?" I ask, studying her.

She looks so damn hot when she's embarrassed. Her cheeks flush, her eyes dart from one side to the other, avoiding my gaze, and her nose scrunches slightly even though I'm sure she doesn't even realize she's doing it.

I hadn't noticed how casually dressed she is when I came inside. I was too angry to pay attention to anything else, but now that I'm looking at her–really looking–I see that her hair is tied up in a messy bun on top of her head, she's wearing a ragged Rolling Stones T-shirt that probably belonged to her father, and flannel pants. I realize I'm fucked.

Every time she looks up at me with her beautiful cornflower blue eyes, I have to tell myself over and over that she is not mine. She was, for one single night, one that I can't fucking remember, but that was it.

This is going to be a nightmare. Maybe she's right. Maybe this plan sucks. How am I supposed to live in the same house as her and stay away from her? How am I supposed to see her every night when I come home and not be able to touch her or take her in my arms?

If I have to see her walking around the house looking like this every day, I might not be able to keep my hands to myself.

Yeah, this will be fucking excruciating.

That's going to be the real challenge, not facing Mateo. It'd probably be much easier to fight a war with him than convince my body that I can't have *her*.

"It is too fast," Chloe argues, although her voice is softer this time. "I have Ellie. She's still adapting to *this* house."

Now, she's just making excuses.

I smirk at her. "Come on, Chloe. That's stupid. I'm sure your one-year-old daughter will adapt just fine to my house," I retort in a teasing tone. "It won't be that hard. Trust me."

She gulps, looking away from me again.

When she doesn't say anything else for a whole minute, I decide it's time for me to go. I have work to do, and I'm not going to convince her of anything else today. If she didn't want me to take charge of the situation, she shouldn't have come to me in the first place.

"Well, I guess I'll see you tomorrow, then." I turn to leave, but then remember something I didn't mention and turn on my heel. "Ah, one last thing. Your mom is not invited to move in." And without another word, I guide myself out of the house.

I half expect Chloe to grab her gun again and shoot me in the back, but when I'm out of the house and safe, I grin to myself.

Somehow, I feel pretty good about this new plan. I had no idea what to do when I came here to confront her about Mateo, but thinking clearly now, I realize this *was* the best solution. It could actually work.

I walk to my car and climb inside, reaching for my phone and dialing Sal, who now works for me in New York City. It takes him a while to pick up, and I'm about to give up and have someone else do the task for me when I hear his voice on the other end of the line.

"Yes, Boss? Sorry, I had a little *situation*," he says as a way of greeting.

"All good over there?" I ask, hearing some guys yelling in the background.

"Yep, the problem was dealt with. Nothing to worry about. What can I do for you?" he asks, his voice more cheerful, yet still professional.

"I have a task for you," I inform him. "Shake down one of the court clerks on our payroll to have a marriage license ready for tomorrow morning. Do not accept any excuses, hear me? I need it done and dealt with by ten A.M. tomorrow."

"Consider it done, Boss."

I hang up and lean my head back against the headrest.

God, what did I get myself into? If someone told me two years ago that one day I'd be fake married to Chloe Bertolucci, I would've laughed in their face and told them there was no way in hell that could ever happen.

But my life is never simple. Never predictable.

Tomorrow could be the beginning of a new life for Chloe and Ellie—or the end of life as we know it. Or, perhaps, both.

11

PLAN INTO ACTION

Chloe

THE FIRST RAYS OF SUNSHINE COME THROUGH MY WINDOW, AND I grumble, turning on my side so I'm not blinded by the light. I frown, my eyes still closed, and I feel sleepiness embracing me again. But then I hear a scream coming from downstairs, and I sit up in a flash. My brain takes a few seconds to make sense of what I'm hearing, but when it does, I frown.

Is my mother yelling at someone? She'd know better than to do that when Ellie is probably still asleep. What time is it anyway?

I look to the side and grab my phone off my nightstand, seeing it's still 6:25 A.M.

"What is he thinking?" My mom's muffled voice continues.

I throw off the blanket and swing my legs out of bed. Something bad must have happened for her to be screaming like this so early in the morning.

Before I check what's going on, I stop by Ellie's room at the end of the hallway to make sure she's all right. I open the door a crack and peep inside, finding her sleeping like an angel in her crib. I let out a sigh of relief but close the door immediately so the next outburst from my mom doesn't wake her up.

I rush down the stairs, running into quite... a peculiar scene.

My mother is jabbing her index finger with her long red nail into Armando's chest. He looks as if he'd rather be anywhere in the world but here.

"This is not happening. You can go and tell your *boss* that he might be running the Saints, but he doesn't get to do everything he wants. Not inside my house. If he plans on marrying my daughter, he should come here himself and ask for *my*... fucking... blessing," my mother snarls, pressing her finger harder into his chest as she emphasizes each word.

"What is going on here, Mom?" I ask in a hushed voice. "Can you stop yelling? Ellie is sleeping," I scold her, looking from her to Armando, still frowning.

Is she making a scene because of Tony's plan to keep Mateo away from us? I don't know what Armando told her about it, but she should know that this is all just pretend.

Her head snaps back to me, acknowledging my presence, but it's clear she doesn't intend to give me any of her time or attention. If it were possible, her eyes would be firing bullets at me.

"If Tony thinks I'll allow my only child to get married at a courthouse, and not in a church, he couldn't be more mistaken in his damn life," she carries on as if she wasn't interrupted, turning to face Armando again. Her voice is quieter, though, so for that I'm grateful.

I look at Tony's second, who seems relieved to see me. Poor man. Only my mother would be able to turn a big, tough guy like him into a scolded, wide-eyed kitten.

"You should know better than to come here and do what that man says, Armando. Tony should know better!" My mother hisses, crossing her arms under her chest. She's still wearing her nightgown, but thankfully, she put a robe on over it before she answered the door.

"Mom, can you please calm down and tell me what's going on?" I ask calmly, walking toward them.

Armando steps past her, approaching me. "You need to get your purse and come with me, Ms. Bertolucci."

"Why?" I crease my forehead at him, although I'm certain he won't tell me.

I look at my mother, who has now stepped to the side but still looks grumpy and angry. Armando is staring at me, his stoic expression back now. He raises one eyebrow at me as if to tell me to do as he said, but I can't make myself do it.

I can't believe Tony meant it when he said we were getting married. Over night, I'd convinced myself that he wasn't serious about going to this extreme to keep Mateo away from me. But, apparently, he was. Knowing Tony since he was a kid, I should have realized that he wouldn't change his mind once he had made it up.

My body screams at me not to do this, to insist that Armando tell me where he wants to take me first, but that isn't happening. He was probably ordered not to mention anything to me, even if I begged.

My heart knows this is all part of Tony's plan. And even though I trust him–otherwise, I wouldn't have gone to him for help in the first place–my body still feels torn.

"You are not going anywhere until I have a word with Tony," my mother says, stepping in and grabbing my arm.

I sigh, closing my eyes for a brief second before turning to face her. "Mom, you know better than to refuse this. Tony is the boss. We don't have a choice right now."

"What the hell are you saying? Did you know about this?" she asks, sounding offended that I might not have told her.

"He brought it up yesterday, but I didn't think he was serious. Look, Mom, Tony might be right," I tell her, not at all convinced this is the best idea. But I need her support with this. Otherwise, I won't believe that I'm doing the right thing by agreeing with this nonsense. "This might be the best way for him to keep us protected. Mateo won't go after a mob boss's wife, or at least, he'll think twice before making a move."

Or that's what I hope. I want to believe that's the case so badly.

"Won't he even put a ring on your finger? This is so unacceptable, even for him," my mother murmurs, as if that's the biggest concern she should have right now. She glances at Armando again, who simply shrugs, clearly not wanting to be dragged into this unnecessary drama.

Mom grimaces and curses to herself as she wrenches off her own engagement ring that Dad gave her nearly forty years ago and slips it onto my finger. I look up at her, too astonished to speak, then notice the tears welling in her eyes.

I don't understand why this is so important to her, but if accepting it means she will be less angry at me and this situation, so be it.

I nod at her, silently thanking her, and offer her a soft smile.

"I'll take Ellie to brunch with the other wives today." Mom sniffs, changing the subject. "You go do what you have to, and I'll bring her back to you later tonight."

I nod again, grateful that she didn't argue any further. I don't think I'd have the energy to try and convince her that this is for the best. Right now, I'm trying to convince myself. It's a good thing to know Ellie will be with her so I don't have to deal with this shitshow while worrying about her.

And I'm also glad that my mom has a group of friends to lean on. Sure, I don't doubt she will blab about what's going on, and everyone will have something to say about it, but well… what can I do? People will know about it anyway. If I'm suddenly moving in with the boss and playing house with him, the word will be out before we even say, "I do."

I'd just be avoiding the inevitable anyway.

Knowing my mother, though, I'm sure she won't spill the truth. She will spin this to her advantage, probably making up a story about how Tony and I have been in love for years and that we couldn't wait any longer. She'll never let anyone know I'm marrying him because I need to escape my psychopath of an ex.

"I'll just get my stuff from upstairs," I say to Armando. "I'll be back in a minute."

I don't have time to get dressed the way I'd like to since Armando told me not to take long because Tony is waiting. So, I just brush my teeth, put on the first jeans and shirt that I can find, and grab my purse.

I still don't know what the plan is or where I'm going by the time I get into Armando's car. He starts the ignition and storms out of my driveway. It takes me a while to realize where he's taking me. It's only when I spot Manhattan on the horizon thirty minutes later that I understand we're going to New York City.

"You seriously won't tell me where you're taking me?" I try for what seems to be the third time since we left my house.

Armando doesn't even look at me, his eyes on the road ahead as we cross the bridge. The traffic is already chaotic, even though it's still early, so it takes longer than I imagine he was expecting. Armando huffs to himself, honking angrily whenever someone takes too long to move out of his way.

I let out a sigh of relief when he pulls up in front of a fancy hotel on Fifth Avenue. He helps me out of the car and walks me inside, handing me a room key.

"Since our arrival was delayed, you only have," he looks down at his watch wrist, "thirty minutes to get dressed and ready."

"How am I supposed to get dressed if I have nothing with me?" I ask, feeling dumb. He didn't tell me to bring anything along, other than my purse.

"Just go up to your room, Ms. Bertolucci." He ushers me away, gently pushing me toward the elevator. "The boss has already provided everything for you. You should get used to that. He will always make sure you have everything you need."

Holy shit. What did I get myself into?

1 2

TYING THE KNOT

Tony

I CHECK MY WATCH FOR THE FIFTH TIME IN LESS THAN TEN MINUTES, too anxious to pretend to be anything else. *Where the fuck are they?* I told Armando they should be here before 8:00 in the morning. The courthouse will open to the public after that, and my plan will be damned.

I'm in the backseat of one of my blacked out SUVs, this time not the one I usually take, in front of the hotel where Chloe is getting ready. I look out the window, noticing a few guests stepping out of the hotel entrance, but there's still no sign of Chloe or Armando.

"Shit, what is taking them so long?" I hiss to myself.

"Should I go and check, Boss?" Franco offers in response from the driver's seat. He's been my driver for the past four years, and he's as reliable, discreet, and tight-lipped as I need him to be. He is so quiet that I had almost forgotten he was here.

That's when I see Armando stepping out, leading Chloe toward us. I'm fucking mesmerized by the sight, so focused on her that I forget I know how to speak for a moment. She looks flawless, with a classy style that makes it seem like she didn't put in much effort at all.

She is the only woman I've ever met who doesn't seem to try too hard. And she fucking knows how to pull it off.

I make a mental note to myself to give a large tip to the team I hired to get her ready. They fucking knew what they were doing.

Chloe is wearing a white pantsuit, custom-tailored for her. I didn't think I'd be able to guess her exact measurements, but man, was I wrong. The fabric embraces her curves perfectly. Her smooth, shiny hair is neatly swept into a bun at the nape of her neck. Her cheeks are rosy, as if kissed by the sun, her blue eyes accentuated by a touch of thin black eyeliner, and her lips... fuck, those pink lips will be the death of me.

I shake my head and open the door, forcing myself to move and stop looking like a fucking teenager who's never slept with a woman before.

"No need. They're here," I tell Franco, finally answering him. I step outside, holding the door open for Chloe. But as she gets close to me, she doesn't acknowledge me, climbing into the vehicle without even glancing at me. I watch as she sits and scoots to the side, but not fast enough for me not to notice the golden ring glimmering on her finger. It feels like a punch straight to my gut.

I recognize it. That's Nicky's engagement ring. She's had it on every time I've ever seen her.

Armando clears his throat, drawing my attention to him. "Her mom wasn't very happy when I went to pick her up, Boss," he tells me in a hushed voice. "She almost hit me when she heard I was taking her daughter to the courthouse. She said you should do things the right, traditional way."

I inhale sharply. "I figured as much." Then, after nodding at him, I get back inside the SUV. Armando will follow us in his car since I need a witness for this, and I didn't want to involve more people than necessary.

The ride to the courthouse is fast, however, not pleasant in the least. Chloe doesn't look at me or talk to me at all. It gets me thinking how I'm already doing everything wrong—backward. I didn't even get her a ring. Nicky giving hers to Chloe only serves to prove how I'm not made for any of this.

Nonna will be fucking disappointed and pissed at me when she finds out about this. As my only living relative, she must expect me to marry someone with high social standing, to build a happy family, and give her great-grandchildren one day. But I can never give her that.

She will understand when I explain to her that this was all for the safety of three innocent people, one of them being a little girl, but I know she'll be upset either way. But I have no choice. Even if Chloe hates me for it, even if Nonna kills me, and even if Nicky will talk my ear off because of it, I need to remind myself–and them–that this is for everyone's safety. The only other option would be putting the Bertolucci women into hiding, which could last for years, and none of us want that.

This thought doesn't make me feel less guilty, though. Not when I feel the aura of dismay emanating from Chloe. I'm partially mad at her for not dealing with this in a more mature way since she was the one who fucking asked for my help, but I can't blame her either. She went through so much; being forced to marry me must not be easy for her.

When the SUV finally gets to the courthouse, I quickly take Chloe inside through the back entrance, the one for employees. Sal had to pull some strings for me, but it worked. The young clerk waiting for us doesn't seem happy to see me . In fact, he looks slightly terrified, if his pale face and trembling hands give any indication.

Chloe and I move into our spots in front of him as he reads a bunch of useless laws and far-fetched terms about union and companionship, as if life is a fucking fairy tale. I don't pay any atten-tion to it, only answering when I have to.

When I slip Nicky's ring off Chloe's finger and replace it with a delicate white-gold wedding band adorned with an array of gleaming, small, round diamonds, she looks up at me in surprise. It's the first time our eyes have met today, and I feel trapped as if she's cast a spell on me or has hypnotized me or some shit.

"How did you know my ring size?" she asks softly, her voice almost a murmur.

I shrug, swallowing down the feelings her blue eyes have brought to the surface. "I wasn't drunk enough to have forgotten how your fingers felt in my hair or on my body that night two years ago, but I guess this was just a lucky guess," I tell her with a grin on my lips.

The grin turns into a smirk when I see her blushing furiously. She is so hot, even without trying to be. I *was* drunk enough to have forgotten most of our night together, but I still have flashes of memory of how she made me feel under her touch. I hate myself to this day for not being able to remember more. Or all of it.

The clerk clears his throat, looking as if he's about to throw up. He wraps this up in record time, which I'm grateful for, and slides the certificate across the counter for us to sign. His hands are still shaking as he hands over the pen to us. Chloe doesn't make a move to grab it, so I do it instead, being the first to sign the document. I just need this to be over and done with as quickly as possible.

Once I've signed, I pass the pen to her. I hate the look on her face. I hate how her fingers are cold as they brush over mine when I hand her the pen. I hate how she looks like an animal trapped in a cage.

Maybe I'm being too hard on her. Maybe I shouldn't have forced her to marry me. Maybe I should have thought more about it and come up with a different solution. No woman dreams of having this kind of wedding. Chloe even less. Knowing what she's been through, I should've been more thoughtful. I should've been more considerate of her.

"You may kiss the bride now, Mr. Bellini," the young man tells me, his voice cracking a little.

Shit, I was hoping we'd be able to skip this part.

I turn to face Chloe, who's still not making eye contact with me, and lean forward. But I don't do what I want to, despite my body screaming at me to take this opportunity. Instead, I kiss her on the cheeks, my lips lingering a bit more than necessary on her soft skin.

My entire being begs me to take her in my arms and kiss her like she's never been kissed before in her life. But I can't.

I don't need her to hate me more than she probably already does.

Then I pull back, not daring to look at her again. I don't want to see the hurt and suffering shadowing her beautiful features.

When the clerk dismisses us, I nod to Armando to pay him for his *services* then whisk Chloe out the back to the SUV. We both climb inside, and when I close the door, Armando knocks on my window. I roll it down, looking up at him.

"What do you need me to do now, Boss?" he asks.

"Get to Staten Island and have Chloe and Ellie's things moved to my house," I order.

"What about Mrs. Bertolucci?" Armando wants to know.

Chloe remains quiet beside me. I give her a sideways glance, noticing she's twisting her new ring, her head down. I don't know if this is a good sign or not, but I know she's hearing our conversation, so I turn my attention back to my second, being cautious with what I say next.

"Nicky is welcome to come over to the house whenever she wants. And if she really fucking wants to, she can plan a small wedding party. *Small*," I emphasize.

I feel Chloe tensing up by my side, but I don't address her or make her aware that I've noticed. Armando nods and turns to go to his car.

Then I roll up my window, lean back against the headrest, and close my eyes. "Go, Franco," I order, feeling a massive headache starting to make its appearance, and it's not even fucking 9:00 in the morning yet.

I need coffee to get through the rest of this day. Or whiskey. Maybe even a cigarette. Whatever can help me forget about this fiasco.

13

NEW ROLE

Chloe

I REMAIN SILENT THE ENTIRE TIME AFTER WE LEAVE THE COURTHOUSE. I have no idea where Tony is taking me now, but just as before, I already know he won't tell me a thing if I ask, so I keep my curiosity to myself.

Besides, I don't trust myself to speak now. I have so many conflicted feelings going on inside my head and heart that I just can't express how I feel.

I'm aware of Tony's strong presence next to me, and I can't help but feel tense and uneasy. This shouldn't be like this. This is not what I wanted… not like this anyway.

But like everything else in my life, I didn't have much of a choice.

I must confess, I wasn't expecting him to be so kind as to give me such a beautiful ring. Sure, it's all for appearances, but the piece he picked is so… *me*. Simple but classy, sparkly but discreet. He knows my style and what I like. And it fits my finger perfectly.

What he said to me in the courthouse about our night together two years ago got me blushing so hard that I feared I'd burst into flames right in front of the clerk.

How can he be such a flirt in a situation like this? Doesn't he know the effect he has on me?

Apparently not. Or maybe he does, and he likes to provoke me and see me look like an idiot.

I wish I could have controlled my beating heart at that moment, but I was caught off guard.

Now, I can barely look at him.

We arrive in the Upper East Side, and the driver stops in front of this cozy breakfast restaurant where the cheapest side dish must cost more than a hundred dollars. I never dared come here when I lived in New York. Even for my family, it was too much.

I ponder resisting Tony's silent invitation for breakfast here. I don't want him to spend more money on me than he already has. The ring on my finger must have cost him a fortune. And even though he's extremely wealthy, I don't want him spending his money on me.

But knowing him, he will fight me until he convinces me, so I simply take the hand he has extended to me and climb out of the car, allow him to guide me inside. The restaurant is empty, as if he has reserved it just for us. I like that we don't have an audience, other than the staff, but it also makes me feel a bit awkward to know he's done all of this only for me.

We are guided to a table in the back, away from windows and prying eyes of passersby. Tony pulls the chair out for me and then sits across from me, accepting the menu the waiter offers him. I look down at mine, opening the first page and suppressing a gasp. I knew this place was expensive, but this is way more than what I was expecting.

Why is everything so unbelievably expensive? It's just... *food*. Foodies would kill me for saying that, but I don't have such refined taste as to notice the difference between a fifty dollar steak and one that costs five hundred dollars.

"You can order whatever you want," Tony tells me as if he can hear my thoughts. Or maybe I wasn't good at hiding my shocked expression.

"I'm not really sure what to order. I'm not that hungry," I say. To be honest, I'm afraid to eat. I feel so all over the place right now, I might throw up whatever goes down my throat.

Tony hums to himself and nods. "Should I order for you then?" he offers.

"Sure," I reply quietly.

Thankfully, he doesn't order anything heavy or that might make me even more nauseated. After the waiter writes everything down and leaves, Tony looks at me. He clears his throat, his beautiful icy blue eyes pinning me to my chair.

"Look, I'm really sorry it has to be this way," he starts, his tone filled with sincerity.

My eyes widen slightly in surprise. Is Tony really *apologizing* to me? I've never heard him apologize to anyone in his life before.

I gulp, unsure of what to say.

"I wish things could be different, too. Trust me," he adds.

Of course, he does. He's stuck with me and a one-year-old baby who just moved into his house. I don't blame him. I tried telling him we could find an alternative, but he insisted on marrying me in less than twenty-four hours, so he doesn't get to be bitter about it.

"So, what happens now?" I ask, grumpily. "Are you taking me home and consummating our sham marriage?" I didn't mean to sound defiant, or maybe I did, but I regret it as soon as I see the smirk forming on his lips.

"You'd probably like that way too much, wouldn't you?" he asks, leaning back in his chair, unbothered. "Since you asked, I'll tell you what the plan is moving forward."

I straighten up in my chair, but Tony waits until the waiter sets down the drinks he ordered for us and leaves our table to continue. "You can get whatever job you want, *if* you want one, but you don't have to worry about anything else. I'll take care of whatever you and Ellie need. You will have a credit card, a new car, a personal driver, and a four person security detail. That's non-negotiable," Tony adds when he sees I'm about to protest. Not that I don't think I need security, but four sounds a bit extreme.

"Okay, is that all?" I cross my arms under my chest, fully aware that I don't have much say in this.

Tony shrugs. "You can move around as you please, if that's what you're concerned with. Get a gym membership, go to yoga class, sign Ellie up for swimming class… do whatever rich wives in Staten Island do. You're not only a mafia wife now, but the boss's wife, so–"

"That comes with unique responsibilities, doesn't it?" I ask, cutting him off. "I need to play the role of the perfect wife…."

"It will be a piece of cake for you," he assures me, the smirk still present. "You were born into this life. You know what to do. Hang out with the other wives, get everyone together for dinner a few times a month, just take care of everyone, I guess."

Including you, I want to add, but I don't.

Some might think this is a boring life, but I've always wanted this. I never felt like I belonged with the other women in the Saints. I don't care for the superficial life of buying clothes, getting my nails done, not doing anything productive with my day. I like taking care of others. I like to feel useful.

And more than that, I've always wanted a family. I wanted a loving husband. I wanted to be there for those who need me. I wanted to have people to celebrate holidays with, especially Christmas, my favorite time of the year.

What Tony is offering me is not exactly what I dreamed of having, but it's the closest to it that I can get—being a single mom to a man who doesn't love me.

At least I'm not with Mateo. Anything would be better than that at this point. Tony will take care of me and Ellie and provide for us. What else could I ask for?

"Chloe?" Tony murmurs, his tone a bit suspicious. He's studying me as if he is trying to read my mind. I offer him a warm smile, not wanting to show my ungratefulness. I wasn't nice to him on the ride here, but I guess I should be thanking him for doing what he could to protect me and my family.

"I can do that," I finally tell him with a determined nod. If that's all I have to do, so be it. I will be the best I can be.

The waiter comes again and places our food in front of us. I'm still not in the mood to eat anything, but my stomach is threatening to growl at any minute, and the last thing I need is to embarrass myself in front of Tony. So I start with the eggs Benedict, although I'm really craving the lemon blueberry scones on the side. The french toast also looks divine, and soon enough, I have my plate cleaned.

And I thought I wasn't hungry.

Tony looks at me with an amused expression as I lean back in my chair and sigh, too full to even bother looking elegant.

"Are you ready to go, or should I get you something else?" he asks in a cheerful tone.

"No, I'm good. Thank you," I reply with a shy smile. He knew exactly what to order to satisfy me, and I don't know how I should feel about this. He seems to know me so well that sometimes it makes me uneasy.

Tony pays the check and guides me outside to the car waiting for us. He opens the back door for me, and I slide inside, making room for him to sit beside me. But he doesn't. Instead, he closes the door.

I frown and roll down the window as he turns to talk to his driver. "Take her back to the island, Franco. To my house. *Our* house," he orders, glancing at me.

"You're not coming?" I ask, confused.

Tony shakes his head. "I have some things to handle in the city first. I'll be home later tonight."

For whatever reason, I feel… disappointed at his response. I hoped —no, I thought—he was coming back with me. But of course he has things to attend to. Today is not a special day. Our marriage is a farce, and I need to remind myself of it over and over so I don't make the stupid mistake of thinking he owes me any explanation. Or his time for me, for that matter.

So I simply nod at him, accepting his lame explanation.

Tony reaches for the phone in his suit jacket pocket that apparently is buzzing with an incoming call and picks it up, gesturing for

Franco to go. The car starts moving slowly, and I roll the window back up. But before we get too far, I hear Tony saying to whoever is on the other end of the line, "Start spreading the word."

My heart drops to my stomach.

He wants Mateo to know I'm married—that *we* are married.

But why? What is his plan? Is he trying to lure Mateo here? Why would he do something risky like that?

14

———

MOVING IN

Chloe

Tony's mansion is beautiful. I'm in awe as I stare out the window of the car. We enter through tall iron gates out front, and stoic brick walls with massive windows and sharp-looking hedges welcome us. The house is enormous, towering pillars leading the way to the front door. It feels almost intimidating.

Franco parks the car and opens the passenger door for me, offering his hand to help me out.

"Are you okay to go in by yourself, Mrs. Bellini?" he asks. I'm caught off guard by him calling me by Tony's last name, and I blink a couple of times, simply staring at him. "Mrs.?" he calls again, eyeing me expectantly.

"Yes, sure. Don't worry, Franco. Thank you," I finally reply.

He types a password into a digital keypad, making sure I see the code as well. Then he swings the door open and steps aside, making way for me to pass. I walk into the grand foyer, and my jaw drops to the floor. I've been inside mansions before, but this one is simply magnificent.

"Will be right out here if you need anything," Franco informs me before closing the door behind me.

I take advantage of the empty house to take a tour and get familiar with everything. There's a huge kitchen, dining room, living room, a pool out back, and a large wooded backyard. On the second floor, there are five large bedrooms and two offices—one already occupied by Tony's stuff.

Even though the place is beautiful and well-decorated, I can't help but notice it looks slightly dated. The first idea that comes to my mind is that the right thing for me to do as the boss's wife is to redecorate. Bring some life and personality to this place. Make it feel like home. Sure, Tony must not spend too much time here, but I want all of us to feel like we belong. Especially Ellie.

The last door I open is at the end of the hallway, and as soon as I peep inside, I realize this is Tony's suite. And it looks a bit... untidy. He doesn't seem like the type of man to be sloppy. I'm sure he has housekeepers to keep this huge house clean and organized, but they certainly haven't gotten to his room yet today.

Clothes are spread all over the bed and floor, and his shoes lay like they were kicked off haphazardly near the door. Despite the mess, the room still reflects Tony's sharp taste. The black leather armchair near the window looks inviting. I wonder if he sits there every night before going to bed. A subtle hint of cologne hits me, and I'm instantly reminded of the night we spent together. His scent is still the same as I remember.

Since I have nothing else to do, and my stuff isn't here yet, I decide to make myself useful. I start gathering the clothes strewn on the floor, and finding a laundry hamper in his bathroom, throw every-thing in there to take to the washing machine.

When I grab the last pieces from his bed, I notice a lace, black bra hanging on the headboard of his unmade bed. My heart sinks to my stomach, and my throat closes with disappointment. But what was I thinking? I should get used to this. Yes, we're husband and wife now, but this is all pretend. Of course, Tony won't be faithful to his vows. They're not even real. I don't think he'll keep bringing his mistresses here, not with me and Ellie living here now. He's not that disrespect-ful. But he will keep having them anyway.

I don't have a claim to him or his heart. And I can't allow myself to fall into the illusion that this could be any different. For years, I thought that maybe–just maybe–Tony might have wanted me the same way I wanted him. But our night together was nothing but a drunken haze. It had nothing to do with love. On his end, at least, it didn't.

It'll be even harder now to tell that to my heart and brain when I'll have to see him every day, to act like his wife whenever there're people around us... how am I supposed to do this?

I sigh, taking the laundry hamper with me and stepping out of his room, making sure I don't touch the stupid bra and leave it exactly where I found it. I get to the laundry room and start the washing machine, placing Tony's clothes inside and adding the soap and fabric softener. I don't want to ruin his expensive clothes on my first day as his wife, so I'm extra careful while handling them.

As soon as I'm back in the living room, considering what to do next, I hear several cars pull into the driveway. I have no time to even guess who it might be as I open the door, and my mom barges inside with Ellie in her arms.

"Mom? Weren't you going to brunch?" I ask, puzzled. Ellie seems thrilled to see me, repeating "mama" over and over until I take her from my mother and give her a kiss on the cheek. "Oh, hey baby. Did you miss your mama?" I add softly, rocking her gently back and forth.

She babbles something that tells me she did, and I turn to my mother, who's already pacing back and forth, taking in her surround-ings, and I'm sure, considering what has to be done with the place. If I noticed the house needs some remodeling, I can only imagine the way her brain must be working hard right now to think of all the solu-tions for it.

"It's already three in the afternoon, Chloe. Brunch was over hours ago," she tells me impatiently, grimacing at a vase in the corner of the room.

I was so busy exploring the house and getting Tony's room presentable that I didn't even notice the passage of time.

Several men wearing suits, bringing boxes in their arms, stop at the threshold as they clearly await for instructions.

"Where should we put this, Mrs. Bellini?" They are looking at me, but I haven't even thought about anything yet. I don't even know what's inside each box.

"Come with me, the two of you," my mother orders, pointing at the two men on the right who have boxes labeled with various rooms. She hurries the other three down the hallway, directing them to the kitchen. "Leave those over there," she instructs them before disappearing upstairs with the other guys on her tail.

I follow her with Ellie still in my arms. She looks tired, her cute little eyes closing slowly as she plays with a strand of my hair. My mother goes from one side of the house to the other as fast as a mouse, knowing exactly where to put everything as if she's been living here for years. This has to be her first time here, just as it's mine, so I'm astonished at how easy this is for her.

"Mom, I can do that," I argue weakly, since I'm not really convinced of it myself. I mean, I can do it, but it will probably take me more than a day to finish everything. And looking at how fast everything is being unpacked, she will likely be finished by the end of the afternoon. The guys don't look particularly delighted to have to do these chores, but they don't complain about it either.

I'm positive they would rather be out there in the streets, chasing down the enemy and earning more money for the family, but well… this is part of the job, I guess. Tony must have ordered them to do whatever we needed, and my mom sure knows how to take advantage of that.

"Sweetie, we both know it'd take you weeks to organize everything. Besides, I don't mind helping. It keeps me occupied," Mom tells me, gesturing around. "Can you get Val to come here? She's downstairs somewhere. I need her to help me make a list of things that need to be done to this place. It looks like a museum," she grumbles, scowling at a portrait that was probably painted sometime during the 1800s.

"It's not that bad, Mom," I retort, rolling my eyes.

She dismisses me with a wave of her hand, rushing me to go do what she told me to.

I didn't even know Val was here. I feel like a lackey following my mother's orders, but since I'm apparently not allowed to share my opinion, I go downstairs and find Val in the kitchen, organizing the ceramic pots my mother brought from our home in Miami.

"Hi, Val. My mom is asking you to meet her upstairs," I inform her, feeling Ellie lay her head on my shoulder, tired of playing with my hair. Her breathing is calm, and even though I can't see, I know she's almost falling asleep, so I lower my voice. "Can you please not let her change the entire place? This is Tony's house."

"Oh, honey. It's your house now, too. You should be able to make it your own," she tells me, patting me on my free shoulder.

Damn. Of course she doesn't know this marriage is fake. I should play the part, even with Val. No one is supposed to know the truth. I'm glad my mother didn't tell Val everything.

I clear my throat, a bit uncomfortable. "I know. But still, I don't want to change everything without talking to him first. It doesn't feel right. It's his house, too."

"As sweet as that may be, I don't think Tony cares about any of that," she jokes, gesturing around and grabbing an old, classic porcelain vase from the shelf. I personally think it looks good there, but I see her point. Maybe Tony *doesn't* care about any of it. "Well, let's see what your mom wants me for. Excuse me."

I take Ellie back to the living room and sit on the couch with her on my lap since her crib and her room are not ready yet. I feel slightly annoyed that my mom didn't allow me to be the housewife she desperately wants me to be, but I guess I can change whatever I don't like afterward.

Although, she does have good taste.

It takes them almost two hours to finish everything, and my arms are numb from holding Ellie for so long.

"Her crib is ready, Chloe. You can put her there if you'd like," Mom tells me as she descends the stairs with Val by her side.

I get on my feet, as carefully as possible so as not to wake her, but Val steps forward, her arms reaching for Ellie. "Here, let me take her for you."

As soon as Val disappears upstairs again, my mother turns to me with a serious expression. She takes a deep breath and grabs my hand, squeezing it in hers.

"Listen to me. You need to take this seriously, hear me? Tony is the boss and your husband now. Yes, things were not done the way they should be done, but what can we do now, right?" she says with resignation. "Now, we can't make a single mistake."

I nod in agreement.

"Let me tell you what the schedule's like for the week," she continues, dragging me to sit beside her on the couch.

"I thought I was supposed to be the one calling the shots now?" I joke softly, chuckling to show her I'm just teasing, though I also mean it.

"Very funny," she mumbles, not the least amused. "So, tomorrow morning we're going to the club." That's the country club owned by the Saints where the wives normally meet while their kids are at school.

"Fine," I concede, fighting the urge to roll my eyes. This sounds so boring already. "As for the weekend, we're having your wedding party here."

I don't even try to fight her on this. Since Tony gave her the green light, this is a lost cause for me. "Can you please just make it small?" I plead, my shoulders slumping.

"Oh, please, sweetie. You'd know better than to ask me that. We need the world to see you're the Saints' queen now," she retorts dismissively. Then she gets to her feet as soon as Val shows up again. "Well, we'll leave you to it now. I'll get to the grocery store and get some stuff to stock your fridge and pantry. This place looks like no one has lived here for decades."

The house is back to its peaceful silence as soon as they both leave.

The only noise comes from upstairs where two of the guys are still finishing up with the last boxes.

"Mrs. Bellini, where should we put your stuff?" one of them comes to ask me, standing at the top of the stairs.

Well, that's a good question. Telling him to put it in a guest room would be suspicious, especially after just getting married. However, I have no plans of sleeping in the same bed as Tony, and I don't want to have to move everything out of his room once they leave. So, I decide he can think whatever he wants when I say, "Take it to a guest room, please."

15

———

HOME

Tony

When I finally park my car in my driveway, I turn it off and lean back, exhaling sharply and closing my eyes for a minute. This has been a fucking busy, long ass day. After I parted ways with Chloe this morning, I had my men spread the word to every syndicate in New York about the head of the Saints being a married man, hoping the news will trickle down the eastern seaboard, all the way to Miami. I want Mateo to fucking know Chloe is mine now.

I must confess it kind of makes my blood pump faster with adrenaline at the thought of seeing the cartel's reaction to this.

It also makes my skin crawl when I think about how Miami is such a tough territory, and I know what Mateo is capable of. But there isn't much he can do from so far away, and I'm not playing around here either. Not when he's messing with Chloe.

If anything, I want to be the one to make him pay for all the atrocities he's made her suffer through. The bruises I saw on her arms still haunt me in my sleep as does the fear in her eyes when she came to me for help. If I have the opportunity to reciprocate, Mateo will see what I'm capable of.

Even though this day feels like it has no end in sight, I haven't been able to shake the image of Chloe from my mind. Her eyes sparkling as she noticed I had gotten her a ring this morning, her cheeks flushing furiously when I flirted with her…God, this woman is driving me insane.

And now I get to call her my wife. It kills me to admit I like the sound of that, even though I have to remind myself this is all business. None of this is real and never will be. Chloe doesn't see me that way, and in all truth, I don't dream about having that life either. The thought of going through what Eleni and Dante went through leaves a sour taste in my mouth.

I guess the one good thing to take from all of this is that I'm off the hook with any of the mafia wives who want to throw their daughters on my lap.

Taking another deep breath, I step out of the car and into the house where I'm instantly greeted by a familiar scent. The place doesn't smell like lemon-lime cleaning solution and empty, musty rooms anymore. In fact, it reminds me of those days when I used to walk into my Nonna's house after a cold, wet winter day at school and ziti was in the oven.

It also doesn't sound like I live in a mausoleum. There's a faint chattering coming from the TV in the living room, and the noise of something being stirred in a stainless steel pan in the kitchen.

I pass by the foyer and head toward the main area where the living room opens up to the kitchen, and the sight is breathtaking.

Chloe is stirring something on the stovetop, her hair pulled back into a messy bun, some strands falling loose and framing her face. She huffs and blows the locks of hair out of the way, angrily pushing them aside with her arm, her hands occupied with the pan and spatula. She's wearing an apron over her light blue sweater, and there's a reality show playing on the TV.

Her cheeks are slightly pink from the heat of the stovetop, and her forehead is creased as she concentrates on whatever she is preparing.

It's endearing. I could stay here the entire day just watching her do this.

She looks up, and that's when she notices me. For a surprising moment, I realize I wish I could have been greeted with a smile. That would certainly have made my whole day worth it.

But she glances down almost immediately, looking somewhat anxious. "Oh, hi, um… dinner will be done in a few minutes," she informs me.

I hate how it makes me feel. Does she think she *has* to do this for me? It's not her obligation whatsoever.

"It's almost ten. Shouldn't you be in bed already?" I counter, approaching while still watching her.

She shrugs at my question, not the least bit bothered by it. "We used to eat late back at home since Dad worked odd hours. I think it eventually became a habit. Ellie is already sleeping, and I'm not tired yet, so…." She trails off, fixing a plate with pasta and pouring Bolognese over it. It looks and smells delicious.

I sit down at the table where she sets down my plate, my mouth watering already. But when she turns to start cleaning up the dishes instead of fixing herself a plate to eat with me, I grimace.

"Aren't you eating, too?" I pry, wondering why she's not taking a seat to share a meal with me.

Is she still mad at me for the forced wedding this morning?

"I am not really hungry, and I ate something before putting Ellie to bed," she explains from her spot by the sink.

I bite my tongue to keep from complaining about her being so distant and uncooperative. I take the first bite of the pasta she prepared, and it tastes divine. I wonder who taught her how to cook like this.

"This is delicious. I dare to say it is better than my Nonna's. Although, I could never tell her that. She'd kill me," I add, noticing the way her lips curl slightly up at my compliment.

"Thank you. That's really sweet," Chloe says quietly.

"Can you at least sit here and talk to me? It's a bit bothersome to see you working while I eat," I say.

Chloe turns off the tap and wipes her hands on the apron while she approaches me in silence.

"How's Ellie doing?" I ask, hoping this subject will shift her mood.

Thankfully, I'm right. Her face brightens up immediately, the smile I was so desperate to see finally making a shy appearance.

"She's fine. A bit overwhelmed with everything, I suppose. But she's getting to know a lot of people while going out with my mom, and that seems to be good for her," she tells me excitedly.

I hum, swallowing a mouthful of pasta. "What is her life like? Do you plan on sending her to preschool soon or anything like that?" I add curiously. Surprisingly, I feel like knowing more about their daily lives and about Ellie's habits.

Chloe shakes her head. "Not yet. It's a lot of change for her, so I don't want her to have to deal with adapting to school so soon. Maybe next year?" she replies with a shrug. "She is awfully young, too, though I suppose some people do start their children in preschool as toddlers."

She then proceeds to tell me a little more about what Ellie likes and dislikes, what it was like when she started crawling and said her first word–*mama*. I feel a strange warmth spread through my heart while listening to her, but I ignore it. I don't want to interpret what it means.

Then I'm hit by a curiosity that I shouldn't have. But before I can hold my tongue, the words burst out of my mouth. "How did you end up with Mateo?"

Chloe looks momentarily surprised by my question, but then she pulls herself together, clearing her throat and fiddling with her fingers on top of the table.

"I met him at a pool at one of the resorts my dad had a member-ship at in Miami," she begins in a low voice. "He was just... nice. Handsome, funny. He really wooed me."

I swallow the jealousy that hits me in the gut and nod for her to continue.

"We started dating, but I knew he wasn't being exclusive. When I tried breaking up with him for the first time, he, um… he hit me," she tells me, looking embarrassed to admit it.

I clench my fingers so hard that my knuckles turn white. And all I can see is red. That motherfucker.

Thankfully, Chloe continues, unaware of how I'm feeling inside. "That's when I came to New York to visit my friends. I-I needed some time away from everything. But when I got back to Miami, I found out I was pregnant, and things just went south. My parents threw a fit, and I was afraid they'd want me to marry Mateo and force him to take responsibility. But my dad forbade it."

I don't know what annoys me the most. The fact that she pretended our night together never existed, not even mentioning it, or the fact that Mateo had any responsibility over Chloe and Ellie.

"My father never liked him, and from that day forward, I found out who Mateo really was. He wouldn't leave me alone. He became possessive over me, thinking I belonged to him and that he had power over me and Ellie. I couldn't escape him, no matter what I did." She sniffs, her voice cracking.

I fight the urge to break everything around me, needing to vent my anger. I swear if this guy was in front of me right now, I'd kill him without batting an eye. I'd make sure that he suffered first. A lot.

Guilt threatens to swallow me whole while I listen to her story. Chloe had to go through all of that by herself, endure everything Mateo did to her because she was afraid he'd get to her daughter. Carlo was the only one able to protect them, but he's gone now, and that's why Chloe had to come to me for help.

A loud cry echoes from upstairs, and Chloe stands in a hurry. But before she can rush to check on Ellie, I grab her wrist, making sure I don't scare her or squeeze it too hard.

She looks down at me, puzzled.

"Listen, I'm sorry you had to go through all of that, but I'm here now. I will take care of you both. You can rest assured, he won't ever touch you again," I promise.

Chloe nods, blinking away her tears, looking withdrawn. And without saying another word, she walks away from me.

16

AN OLD FRIEND

Chloe

THE FOLLOWING WEEK IS BUSIER THAN I EXPECTED. HOWEVER, I'VE
managed to set up a new routine for both Ellie and me. As a toddler,
it'd be bad for her not to have some sort of routine, and I'm glad I got
to give her a sense of normalcy after a few bustling days in the city.
I'm happy to have my mother's support during all of this. Otherwise, I
wouldn't know what to do by myself. I'm definitely not ready to put
Ellie in a preschool or a daycare center yet, especially knowing Mateo
is still lurking around.

The mafia wife duties aren't easy either, and they sure consume a
lot of my time. Every evening, I leave dinner ready for when Tony
gets home from work, knowing he won't prepare anything for
himself after midnight. It's also a guilty pleasure of mine. The way he
seemed to have loved my food the first night I prepared it made my
heart beat frantically in my chest. I sort of want to do that for him.
After what he did to protect me and Ellie, it is the least I can do.

Having to keep up with the house and the other wives is also
exhausting.

Not to mention, I had to go shopping and refresh my entire closet. In my mother's words, "You have to look flawless, showing the world that your husband gives you unlimited access to his credit card. You can't walk around with clothes that don't match your status as the mafia queen of Staten Island."

I didn't mind getting some new pieces of clothing, I'm not *that* humble, but still… it felt a bit excessive to buy an entire closet full of new clothes.

Since day one, I haven't slept in the same bed as Tony. He never asked me about it–not that I expected he would–but if he was bothered by it, he didn't show it. I had my stuff moved to one of the guest rooms, but most days, I end up sleeping in Ellie's room instead. I guess I still don't feel completely safe or assured that no one will get to her while I'm sleeping peacefully somewhere else.

I know the odds of someone barging into Tony's mansion are minimal, if not nonexistent, but still….

Despite having everything I could ever wish for, I feel alone. Yes, I have my daughter, my mother, and the other wives , but I miss my friends. I miss having… *someone* with whom I can share anything and everything. Most of my old friends from the city are unmarried and carry on a completely different life, so it's hard for us to meet or even find the right moment to see each other. A lot of them don't even know I'm back, for that matter. I figure it's better to keep it a secret for now. I don't want them to be thrown into the crossfire.

However, this morning I woke up with a text message from Lucy. She's been my friend ever since I can remember, and she also grew up in the underworld. She lives in New York now with her boyfriend, Andy, who also works for Tony. That's why I am not surprised that she knows I'm back in town. Andy must have told her.

She, on the other hand, seems to be freaking out over the news. I chuckle as I read her text that says, 'Why the hell didn't I hear from you that you're back in town? We need to meet ASAP.'

I reply to her saying that I was going to contact her once I settled down, but she doesn't let get away with that. She insists we meet for lunch in her apartment and texts me the address, saying she won't accept no for an answer.

So, I get myself and Ellie ready and call my mom to see if she can watch her while I'm out. After that, I call Rocco—the driver Tony assigned to me, who is also my personal bodyguard. Rocco seems to be about my age and worships the ground Tony walks on. It would be cute if it wasn't a bit annoying. He doesn't let me go anywhere without following me like a shadow. Tony's orders, he keeps telling me, as if I don't already know.

"Hi, Rocco. Could you please come pick me up? I need to drop Ellie at my mom's and head to the city," I explain to him over the phone.

"Sure, ma'am. I'm just filling up the car and will be there in ten," he informs me before hanging up.

"Okay, baby girl. We're going to spend the afternoon at Grandma's, okay? Mom will be here later tonight." I turn to Ellie, fixing the little bow in her hair and straightening her dress. She giggles at me and hands me a fluffy toy she's holding.

When Rocco arrives, he helps me with Ellie's bag while I climb inside the car and buckle her into her car seat. He drives us to my mom's house where I drop Ellie, and then we head toward the city.

Rocco is not one to chit chat, so the ride is quiet and peaceful. However, I feel like I should get to know him better since we're going to be together every day from now on. I start by making small talk, asking superficial, non-personal questions. After a few minutes, he seems to loosen up a bit, and by the time we reach the bridge, he's talking freely about all sorts of different topics.

He seems to be a nice guy. He came from a broken family, had to work since he was a kid, and the grandmother that ended up raising him died a while ago, leaving him completely by himself. I feel sorry for him, but hearing him say how Tony took him off the streets and gave him a job makes me better understand why he adores Tony so much.

Then I decide to pry a little, hoping he can tell me more about what his boss has been doing out so late every night.

"Oh, I don't know, ma'am. He was at Aphrodite's Lounge last night, but that's the only thing I know," Rocco tells me, glancing at me through the rearview mirror.

I nod and look away, biting my lower lip so as not to make a face. I have no reason to feel jealous, but I do. Aphrodite's Lounge is known for its women and cards, and I shouldn't care why Tony is spending his nights there, but I can't help it.

After that, I decide to remain quiet for the rest of the trip. I don't want to hear anything else about Tony. Rocco said he doesn't know much, but just in case he reveals more than I can handle, I stop with the prying questions.

When he parks in front of Lucy's apartment building, he steps out and opens the door for me.

"I will accompany you upstairs, ma'am," Rocco informs me when I start walking away.

"Why?" I frown, turning to look at him.

"Boss's orders." He shrugs, not giving me much of a choice.

And sure enough, he only leaves me when Lucy opens the door, and I step inside her apartment, greeted with a tight hug and a squeak in my ear.

"Oh, my God! I can't believe you're here. It's been, what, two years since we saw each other?" she asks, pulling away while still holding me by the shoulders.

Lucy still looks the same as I remember. Her straight black hair is shorter, a little below her chin, but other than that, her delicate features and confident posture remain the same. Her dark eyes roam over me, stopping at my left hand.

"Okay, so you need to tell me how the hell you ended up marrying Tony Bellini," she says, pulling me by the hand to sit on her fancy, velvet couch. Out of nowhere, she hands me a glass of white wine, and although I ponder if it would be wise for me to take it, it looks so inviting that I figure it won't hurt to have a glass. Rocco will be waiting to take me home afterward anyway, so there is no harm in accepting it. It's not like I'm going to get drunk and make a fool out of myself.

I take a sip, enjoying the way the cold liquid slides down my throat. Lucy does the same, leaning back on the couch and bringing her legs up. She crosses them and turns to face me, her eyes studying me expectantly.

"So, judging by the ring on your finger, the rumors are not just rumors, right?" she presses with a grin on her lips. "What happened? Last time I heard, you were with Mateo." Lucy grimaces at the mention of his name.

I can trust her. She knows a little bit about what I went through with Mateo, and she never said a word to anyone. She helped me a lot when I needed to confide in someone, and I used to text her every now and then with updates on my relationship. She also knows about the night I spent with Tony, so if anyone knows anything about how screwed up my life is, that someone is her.

"The rumors *are* true," I confess, lifting my hand and turning it for her to get a better view of my ring. "But this was just to keep me and Ellie protected. Mateo wasn't happy about me leaving him, so Tony thought this was the best way to keep him away from us."

"And is it?" she asks, her brows raised at me. "The best way, I mean."

"Well, Mateo hasn't shown his face yet, or tried to contact me again, so I suppose it has its pros," I reply, unsure. "I didn't get a say in any of this, but I'm getting used to it. Tony is giving me and Ellie everything we need, more than that even, so I'm looking at the bright side. At least Ellie will have a good life and will be taken care of. I'm grateful."

"Of course, you are. It can't be that bad to be married to a man as hot as Tony," she jokes, nudging me in the shoulder. "I mean, my boy Andy is a hottie, but your man is another thing entirely."

I laugh, taking another sip from the wine. She isn't lying. Even I believe Tony is from another world sometimes. It should be a crime to be as handsome as he is.

"It's not like that," I counter, feeling my cheeks burn with embarrassment. Lucy knows I slept with Tony, but it doesn't mean I want to talk about it with her again.

"What isn't?" She sounds confused.

"I am not... *with* him," I explain.

"You mean you're not sleeping with him?"

I shake my head, chugging down the wine. My throat is suddenly as dry as the Sahara.

Why not?" Lucy squeaks.

"Because... that is not what this marriage is about." I don't want to share all the details of my marriage with her. I trust my friend, but the less she knows, the better. For her safety.

"Girl, please. How can you resist that man living under the same roof as you? It must be a nightmare," she points out. And she has no idea how right she is.

"I barely see him. He gets home so late every night, and he's already out of the house when I come downstairs with Ellie in the morning."

That's not a lie either. I barely see Tony, and I suppose that's a good thing. It makes my life less excruciating not having to resist the need my body seems to have for him whenever he is near me.

"Well, let's hope you can change that soon. You should be happy, especially after everything you had to endure with Mateo. Tony might lead a dangerous life, but aren't we all used to it by now?" Lucy shrugs, leaning forward to grab the wine bottle to refill our empty glasses.

I should say I am used to it, but I'm not. I don't think I ever will be. If I had the chance, I'd escape to an unknown country and start over with Ellie. But I can't do that.

Because I know Mateo will find me wherever I went. It'd be just a matter of time.

And right now, the only place I'm safe is here in New York. With Tony.

A few hours, two bottles of wine, and three boxes of Chinese food later, my phone buzzes in my purse with a message from Rocco.

'We need to go now, ma'am. I have somewhere to be after dropping you at home.'

"I'm afraid I have to go," I tell Lucy, setting my glass down on the coffee table in front of us.

"Already? It's still so early," she whines.

"I've been here for most of the afternoon," I chuckle, getting to my feet.

"Fine, fine," she concedes. "But let's make sure we do this again soon. Andy and I are moving back to Staten Island in a few weeks, so we'll be living closer to each other."

"Oh, really?" My eyes widen in surprise. "It will be so nice to have a friend living close to me."

Lucy nods and smiles at me. We say goodbye, and I head downstairs, finding Rocco already waiting for me in the same place he parked earlier to drop me off.

17

TROUBLE IN PARADISE

Tony

As much as I hate to admit, the married man's life isn't as hard as I imagined it would be. Not for the reasons I expected, anyway. Sure, it fucking kills me to have Chloe living under the same roof as me and not being able to touch her, or get close to her whatsoever, but her presence—and Ellie's for that matter—is like a balm to the soul. One I didn't realize I needed.

Not to mention the delicious food Chloe leaves prepared for me every night. She doesn't have to, and I made sure to tell her that, but she makes it anyway. I can't say I don't like it. She might not be doing it because she wants to make me feel good or anything, but my ego is not so big as to refuse a nice meal after a hard day's work.

Today is one of those days, and my mouth is watering just from thinking about what I might find when I get home.

I'm currently in my office at the deli, surrounded by Armando and some of my men who seem to have nothing better to do than smoke cigars and play poker on my coffee table. It's my fault they are here since I told them to take some time off after what we had to do last

103

night. They worked hard getting rid of a stupid son of a bitch who thought he could outsmart me in my own business.

He should know better than to try and mess with me. If there is one thing I don't take lightly, it's a motherfucker trying to steal from me. Handling him was tough, but my guys did a great job sending him to visit Davey Jones at the bottom of the Hudson, so things are okay now. I wanted to do something nice for my men, so I bought them some bourbon and Cuban cigars and told them to take the afternoon off.

I was hoping they'd go home, run whatever errands they had to at home, but they chose to stay here instead in case I needed them. The bastards are fucking loyal, that much I can say about them.

However, it's annoying as hell to have them chattering and laughing in my ear for hours. I wanted some peace to get shit done today, but they are distracting me.

And it doesn't get better when Rocco shows up at my door. I asked him to come here so he can check on a few things for me. Since he was dealing with these business deals before I assigned him to work for Chloe, he's the only one up to date with its progress.

Also, I'm eager to ask him about Chloe and what she's been up to. Since I barely see her at home, I can only count on him to keep me updated on what's going on in her life.

"Boss," he greets me as he steps inside, glancing suspiciously at the men spread around the office.

I gesture for him to come to my desk, the others barely acknowledging his arrival. Good, I don't need them prying in my personal business. As soon as he gets closer, I hand him some papers with new information on the deals he needs to check on for me.

"How is Chloe?" I ask bluntly, not bothering to walk him through what I need from him. He already knows.

"I just left her at home, sir," he informs me, his tone professional. "She spent the day at Ms. Lucy's apartment in the city."

I nod. Lucy is Andy's girlfriend, so I'm not concerned. She's also been friends with Chloe since they were young, so I have nothing to worry about.

"Anything you need to report to me?" I ask him before I dismiss him.

Rocco remains quiet, visibly uncomfortable while shifting from one foot to the other. I raise my eyebrows at him and lean back in my chair, studying him.

"What is it?" I press, folding my arms across my chest.

"Um... it's not a big deal, sir, but I thought you might want to know," he starts, avoiding my eyes. "Mrs. Chloe didn't seem very happy to know you were at the Aphrodite's last night," he tells me.

I feel my heartbeat plummet to my stomach. "How does she know I was there in the first place?" I counter, my voice firm and grim.

"I told her, Boss. She asked me what you've been up to lately that you're getting home so late every night, and I didn't want to lie to her," he explains, clearly regretting his choices. "Now, I realize what she must have thought, but it wasn't my intention to cause you any trouble."

The guy looks distraught enough, so there's no need for me to scold him for this. Also, it's not his fault. I didn't ask for secrecy or anything of the sort. I haven't been doing anything wrong, anyway, not what Chloe must think I've been doing, anyway.

I was dealing with a situation, the same one that ended with the guy swimming with the fishes. She doesn't need to know these details, so why bother her with it?

I do like to know she didn't look happy about it, though. Is she jealous? Or am I reading too much into it?

"It's fine, Rocco," I assure him. "Did she say anything else?"

He shakes his head at me. "No, she was quiet the rest of the ride to her friend's apartment."

"All right, you can go now. Keep me updated on that." I point at the files in his hand, and he nods eagerly at me, excusing himself with a subtle bow.

As soon as he's out of the room, Armando approaches me, the other guys still entertained with whatever game they're playing now.

"Trouble in paradise, Boss?" he asks, a note of sarcasm in his voice.

Apart from Nicky and Chloe, he's the only one who knows about my sham marriage. Most of my capos know the version Nicky spat around—that Chloe and I were in love for a long time and couldn't wait any longer to get married. And now that she's returned to New York, nothing was stopping us.

This obviously isn't the truth, but it's not absolute nonsense either, taking into consideration I've been interested in her for years now.

Armando's question reaches the curious bastards' ears, so now I have some of them throwing glances at me, probably wondering what the hell is wrong between me and Chloe after just a couple of weeks of being married.

"Everything is fine," I reply loud enough for everyone to hear, although my jaw is clenched with suppressed annoyance. "Can you guys excuse us for a moment?" I ask, looking at them.

Then I throw a death look at Armando, hoping it will keep his mouth shut until everyone is out of the room. The men start moving around, getting up from their seats, fumbling with their half empty glasses, in a hurry to get out of my sight before I yell at them. At another time, I'd have rushed them, but I don't want to raise suspicions about my marriage, so I simply wait while I watch them embarrass themselves while leaving my office.

Once the place is clear, I turn my attention back to Armando. "If you do that again in front of them, I'll fucking punch you in the face and leave you with a broken nose," I growl in a low voice.

But my threat is nothing but amusing to him. He snorts at me, plopping himself on the chair across from me.

"You'll excuse my bluntness, Boss, but if you don't want them to find out, you should put more work into it. I'm not the one making them question the validity of your marriage with Ms. Bertolucci," he tells me.

I bite my tongue to prevent myself from cursing him. I hate when he's right.

"Whatever. And it's Mrs. Bellini now," I correct him, pointing my finger in his face.

Armando grins at me and nods. "Sure. If I can give you a little piece of advice, and I know you didn't ask for it, you should take Mrs.

Bellini on a date tonight. From what I heard, she seems to be a little upset with you."

"I have a meeting in New York with Cal tonight," I retort bitterly, looking at my computer screen instead of his annoying face.

"I'm sure that can be rescheduled," Armando notes, a tone of amusement in his voice.

"Since when are you so nosy when it comes to my personal life, huh?" I counter, getting to my feet and narrowing my eyes at him.

He throws his hands up in the air, feigning surrender, and smiles at me. "Sorry, Boss. Just thought you'd like advice from someone more experienced in the world of married people."

I grumble, grabbing my wallet, phone, and car keys from the table and shoving them into my pockets.

"Don't you have work to do?" I ask, still angry at him for prying… *and* being right. "I'm going home."

I head for the door, and before I'm out of the office, I hear Armando musing, "Make sure to take her to a nice restaurant."

I consider turning back and giving him the punch he seems so desperate to receive but decide against it. Instead, I head for my car, wondering if I should really follow his advice. Would Chloe even accept my request for a date?

We've barely seen each other since the wedding, and I'm not sure if she would misinterpret things. I could always tell her it's all for show, but would she believe it?

Do I want her to believe it?

I scold myself for being such an indecisive man. I was never like this before. I shouldn't be overthinking everything related to Chloe. If anything, I could just order her to come with me. I wouldn't like to force her to do it, but if it meant I get to maintain this facade, and keep both her and Ellie safe, I'd do it.

It takes me a while to get to the house, but when I do, I'm instantly met with the feeling of blood boiling in my veins, and my grip on the steering wheel tightens when I spot a familiar car in my driveway.

18

CONFRONTATION

Chloe

AFTER ROCCO LEAVES ME AT HOME, I GET INSIDE AND PREPARE A NICE, hot bath since Ellie is still with my mom, and I have the entire place to myself. I can't remember the last time I've been by myself, so I plan on making the best of it.

I rush to my bathroom and gather all the expensive products my mother made me buy while we were shopping, saying I should take care of myself more. I pour in several scented oils and salts, and get inside the tub.

I don't know how long it takes, but at some point, I end up falling asleep and only wake up when my phone rings with a message from my mom asking if Ellie can sleep over with her tonight.

At first, I'm hesitant. I'm not used to sleeping away from Ellie, but I trust my mom, and I know she has bodyguards stationed around her house, too, so it shouldn't be a problem. It'd be nice to have some time to myself as well, so I tell her that's fine.

I need to learn to chill out a bit. Otherwise, I'll become paranoid. More than I already am.

After I set my phone aside, I finish washing my hair and body and step out of the tub. I blow dry my hair and change into some comfy pants and a sweater, not bothering to put on anything elegant. I don't need to be the mafia queen while I'm at home alone.

When I consider what to do with my free time–maybe a movie, or even a book–I hear a car parking outside in the driveway.

I frown, wondering who it can be. I look at my phone screen to check the time and realize it's too early for Tony to be home already. Then the doorbell rings and I freeze.

Okay, if this were Mateo, he wouldn't be ringing the doorbell to announce his arrival. Neither would his men. Also, Tony's soldiers are outside, so whoever it is, they let them in. They can't all be dead, can they?

I shake my head, pushing away the intrusive thoughts. It shouldn't be a problem to answer the door.

The bell rings again, and I fight the urge to groan with annoyance. *What's the rush?*

"I'm coming!" I yell, yanking the door open, the gush of wind blowing my hair over my shoulders.

I am met with the brightest pair of green eyes I've ever seen. Tanned skin, toned legs and arms, and long, straight black hair cascading over this woman's back, reaching her waist—she leaves my mouth agape.

I don't remember ever meeting a woman so beautiful in all my life. And I've met a lot of people. Her eyes scan me up and down, and the sneer plastered on her lips doesn't go unnoticed.

"Can I help you?" I ask, trying to sound polite. My gaze darts behind her, as I'm trying to spot Tony's soldiers, but they don't seem to be anywhere in sight.

"So, you're the little gold digger who stole my Tony, huh?" she squeaks in a pitched tone. "You should know better than to do that," she adds, pointing an accusatory finger at me. "I will make sure Tony knows who you really are."

"What the hell are you talking about? Who are you?" I hiss, fighting to control myself so as not to jump down her throat.

Who does this lunatic think she is to come to my house and accuse me like that? If anyone here is a gold digger, it's clearly her. Judging by the luxury car she drives and the tiny designer dress she's wearing, I can't imagine who paid for it. Not her, I'm guessing.

I don't like how my stomach twists at the thought of it.

"Who am I?" she snorts, flipping her hair over her shoulder. "I'm Estella, Tony's girlfriend."

I swallow hard, ignoring the bile threatening to come up my throat. If she really is his girlfriend, he should have warned me about this. However, I know her type, and she doesn't seem to be convinced of what she's saying either. She seems to be feeling more threatened and desperate than anything else.

"Yeah… I don't think so," I retort, giving her a mocking smile.

Her jaw clenches, and her knuckles turn white because of how hard she's bawling her fists. Estella takes a step forward, but I don't budge. I might be small, but I'm not weak. I can handle a fight.

"Either you get out of my doorway, or I'll have you thrown out," I warn her in a hiss.

Estella chuckles, not moving away from me. "What did you do to bewitch him, huh? It can't be sex because I know what he likes better than anyone in this city," she notes in a mocking tone, and I feel like vomiting all over her. "You don't look like his type either. I'm sure he's just enjoying a new toy for a change. But it'll be a matter of time before he comes rushing back to me and—"

"I told you to get out," I snap, having heard enough.

Maybe it's all the emotions I've been burying during these past few months, or maybe I'm just pissed at her rudeness and sense of entitlement, but the next thing I know, I'm throwing myself at her.

I don't know how I end up with my fingers wrapped around her long hair, pulling her head backward, but I'm aware that I seem like a wild animal that just escaped its cage at the zoo.

But the next thing I know, an arm is pulling me away from her, wrapping around my waist from behind and putting some distance between us. I'm panting and yelling at her to leave my house, and Estella is looking at whoever is holding me with wide eyes, her face contorted as if she's faking that she's in pain.

The bitch is such an actress!

"Tony, she attacked me!" Estella whines, smoothing her hair with her hands in a dramatic way.

She is so full of shit...

"Get out, Estella!" he orders from behind me, his arm still around me. His voice is firm, hoarse, and angry. I don't have to look at him to know he is not happy that she's here.

I release myself from his grip, turning to look at him. Tony seems wary as I step away from him as if he's expecting me to jump on her again at any moment.

Estella huffs, her eyes pleading as she pouts at him. "Tony, baby, she–"

"I told you to leave." He cuts her off, taking a step forward and heading for her car. He opens the driver's door and angrily gestures for her to get inside. His gloomy face and dark eyes are a clear sign that he's pissed off.

Whether that's because she came here, or because I made a scene in front of his house, I'm not sure. Whatever it is, it's not my fault. If he has a stupid lover, he should know better than to let her come here. If he wants to have an affair, it's his problem. But he should respect me. And Ellie.

Estella doesn't say anything. She simply stomps away from me and heads for her car. She glances at Tony one last time, but since he doesn't look at her, she jumps inside her car and drives away, fuming.

"You can just go with her," I snap at him, still angry. "I know our marriage is fake, and you have every right to have however many lovers you want. But your fucking strippers, dancers, or whatever the hell she is, aren't allowed in this house. *Our* house," I emphasize, hoping he understands the limits I'm setting for this sham marriage to work. "I will not tolerate being disrespected like this."

Then, without waiting for him to answer me, I turn on my heel and rush back inside the house, not bothering to slam the door in his face. For a second, I expect to hear his car driving away as he goes after Estella, but when the door closes gently behind me, I turn around to find him staring at me.

His expression is stoic as ever, and I can't interpret it. I'm still fuming, my breathing erratic as I watch him step closer to me.

"Where is Ellie?" he asks.

I blink a couple of times, bewildered with the sudden change of topic.

"She's with my mo—"

I'm cut off when he takes another step forward, standing right in front of me, his face only inches away from mine. His scent is so strong, his cologne so intoxicating, that I take a deep breath involuntarily. His eyes roam from mine to my lips and back up, and I need to tell myself not to make a move. Otherwise, I'll regret it.

However, my entire body is on fire, urging me to close the distance between us.

"Do you really think I'm that kind of man, Chloe? You've known me for years now. Do you think I'm the type of guy to be disloyal to his *wife*?" he whispers.

Shit, stop looking at me like that!

How is it possible that this man still holds this much power over me and my body? If he knew how he makes me feel whenever he's this close, I'd be screwed. It's irritating to be easily affected by him, unable to control my feelings and desire.

"I'm not really your wife." I shrug, acting casually so he doesn't notice my knees threatening to buckle beneath me.

Tony scoffs. "That ring on your finger says otherwise. You're my wife, Chloe, whether you want to accept it or not. We might have made our vows in front of a clerk instead of a priest, but I meant every word I said there," he tells me, his tone firm and serious. His eyes never leave mine as he speaks, and I'm the one left speechless. "Now, go get dressed," he orders then steps away from me so quickly that his sudden absence bothers me.

"W-why?" I stammer, struggling to compose myself. "Get dressed for what?"

Tony turns to me again while pulling his phone out of his pocket. "I'm taking my wife on a date."

What?!

19

DATE NIGHT

Chloe

I NEVER EXPECTED THAT BEING IN A FERRY HEADING TO THE CITY WITH Tony for a date would be the way I'd end this day. My life was never predictable before, but I never would've imagined Tony would ask me on a date. Sure, he didn't have to say outright that this is all just for show, and I didn't feel the need to clarify that with him either, but I can't help but wonder if there's more to it than he's letting on.

I'm probably kidding myself, But as we stand side by side, leaning on the railing and overlooking the moonlight reflecting on the water, my mind goes back to that day two years ago when we were in this same place, and my heart betrays me. Again.

I still remember exactly how I felt when I saw him. When he shattered my phone and ruined my purse. And when I boldly—sort of—invited him on a date. I was so intoxicated by his presence back then that I still don't know what came over me.

We never talk about that day, and I wonder if he still thinks about it as frequently as I do. Or did it mean nothing to him? I don't know why he never brings it up–except for when he briefly mentioned it at our wedding–but I know why I don't. I'm too scared he will tell me he doesn't remember much. Or worse, that it meant nothing to him. I don't know what would hurt more.

And that's still the same reason why I don't talk about it now. My mouth opens and closes a few times before I decide I'm not bold enough. I don't know why I felt encouraged back then, but I'm certainly not that girl anymore.

Tony seems to notice my uneasiness and steps over, getting closer to me. I wish he hadn't. Now, with the night breeze blowing his musky scent toward me, I can't focus any more than I could a second ago.

His eyes roam over my face and his brows crease slightly. "Is everything okay?" he asks, concern lacing his voice. "I know it was a last minute thing, but I thought it would be nice for us to have a moment alone. Armando told me the guys were starting to suspect the truth."

Ah, so that is the reason why he's taking me on a date. Of course....

"Yeah, don't worry. It's completely fine," I assure him nonchalantly. "And I agree. If we want to make this work, we both need to play our parts, I guess."

"I..." he continues, dragging the word out as he seems to consider the right one to use next, "I heard the party to celebrate the party is scheduled for Sunday. Did your mom tell you about it?"

I nod, letting out a sigh. That's all she's been talking about ever since Tony gave her the green light to organize something. It was supposed to be a small gathering at our house, mostly a meeting for the wives to make a big deal out of nothing like they always do. But knowing my mom, I'm positive it will be far more than that.

"Judging by that sigh, I am assuming you're not excited about it?" Tony asks in an amused tone, a smile plastered on his face.

"Yeah, well, you know my mom. She'll turn this into the event of the year," I reply, rolling my eyes.

Tony chuckles. "Judging by how much she's spent, you're right about that."

"Oh, God. I am so sorry about that. I tried to convince her to do something small, but she never listens to me," I whine, embarrassed by her actions. She shouldn't be spending Tony's money like that, no matter how much he has.

"It's okay. I don't mind—really. Although, I must agree with you. I'm not much of a big party guy myself, but Nicky is a tough nut to crack."

"That she is," I muse with a laugh.

We remain in silence for a minute until I say, "Now that I think about it, I don't think I ever pictured myself having a huge wedding. It was always her dream, not mine."

Tony nods at me, his icy blue eyes glooming as he stares at the darkness ahead of us. "I never wanted to get married."

I ignore the way his words feel like a knife to my heart. Sometimes I wish he wasn't so honest with me.

"Is that because of Dante and Eleni?" I ask. I can understand how their love story might have given Tony a sour taste on what married life is supposed to be like. His job is certainly not fit for family life. But he also needs to understand no one should live alone, without someone to take care of them and be there when they need someone to lean on.

"Yeah," he finally answers me, and our eyes meet. It's like a current of electricity travels through my spine, down to my core. I can't stand to look at him, but I also can't peel my eyes off him.

We don't say anything else after that, focusing on the city lights dotting the horizon. An hour later, we're sitting in a restaurant I've been to a couple of times before on different occasions. It's not crowded, and it is a secluded place, so I'm grateful for the privacy it offers.

The dimly lit atmosphere is more romantic than I'd like to admit, but I don't mention that to Tony. I didn't feel like this the other times I've come here, but with him it just feels… different.

The waiter comes and hands us the menus, and I quickly pick what I want. Tony does the same and orders us some wine to go with our meal. I was planning on having some by myself tonight, so it's nice to be able to stick to at least a small part of my plan.

The glasses of wine come soon enough, and I rush to grab mine, taking a huge sip. I hadn't realized how tense I'd been the entire way here. Being around Tony makes me so stiff, I feel my muscles need some relaxing right now.

"So, I've been meaning to ask you... is everything back home to your taste? Does Ellie need anything? Or you?" he asks bluntly.

I swallow the wine in my mouth and nod, surprised by his question. "Of course. Everything is more than perfect. What else could I possibly want?"

He shrugs, sipping from his own glass. "I don't know. Maybe someone to cook? You don't have to do that every night for me."

"I know. You've said that a couple of times already, and I told you I don't mind. I like cooking, and it makes me feel somewhat like a dutiful wife." I smile at him.

"You were the one who said we're not really married, so..." he notes, raising his eyebrows at me.

Damn, he's so effortlessly sexy. Under this dim light it's even harder to pretend he doesn't stand out from everyone around us.

"Still, I don't know what else to do with my free time anyway. I'm still not sure if I want to work outside the home, and until Ellie goes to school, I think I'll just hang around the house," I explain casually. "I'm sure you figured out by now I'm not the best Saints wife material." I chuckle.

"I'll have to disagree with that," he tells me seriously. "I like the way you care about others. I don't see a lot of other women doing that. It's easy to become superficial in this world, and I don't see a hint of that in you. And I like that."

His compliment catches me off guard, and I don't know how to react to it. I'm flattered that he noticed. I would never want him to see me as someone who doesn't care about anything other than money and status.

His eyes study me from over the rim of his glass, and I have to look away so as not to give away how much he affects me.

Someone standing near the bar waves at our table, and I frown, not recognizing who it is. But it becomes clear to me the man is not waving at me when Tony stands up from the table and says, "Excuse me, I'll just greet the owner real quickly. He did me a huge favor getting this reservation for us at the last minute, so I want to personally thank him."

I nod and watch as he heads toward the middle-aged man who shakes his hand warmly. Their interaction is brief, but my eyes are glued to them, especially when Tony smiles at something he says. His smile is like a breath of fresh air. He looks so carefree and young. I barely get to see him smiling, let alone laughing, but I can't deny the sight is mesmerizing.

And that's what makes me realize that my feelings for Tony are still very much present. I never denied they were still here, but being away from him made me bury them in a way that it *was* almost like they never existed.

But living with him now, having him take care of me and my daughter, is doing something to my heart. I never thought Tony would want me. Not in *this* way. Our night together might as well have been a mistake from his perspective.

But even so, I ended up being his wife. Even if it's fake. I've never heard of him doing anything of this sort for any other woman before. And he must have met a lot of troubled women leading the life he does in the underworld.

When Tony returns to our table, I clear my throat, taking another sip from my wine. He's still smiling as he sits down across from me.

"Care to share what was so funny?" I press, watching him curiously while leaning back in my chair.

Tony raises his eyebrows at me. The place is dark, but I can still see the way he blushes a little. It's endearing. And sexy.

"Sure. You want to know?" he asks with a smirk.

My eyes widen in surprise. "Yeah? Why not? Is it something dirty?" I blurt cheerfully.

Tony shakes his head, equally entertained. "Not really. The opposite, in fact. He was just saying he doesn't know how I ended up with someone as beautiful and elegant as you. He used to call me 'man-whore,' although I feel that was totally uncalled for," he grumbles, rolling his eyes dramatically.

A laugh blurts out of my lips, and my head falls back. I wasn't expecting to be amused by the statement, knowing the man was referencing Tony's past sex life–possibly still present–but still, it amuses me more than it should.

Tony looks at me with a puzzled expression, but his lips are still curled up in a grin I can't ignore.

"What?" I ask after composing myself.

"Nothing. I just think you should laugh more often. You look even prettier than usual," he points out, and my heart does backflips, the butterflies in my stomach fluttering their wings so fast I might explode from the inside out.

Oh, God. What do I do with this man?!

2 0

HEATING UP

Chloe

MY DATE WITH TONY TURNS OUT TO BE LIGHTER AND FUNNIER THAN I imagined it would be. I still feel tense and nervous, but mostly because I can't control my own feelings when I'm around him. But the wine helps me to loosen up a little, and by the time we return to the house, I'm feeling much less stiff and robotic around him.

Tony has this dry sense of humor that I love. I also love the way he purses his lips when something isn't to his taste, and the way he's so smooth while talking to people, almost like he knows how good he is at getting them to do what he needs or wants from them.

He told me a little bit about how life as the mafia boss has been tougher than he imagined it would be, and I feel sorry for him. Like me, Tony grew up in this life, so I don't think he had much of a choice, the same way I didn't.

It's past midnight by the time we arrive back in Staten Island. I'm slightly drowsy, but other than that, I feel great.

"Thank you for taking me out tonight," I say as we get out of the car and head inside the house. "I really needed it," I confess.

He nods, offering me a sly smile. "It was my pleasure. Maybe we should do this more often."

"I'd like that," I blurt out. I hope he hasn't noticed the eagerness in my voice. I don't want him to think I'm desperate to go on another fake date with him.

The living room is dark and empty when we arrive, and there's no other noise other than our breathing.

"Where is Ellie?" Tony asks with a frown. "I thought your mom would have brought her back by now."

"No, Ellie is staying with her tonight," I tell him. "It's really weird, you know? I haven't ever slept away from her since she was born. I miss her."

"I can imagine. But I do think you could use this break. To have an entire night of uninterrupted sleep? When was the last time you had that?" he asks me, following me to the kitchen where I grab a glass of water.

"Well, you do have a point there. I don't think I've slept well ever since I found out I was pregnant." The moment the words leave my mouth, I regret them. I didn't mean to share that much with him. I take a huge sip of water and clear my throat, looking around and trying to find another topic to bring to the conversation. "So, I know my mom did what she wanted with the house and all, but I was wondering if there's anything you don't like? We can change it if you want."

He shakes his head, leaning against the counter and folding his arms across his chest. "I actually like what she did with the place. This house never felt like a home before, but it feels cozy now. It makes me want to come home more often."

His words surprise me. He doesn't outright say it, but I can read between the lines. He feels at home with us here. With what we've done with the place. I bite my lower lip, overwhelmed with my emotions and thoughts.

"One thing I'm not happy with is you playing the role of my wife at home, too. It's not what we agreed on, and I don't want you to do that just for me," he insists. He's mentioned this whenever he's had the opportunity, but I honestly don't know why it bothers him so much when I do it out of love. I like it. I like to do something for him, especially after what he's done for me.

"It's the least I can do to pay you back for helping me with Mateo. Besides, I told you I have nothing else to do now, so I might as well make good use of my time," I counter, coming to sit on one of the stools near the counter. I choose to keep a safe distance from him, but we're still close enough that I can see the flecks of darker blue in his eyes and the stubble on his jaw.

His dark hair is still impeccably styled back with gel, but there's a rebellious curl falling over his left eye, and my hand is itching to put it back in its place. I wish I could run my fingers through his smooth, curly hair. I wish I could caress his face and kiss his inviting lips. God, how I wish he would kiss me now.

"You don't have to pay me back for anything," he retorts in a firm voice. "That's not why I did it."

"I know, but still… I don't want people having any reason to say our marriage is a lie. Or that we're going through any trouble," I mention, remembering how he told me his men are starting to suspect us. "I might as well play my role perfectly." I smile smugly at him. Then I remember something, and my mouth works faster than my brain, blurting out, "Or giving reasons for *people* to think they have any right to barge into my house and claim you as their man."

The image of Estella snarling at me that I'm just a toy Tony is using, calling me a gold digger, and affirming I'm not his type is still imprinted in my brain. The audacity of that woman still has my blood boiling with rage. I hate the idea of Tony and her together even more than before. I grit my teeth, forcing myself to think of anything else but that.

Tony chuckles in front of me, and I narrow my eyes at him.

"So, you're talking about Estella, right?" he asks, pushing off the counter and heading toward me. "Still upset about that, huh?"

"Should I not be? The bitch called me a gold digger and said I'm not your type," I grumble. "What's that supposed to mean?"

Tony moves slowly toward me, each step deliberate. A teasing smile plays on his lips, and I gulp, wondering what he's doing. I feel vulnerable, yet thrilled, under his intense gaze. The air between us seems to have been sucked out of the room.

"Is that jealousy I smell?" he teases, stopping inches away from me.

"Of course not!" I argue, but I don't dare move away from him.

"Because that'd make no sense at all. Why would you be jealous of a club dancer as if she's remotely comparable to you? You're on another level entirely. You shouldn't even bother with her," Tony says in a low, seductive voice.

Shit, he must know how my body reacts to him. Otherwise, he wouldn't be teasing me like this.

I shrug nonchalantly, attempting to maintain my unbothered facade. But the smirk on his lips tells me he isn't buying it. Damn it.

"I don't see how you benefit from this, to be honest. You're stuck with me and forbidden to have your women at the house, so…" I trail off, hoping he can see my point.

"I benefit from your safety and Ellie's. That's all that matters to me," he answers in a heartbeat. I'm left speechless, not expecting him to be so straightforward.

His face is so close to mine now that I can barely breathe. Tony leans forward, his lips almost brushing mine. His intoxicating cologne invades my nostrils, and my senses are scrambled. My head is dizzy, and I can't think properly anymore.

What is he doing? Is he going to kiss me? And why do I want the answer to be 'yes' so badly?

He reaches up, his fingers brushing a strand of hair from my face and tucking it behind my ear. The brief contact of our skin is enough to set my body ablaze. Every nerve in my system is enticed, desperate, yearning for more of him.

I'm aware of my erratic breathing, my heart pumping so hard against my ribcage that I wonder if he can hear it since he's standing so close to me.

"You know, there isn't a day in my life I don't wish I could remember more of the time we spent together that night. Not a day goes by that I don't curse myself for being completely wasted," Tony whispers, his eyes trailing to my lips. "That's my biggest regret."

And with that, he steps away from me and turns, making his way out of the kitchen and up the stairs.

My appendages are still shaking, my body still tingling as if he's still right in front of me. My core is on fire, and for a moment, I wish he had taken care of that. Just like he did two years ago.

It takes me a couple of minutes to compose myself, the annoying yearning between my legs hard to ignore this time. I hadn't realized I was so needy until now. Yeah, it's been a long time since I had sex, but until recently, that hasn't bothered me. Especially since Mateo had been my only option for so long.

Now that I'm away from him and closer to Tony than ever, all these feelings seem to be bubbling up, and I can't control them anymore. It's annoying and inconvenient, especially when I need to be able to ignore him and pretend to be his wife. I can't do that well when all I want is for him to make me his real wife—with all the rights that come with it.

2 1

—————

BURNING

Chloe

Two Years Ago

I had my fair share of drinks tonight, but being with Tony was so easy and fun that I couldn't force myself to stop. It was a coincidence that I ran into him on the ferry, and I had been bold enough to sort of ask him out. I don't know what came over me, but by the time my mind caught up to me, I had already done it.

When the drinks started to flow freely and entered my system, I loosened up, my inhibitions be damned. I lost track of time, talking and flirting with him, sharing what life had been like in Miami, making sure to keep the awful details out of it. I didn't need to remind myself of the nightmares haunting my life . Not when I felt so happy and carefree.

By the time I realize the bar is closing, a gloomy feeling comes over me. I don't want this night to end. And I don't want to separate from Tony and go back to my traumatizing life.

His warm hand grabs mine over the bar, his fingers caressing my palm and causing chills to run down my spine. The brush of his skin on mine ignites a fire that drives me insane. When he leans closer, his lips inches away from my ear, I have to gather everything in me not to lose my senses and surrender to him completely, right here and now.

"I think we need to go. Do you want me to take you back to your hotel?" he offers, his husky voice in my ear making me squeeze my legs together.

"I don't want this night to end," I blurt out then grab his collar when he starts leaning away from me. "Will you stay with me tonight?" I ask boldly, noticing the way his eyes widen slightly at me.

"Are you sure?"

I love that he's being a gentleman by not jumping to accept my offer right away, but I love even more the way his eyes burn with desire. It's great to see he feels the same way I do.

I nod, not trusting my voice enough to answer him. Then, with one swift movement, I tug on his collar, pulling him toward me, and our lips collide. He tastes like bourbon and mint, and my brain melts as I feel his arm wrap around my waist, his tongue passionately playing with mine. I'm keenly aware of the few customers still around us, but I don't care.

Tony, however, pulls away from me a few seconds later, clearly hating himself for doing so. But I'm glad he's more responsible than me at the moment, even though he is surely drunker than I am.

"I think we need to go somewhere else before we're kicked out," he suggests. "Where are you staying?"

"The Ritz," I answer. I'm so turned on by just one kiss that I can only imagine what it will be like when Tony and I are alone in my hotel room.

He pulls me up by the hand and guides me toward the sidewalk where he calls a cab.

"What are you going to do about your car?" I ask, confused.

"Trust me, the last thing I need tonight is to get pulled over and arrested for DUI. I have better things to do with my time," he tells me with a grin. "I'll get it later."

My cheeks flush, and when the car stops in front of us, he opens the door for me and gestures for me to get inside. Tony's smart not to drive to the hotel. Judging by the amount of alcohol he's ingested, and his slurred speech, we could very well crash and kill ourselves and other, innocent people.

However, going by cab means we're not alone. I can't stop imagining what it will be like to have Tony's hands on me. His lips. His...

I shake my head and cross my legs in a failed attempt to order my body to get a hold of itself.

What is happening to me? Why can't I control my needs?

We finally get to The Ritz, and it's a good thing the elevator is filled with other people. Otherwise, I'm afraid we would be starting to undress each other right here, despite the cameras.

As soon as we get to my floor, I pull out my keycard and unlock my bedroom door, Tony wraps his arm around my waist, turning me to face him, his lips claiming mine in a desperate kiss. He walks us both inside and closes the door with his free arm, pinning me against it with his body.

I have to give it to him, even with how drunk we both are, he still holds me properly and seems to know exactly what he's doing. His free hand travels up my thighs, causing me to shiver under his touch, while his other arm is still wrapped around me, keeping me flush against his hard chest.

My mouth is occupied with his, but I'm not the slightest embarrassed by the moans escaping my throat. And to be fair, that seems to be turning him on even more.

When he finds the hem of my dress, his fingers wrap around it, and he steps away from me just enough to look me in the eyes as if asking for permission before taking it off.

"Are you sure you want to do this?" he asks in a whisper. His voice is hoarse and restrained with desire. I don't see how he would find the strength to pull away if I told him I don't want this anymore, but since that's not the case, it doesn't matter.

"Yes," I answer with a nod, my eyes traveling to his swollen lips.

That's all the answer he needs before pulling my dress over my head and tossing it somewhere behind him. I'm not wearing a bra, so everything is exposed to him. Then his mouth is on my neck, and I tilt my head backward, granting him the space he needs. He slowly pecks my skin until he reaches the sensitive spot close to my shoulder, sucking gently , causing me to moan and tug on his shirt.

I wrap my arms around his neck, and our eyes meet. There's so much intensity in his gaze that I feel vulnerable being under it. His fingertips graze my thigh as he slowly moves his hand up, reaching my most sensitive spot beneath my lacy underwear.

I gulp, not daring to break eye contact with him. The last thing I need is for him to think I'm not sure of this and pull away from me. I'm so turned on right now that I might combust with just the minimum amount of stimulation from him. I can't be left hanging.

Tony watches me as he starts removing my panties, slowly sliding them down. I kick them off as they reach my ankles and spread my legs slightly, waiting for him to work his magic. His dark gaze is on me, but I can feel his arm tensing around me as his other hand reaches my core, already dripping wet with anticipation.

I hiss as soon as his fingers brush against my clit, and he starts circling it, applying just the amount of pressure I need.

"Shit, you're so wet for me," he mumbles under his breath, leaning down and claiming my lips once more. But I can't focus on his kiss, not when he's touching me like that.

I struggle to concentrate on anything else other than the pleasure he's giving me, but I feel like I need to do something to reciprocate. My hand brushes against the bulge in his pants, and he winces, so I cup him with just enough pressure and stroke him through the fabric. It makes Tony stiffen, then his fingers start working faster, and my vision threatens to blur.

I can feel my orgasm approaching. I'm not nearly ready to end this yet. But I can't seem to be able to stop it either.

"Tony," I murmur, pulling away from our kiss, but unsure of what to say. "I need to…. We have to… bed…" I stammer, trying to push him backward toward the king bed in the middle of the room.

But I don't trust my legs to move. The way my knees are trembling, they'll surely buckle as soon as I push off the door. I squeeze his cock through his pants, and he moans, staring down at me, his eyes dark with lust.

"I can finish you off right here," he offers, his brows shooting up, that sexy smirk playing at the corners of his lips. "And then we can move to the bed."

I shake my head, even though his offer is so tempting. But he ignores me. His fingers slide inside me, and I have to hold onto his shoulders for support. He moves them back and forth, and before I know it, I have spasms running all through my body as I ride my orgasm.

I'm panting as I compose myself, and Tony gives me a moment before he moves me to the bed and climbs on top of me, his eyes still hungry for more. And I can't blame him because, even though I'm already worn out, I can't say I don't want to feel him inside me.

His hands cup my breasts, massaging them and making my nipples harden instantly. I arch my back, begging for more.

And that's when he can't take anymore. He steps away from the bed just long enough to undress. His cock springing freely from his boxers. I spread my legs while watching him climb on top of me.

"You're so fucking beautiful," he whispers, his eyes studying me while he teases me with his tip brushing against my entrance. "I can't believe I get to have you for myself."

Before I have the chance to interpret his words, he slides himself inside of me. His thrusts become faster and harder as we get closer to coming together....

* * *

PRESENT DAY

I JOLT AWAKE, TANGLED IN A MESS OF SWEATY SHEETS.

Fuck! I can't believe I had a wet dream about Tony. Much less about the night we spent together. It happened so long ago, yet it felt as real as if it had happened last night.

"Shit," I hiss under my breath.

Going to bed feeling needy and horny was definitely a bad idea.

I rush to the bathroom to take a shower and rid myself of the sweatiness and the aching longing between my legs. It's like I can still feel Tony inside me.

It takes me a few minutes to pull myself together, and by the time I get dressed and head downstairs, I'm feeling slightly better. However, my cheeks are still flushed, and my body is still hot. I thought the shower would help me feel better, but it didn't.

Tony is already making coffee when I get to the kitchen, and I swallow hard, shoving aside the image of him pinning me against the hotel room door. He's dressed casually with a simple, plain black T-shirt and gray sweatpants. His hair is tousled as if he just woke up, his curls falling over his eyes.

"Good morning," I say in a weak voice, then I clear my throat.

He looks up at me and offers me a cup of coffee, then his brows crease as he takes me in. "Are you okay?" The answer is stuck in my throat as he reaches his hand to caress my cheek. "You're burning up, Chloe!"

"Oh, I... I feel fine," I tell him, taking a step back, away from his touch. I don't trust myself right now around him. Not after the dream I just had.

But he is already shaking his head at me. "Absolutely not. You clearly have a fever. And you don't look fine."

Well, that explains why I'm still feeling hot and weird after the shower. I thought it was because of my dream, but apparently it's not.

"There's no way you can go to a party like this," he insists. "You go back to bed, and I'll take care of the wedding reception your mom was supposed to throw today."

"She will kill me if I cancel this," I argue, but Tony is already gently pushing me toward the stairs.

"No, she won't. I'll take care of it. You just go back to bed and call me if you need anything."

I consider fighting him about this, but to be fair, a party is the last thing on my mind right now. I don't think I have the energy in me to indulge both my mom and the wives tonight. But I'm also afraid to go back to sleep and have another dream about Tony. That will not help me feel better either.

As soon as my head hits the pillow, I fall asleep, this time with no more dreams. Thank God.

2 2

UNDENIABLE SIMILARITIES

Tony

MY FAKE DATE WITH CHLOE WAS NOT WHAT I WAS EXPECTING. IT WAS surprisingly great. Not that I didn't think I could have fun with Chloe because I know I can. She is quieter than most women I know, but her presence is so addicting, I feel almost obsessed whenever I'm with her. I want to do everything to make her talk more, to laugh more. Whenever I managed to get a smile from her last night, it felt like my heart would explode.

Now, more than ever, I want to do everything in my power to give her the life she deserves. I want to be responsible for putting a smile on her face every day.

And that's why I sent her to bed as soon as I set my eyes on her this morning. She looked… awful. Slightly flushed, her eyes glossy, with dark circles under them, not to mention her pale skin.

When I showed up in her room with a tray filled with coffee and some fruit a few minutes later, she was already asleep, so I didn't want to wake her up. I ordered something to be delivered for her to have lunch later.

Nicky and some of the wives ring my doorbell a couple of hours later. I steady myself for the inevitable confrontation I know will come and open the door for them.

Nicky has Ellie in her arms, and the other wives have bags of what I assume are party decor items with them.

"The party is off, ladies," I inform them bluntly before they have the chance to say anything.

Their faces fall immediately, one of them even gasping in surprise.

"What? Why?" Nicky whines. "You said I could throw a party for the wedding and do anything I'd like," she reminds me in a scolding tone.

"I said you could throw a *small* party," I correct her. "But in any case, that's not the reason why I'm canceling it. Chloe is sick."

She widens her eyes and takes a few steps forward, entering the house. Ellie is looking at me from Nicky's arms with a cute expression, her little arms waving at me to scoop her from her grandmother's grasp.

I consider ignoring her. I'm not good with kids, but something about her is so... intriguing, I feel drawn to her whenever she's around. She is one of the cutest little things I've ever seen in my entire life.

So, clumsily, I reach for her, taking her from Nicky's arms, who hands me the girl as if she was dying for someone to take her.

"Where is Chloe?" Nicky urges, worried, looking around the living room.

"She's sleeping upstairs. I'm sorry you all had to come all the way up here, but I didn't have time to let you know sooner," I say, turning to the wives standing at my doorstep. "I'm sure we can postpone it until she feels better."

Most of them nod, some grumble, turning and heading for their cars, but Nicky stays behind, sitting on my couch as if she owns the place.

I wait until everyone leaves and close the door behind them, Ellie still in my arms.

"You're welcome to stay if you want, but I can watch Ellie while

Chloe is in bed," I tell her. "I don't have anything important to deal with today since I cleared my schedule for the party."

"Maybe she'll wake up feeling better, and I can have things ready in a heartbeat," Nicky insists hopefully.

I shake my head at her. "Honestly, Nicky, I allowed this because it seemed to be something important to you, and I also didn't want anyone spreading shit they don't know the truth about, but this is clearly stressing Chloe, so I think the best option is to cancel it. At least until she feels better and is more comfortable with the idea."

Nicky narrows her eyes at me, studying me like I'm a fucking lab rat. I feel uneasy under her gaze, so I turn my attention to Ellie, who's now playing with the little pink bow on her dress.

"Why are you suddenly so interested in Chloe's well-being? Why do you care how she's feeling?" Nicky finally asks, making me snap my head at her again.

Her question bothers me immensely.

"You know damn well I've always cared about her," I reply bitterly. "You know better than anyone, actually, given the fact that your husband was the one responsible for pushing me away from her."

Nicky winces at my accusation, but I don't budge. It's past time we address this.

"Carlo made it very clear when he was alive that he didn't want me near Chloe, so don't pretend you don't know where I'm coming from," I add, holding her gaze. That seems to make her uncomfortable since she looks away, straightening up in her seat.

Silence fills the room after that, the only noise coming from Ellie's babbling and murmuring the few words she knows how to speak. Then Nicky clears her throat, getting up from the couch and adjusting the strap of her purse on her shoulder.

"I can take Ellie back with me for the day so Chloe can rest. You don't have to worry about her. She'll consume your time," Nicky says, reaching for Ellie.

But I take a step back, hoping that's evidence enough I don't want to accept her offer.

"It's okay, I don't mind watching her. It'll be nice to bond with her a little," I reply, looking at Ellie and grinning. "Isn't it, Ellie? Do you want to stay with me until Mommy wakes up?"

She giggles at me as if she understands my question.

Nicky seems hesitant to agree with it, but I don't want her to feel like I can't handle Ellie. I'm not experienced with kids, but I'm not a risk to her either. I've had puppies before. It can't be that different.

"Seriously, Nicky, it's fine," I reassure her. "I'm sure Chloe will be up soon since she didn't have anything to eat this morning. I can handle Ellie for a few hours."

She finally sighs and nods, my reassurance seeming to have worked.

"I promise I'll call if I need anything. And I'll ask Chloe to call you once she's up."

"Okay, great. Thank you," she murmurs. Then she places a kiss on Ellie's forehead and heads for the door.

As soon as she's gone, I look at Ellie, wondering what I can do to keep her entertained. She has several toys in her room, so I head there with her, hoping we can find something cool to distract her.

For the next hour, Ellie finds herself busy with a stuffed pink elephant, a doll, and a colorful cube with geometrical pieces. Most of the time, I watch her play, once in a while engaging with her and participating a little with her toys.

But when she starts to show signs she's getting bored, I freak out a little. What if she's getting hungry? I didn't ask Nicky what she normally eats at this time of day. I also have zero skills when it comes to cooking food for toddlers. Chloe might have prepared something for her and put it in the fridge, but I have no idea what that could be.

"Are you hungry, Ellie?" I ask tentatively, but she shakes her head at me.

How the fuck is this kid so smart? Are babies supposed to understand everything we say when they're only one year old?

"All right, so what do you want to do? Do you want to try and find some new toys?" I try, remembering some of Seb's old stuff locked somewhere in the attic.

I don't know why I thought about him right now, or why I even feel like messing with his stuff, but the words are out of my mouth before I can stop them. Ellie's eyes sparkle as she looks at me expectantly.

It's been a while since I packed those things, so I don't have to touch or look at them, and I'm honestly not sure I'm ready to face them yet. But I can't leave Ellie hanging like this after offering it. So, I take her to the attic, hoping it won't fuck up my mind.

I grab the first box I can find and take it to the living room, since the attic is too dark and musty for us to stay there. As soon as we settle on the living room carpet and I open it, I find a little bear that used to be Seb's favorite when he was a kid. My throat tightens, and I give it to Ellie, who clearly loves it already, her eyes almost popping out of their sockets while she stares at it. Then I focus on the box again, finding an old photo album next.

I skim through it, seeing some pictures of Seb and I at Nonna's house when we were too young to remember it. Some of them were taken on trips we used to make with our family, and lots of them I've never seen before, taken before I was even born. Nonna used to document everything. At the time, I used to find it annoying, but now I can understand why she did it.

Seeing Seb looking so carefree and happy makes my heart crumble in my chest.

"Oh, look, Ellie. This is my mom when she was your age." I turn the album over to her, showing the black and white photograph. "She was cute, wasn't she?"

Ellie doesn't seem interested in what I am showing her, returning to her new toy. I study the picture again, a strange feeling coming over me.

My eyes are drawn to Ellie once more, and then back to the album…

Then my stomach twists into a knot.

What the fuck is this?

They look almost identical.

No, that can't be. This makes no sense. Maybe what they say is right—all babies look the same.

But there is no way I can be wrong about this. Apart from Ellie's eyes–which are the same as Chloe's–her dark hair, her round cheeks, and even her little nose look the same as my mom's.

What the actual fuck?

My mind flies into a frenzy, trying to do the math. Is it even possible for Ellie to be mine instead of Mateo's? Chloe told me she's what... a year and a half? Or a few months older than that? Or is she younger?

She also mentioned that she found out about her pregnancy after she left New York. She didn't go into detail, but it never occurred to me that Ellie could be my daughter.

Everything in my body is screaming at me that I'm right, but it can't be.

Because if it is, why didn't Chloe tell me? If Ellie was mine, she wouldn't keep it a secret from me, would she?

Or does she even know about it?

2 3

THE TRUTH

Chloe

I OPEN MY EYES SLOWLY AND STRETCH MY ARMS OVER MY HEAD, noticing the darkness enveloping my room. A fading beam of moonlight shines through the open curtains, but apart from that, it's pitch black around me. I look at my nightstand clock, realizing it's almost 7:00 P.M. It takes me a few seconds to remember why I'm in bed at this time of day.

What the hell happened to me? I don't feel sick at all, just slightly exhausted, but I simply blacked out after Tony ordered me to return to bed because he thought I had a fever.

It might be that I'm under a lot of stress lately without even noticing it. With everything that has happened—my father's death, moving back to New York, breaking free from Mateo, the sudden fake marriage with Tony, and me having to confront my own feelings for him—it all might have unconsciously taken its toll on my health.

With a sudden start, I remember the party my mother was supposed to throw today. It should be happening already. However,

Tony did mention something about taking care of it himself. I'm sure he tried to cancel it, but knowing my mother, I can only expect she didn't accept it nicely. She was also supposed to bring Ellie back to me, and I can only imagine she had to take her back when Tony informed her I wasn't feeling well.

Feeling somewhat renewed, I climb out of bed and head to the dark hallway. The house is sounds completely empty and silent.

Where is everyone?

I go downstairs, hoping to find someone, but the place seems to be uninhabited. Arriving in the living room, I find Ellie's diaper bag on top of the table, but she's nowhere around. Neither is Tony or my mother. But then a giggle echoes across the house, coming from the backyard, and I head there immediately.

The sight I encounter is not what I'm expecting at all. Ellie is seated on a picnic blanket, playing with some toys I don't recognize. She looks happy and entertained, but the person watching her is not my mom. It's Tony. He's seated on the last stair of the porch, his back turned to me as he watches Ellie playing by herself.

His shoulders look tense and stiff from where I'm standing, and I wonder if he's mad he had to watch her while I was sleeping. Why would my mother even leave her with him?

However, it also occurs to me that Tony is not like that. I've seen the way he looks at Ellie whenever she's near him. He might not be experienced with kids, but he would never be mad because he had to stay with her.

"Tony? Where's my mother? What about the party?" I ask softly, but he doesn't even move from where he's sitting.

In fact, he doesn't even look at me when he replies, "I called it off, and she left."

I swallow hard. Something doesn't feel right. He isn't being rude to me or anything, but something about his tone doesn't sit well with me. He sounds… upset.

"Is everything okay? Why did she leave Ellie here?" I add, taking a few steps forward and narrowing my eyes with confusion. "You didn't have to stay with her. You're always so busy."

Tony shrugs slightly. "I offered to stay with her until you woke up. It wasn't a big deal," he tells me coldly, still not looking at me. "I am her *stepfather* after all. It's only right that I do my part."

He gets to his feet and walks to Ellie, picking her up from the ground and finally turning to look at me. But I almost wish he hadn't. I hate the way his eyes are dark as he takes me in, his jaw clenched and his brows furrowed. He looks more than just upset. He seems mad at me, but I have no idea why or about what. If he was the one who offered to watch Ellie, why would he be mad?

Could it be about the party? Again, I'm not to blame since *he* was the one who authorized my mother to organize it in the first place. And *he* was the one who called it off.

"Is something wrong?" I finally ask, my voice quivering a little.

"Who is Ellie's father?" he asks bluntly, his voice barely above a whisper.

I feel like I've been hit by a bomb. My stomach sinks, my mouth falls agape, but no sound comes out of it. I'm frozen, glued to the floor as if I'm a marble statue.

What does he mean by that question? There's no way he can know the truth. My mother would never tell him, and I sure as hell didn't say anything. Could he have made that connection himself? I never thought it was evident from Ellie's features that she looks like him, but on second thought, *maybe she does?*

No one has ever said anything about it, though, not even a word. I'd assume they would have said something if they thought that was a possibility.

"What do you mean? I-I..." I stammer, but Tony cuts me off.

"Who is her father, Chloe?" he insists, his eyes scanning me like an X-ray machine.

"I told you, it's Mateo," I manage to say.

"Don't lie to me," he snarls in a low voice, through gritted teeth. "I know the truth, but I want to hear you say it. Who is her father?"

No, no, no, no, no. This can't be happening!

How did he find out? This wasn't supposed to happen...

Tony's eyes stare at me hard as he awaits my answer. But no

matter how hard I try, I can't force myself to say anything. I can't give him the answer he wants. I open and close my mouth several times, but I can't get out a single word.

"I found a picture of my mom when she was Ellie's age, and they look exactly the same," Tony continues, struggling to restrain himself from yelling at me. His tone is so accusatory that I can only imagine how much he must hate me right now. "And I did the math. The timeline is so obvious that I don't know how I was so stupid not to notice it before."

It kills me to hear his voice cracking and see the judgement in his eyes. I can barely stand; my knees threaten to buckle under me at any moment .

My world spins, and I can't understand how this happened. How did things fall apart so quickly? I thought after our date last night, even though it was fake, the situation between us would improve. But what was I thinking? Of course, I could never be happy with Tony. Not when our relationship is built on a lie in the first place. And I've been keeping the biggest secret from him for over a year.

I feel weak, exposed, but worst of all, I feel guilty.

"I'm sorry," I whisper, but my voice is so quiet I doubt he hears me.

Tony stares at me for what feels like an eternity, his silence shattering my soul into irreparable pieces. He will never forgive me. I would never forgive me if I were in his shoes, either.

What kind of human am I to hide his daughter from him? When I found out about my pregnancy, I had plenty of excuses that seemed reasonable in my head, but right now, looking at Tony and seeing how heartbroken he is, I can't think of a single reason to explain to him why I did this.

When he realizes I'm unable to say anything else, he nods as if accepting I won't give him the answer he needs. He walks forward and hands Ellie to me, not daring to spare me a glance.

"I'll be back later," he informs me dryly and heads through the back door, disappearing inside the house.

The only noise I hear after that is the front door slamming as he leaves me alone in this huge house with our daughter in my arms. She's the only thing I need to be happy right now, but why do I feel like I just lost my entire world?

2 4

ACCEPTANCE

Tony

I COULDN'T STAY AT HOME. AFTER I SAW THE PICTURES OF MY MOM AND realized that Ellie was, in fact, my daughter, my entire world collapsed. I couldn't think straight. I couldn't understand what made Chloe keep this huge secret from me for so long. How could she live under the same roof as me now, with *our* daughter, and not tell me the truth, not tell me Ellie is mine?

I have missed so much. And the worst part is that it wasn't even my choice. I wasn't given a choice from the start. She had chosen that *for* me. No matter how hard I try to find a reasonable explanation as to why Chloe did this to me, I always end up hitting a dead end.

There is no excuse. There is no reason....

Why would she allow someone like Mateo to be around her and Ellie when she could have come to me sooner? Why did she think she could keep such an important secret from me? What gave her the right?

I feel overwhelmed with emotions I don't want to feel. I don't want to hate Chloe, or question her reasons, but it's hard not to. The entire time I was waiting for her to wake up, I tried to keep Ellie entertained, but I couldn't do it. All I managed to do was stare at her while she played with Seb's toys, trying to make sense of what I just discovered. My brain was a mess.

When Chloe finally showed up in the backyard and asked if everything was okay, I couldn't pretend I was fine. I couldn't keep my doubts and feelings inside any longer. I choked with unsaid words, my emotions boiling over. I had to ask her, to confirm my intuition.

The truth was obvious to me when she couldn't give me an answer. Her stammering was everything I needed to know.

And that's the reason why I'm now in my usual booth at Aphrodite's Lounge with three empty glasses of whiskey on the table and another one in my hand. I couldn't stay at home. I couldn't look at her—or Ellie, for that matter—without feeling like I've been betrayed.

I still don't know how to handle this whole situation, and it kills me not to be in control of it.

There's a very boring strip show happening on stage, but my focus is on my whiskey, my mind miles away from here.

"Everything all right, Boss?" Armando's voice startles me. I snap my head up just in time to see him sit down across from me, unceremoniously. I sip my drink, raising my eyebrows at him over the rim of the glass, but he doesn't seem deterred. Instead, he points out, "You seem concerned about something."

"Do I?" I hiss through clenched teeth. Armando is such a pain in the ass sometimes. "Have you noticed how nosy you've been lately?" I ask, leaning back in my seat.

But the motherfucker only chuckles, mocking me. "A few times, yes. I still think it's my duty to help you with marital advice. Is it something I can help you with? I thought the date last night went well."

It did. But with everything that happened after it, the date seems insignificant now, like it happened ages ago. However, I'm not in the mood to talk to Armando about any of it, especially not about the fact that I just found out I'm a father, so I decide to change the subject instead.

"Any news from the cartel? Are they sniffing around somewhere? Have we seen anything strange lately?" I ask taking another drink.

Not hearing from Mateo and his cartel has been fucking with my mind and my sleep the past few days. I have no idea what he's planning, and I must admit it freaks me out a little. Not because of me, but now, more than ever, I have to protect Chloe and Ellie from him. I've always cared for them, but knowing Ellie is a piece of me changes everything.

"Not yet," Armando answers, his tone apologetic. "But I have ears and eyes on the ground all the way to Jersey, so if they come up here, we'll hear about it, Boss," he assures me.

It's not enough reassurance, but I suppose it's all I can get right now. I nod, chugging down the remnants of my drink and slamming the glass on the table in front of me.

I have to go home. I still haven't decided what to say to Chloe or even if I want to say anything to her at all, but I can't leave things the way I did. She needs to give me an explanation. I'm still pissed off, hurt, heartbroken even. I gave her enough time to think about what she did, and I don't think this conversation can be postponed. We live in the same house now, and we still need to pretend to be married. I won't be able to do that if we don't discuss this.

"I'm going home," I tell Armando, who's looking at me with curiosity in his eyes. "Keep me updated," I order before getting to my feet and walking toward the exit. I ignore the strippers calling me, waving for me to join them in other private booths, and head to my car, my footsteps determined, even though I feel everything but.

I have a massive headache, and during the entire ride home, I can't stop thinking about Chloe's shocked face when I asked her who's Ellie's father. She didn't have to utter a single word to confirm it's me; her eyes were enough of an answer.

I grit my teeth, my knuckles turning white as I tighten my grip on the steering wheel.

"Fuck!" I yell, punching the wheel several times, hoping the pain in my hand will be enough to vent my anger. But it's not.

When I get to my driveway a few minutes later, I lean back on the headrest, closing my eyes and taking long, deep breaths. After I manage to steady myself for the confrontation that's sure to come, I step out of the car and go inside. The house is dark and quiet, except for a beam of light coming from the living room and a murmur of voices from what I assume is the TV.

Chloe is probably still awake.

As soon as she sees me passing by the door, she points the remote control at the TV and turns it off, turning to face me. Her legs are crossed beneath her on the couch, the delicate fabric of her flowered dress sweeping over her thighs, soft and inviting. The vulnerability in her pleading, beautiful eyes almost undoes me right there. My fists ball at my sides, every muscle in my body taut with frustration.

How the fuck can she look so hot when I'm this mad at her? It's not fair.

"Tony," she calls in a whisper, her soft voice rattling me. I curse myself inwardly for being such an idiot to fall for her charm every time. "Can we please talk?" she begs.

"It depends," I say bitterly, grasping for my anger not to slip away from me. I won't let her fool me. Not again. "Are you going to give me a stupid excuse for why you hid the fact that I have a daughter with you? Because if that's your plan, I won't fall for it, Chloe," I growl under my breath, my eyes narrowing at her.

Chloe doesn't seem to mind my rage. Instead, she gets to her feet, coming toward me, her footsteps slow but determined. "I'm truly sorry, Tony. But I did what I had to do to keep myself safe while I was pregnant," she tells me.

I snort. "Are you fucking kidding me right now?" I snap at her, struggling to keep my voice low. I'm sure Ellie is sleeping in her room upstairs, and the last thing I need right now is to wake her up. "I don't recall you being safe with Mateo. In fact, isn't that the whole fucking reason you and I got married in the first place? Is that the only explanation you can come up with?"

This is a mistake. I thought I was ready to hear what she had to say, but I'm definitely not. I can't stand the fact that she is trying to tell me she wouldn't be safe with me while the entire reason we got married is because I am the only one who can protect her from her asshole of an ex.

"I can't do this. This is fucking insane," I add in a hiss, turning and walking away from her.

But before I can even get to the door, her tiny, warm hand grabs my wrist, forcing me to stop.

"Wait," she whispers. "Please, Tony. Just let me explain."

25

OVERDUE CONFRONTATION

Chloe

"I can't do this. This is fucking insane," Tony says to me, turning and walking away.

I grab him by the wrist before he has the chance to disappear from my sight. I've been waiting for him to return home for hours. After he left, so angry at me, I put Ellie to bed and took a shower, taking the time I needed to get my mind in the right place.

Tony was never supposed to find out about Ellie this way. I did plan to tell him eventually, but with everything that's happened in my life recently, I couldn't drop another bomb on him like that. I've imagined how it would be to tell Tony about it so many times during the past two years, but I didn't picture any of them being like this.

Sure, I figured he'd be mad at me, but the look in his eyes when I didn't answer him earlier, and the way he seems disgusted by me right now, is more than I can handle.

"Wait. Please, Tony. Just let me explain," I beg, releasing him.

I'm struggling to fight back tears that are desperate to fall. I thought I cried enough in the shower, but I was clearly wrong.

"What else is there for you to explain, Chloe?" Tony retorts, turning to look at me. If his eyes could fire bullets, I'm sure I'd be dead right now. "You know, I tried to think of several reasons as to why you'd keep this from me, but no matter how hard I tried, nothing made sense. I never thought you'd be capable of something like this."

He sounds so hurt and disappointed at me that I can feel my heart breaking inside my chest. No matter how much I hate it, I have to agree with him. It'd never be something that I'd willingly do. If my life was different, if I didn't have to protect my family, if things were easier...

But that's not the case. My life might have been comfortable, but it has never been easy.

"That time I came to New York and we... slept together," I begin, hesitating a little. I guess that's the moment I've been avoiding for so long. There's no more escape now. I have to get this done and over with. Even if it means Tony will hate me forever.

He probably already does anyway.

"Well, I had broken up with Mateo a few weeks before then," I carry on, lowering my gaze so I don't stammer under the intensity of his stare. "After I returned to Miami, I found out I was pregnant. I knew there was no way it could be anyone else's but yours."

I feel Tony stiffen in front of me, but I don't dare look at him.

"By then, Mateo was bullying his way back into my life, threatening me and my family. If he found out I was pregnant, from another man nonetheless...." I swallow hard, remembering the darkest days of my life. "I couldn't escape from him , so I had to make sure my family would be safe. I didn't know how to get away from him. I didn't know how to escape," I admit.

"Why didn't you come back to New York and ask for my help?" Tony asks bluntly. "Like you're doing now. I would have protected you. All of you."

I sneer, shaking my head. "You're the boss of the Saints. One of the most desirable men in the country. You would never have believed me. I grew up in this life. I know what it's like. I can only imagine how many women pound on your door, saying they are pregnant and demanding you take responsibility," I explain my point of view. "I was just another one-night-stand to you. Why should I assume you'd be—"

"That's not true," he cuts me off, his voice firm and serious. "You know damn well that's not how I see you."

"Come on, Tony." I roll my eyes at him. "We're both grown-ups. I never expected anything from you, and I say this with all due respect. I knew that night was a mistake, an outcome of a bad moment for both of us. We ran into each other unexpectedly, and, well, I guess we just let ourselves get carried away. It's human nature, isn't it?"

"Yes, it is. But that's not what happened between us," he argues, his forehead creased as he stares at me.

"Sure it was."

It wasn't. At least not to me. I always had a huge crush on him, but for multiple reasons, I never thought I had a chance with him. When we finally slept together, I assumed I was just another one night stand to him. But from the way he's speaking to me right now, the way he's looking at me, the way he's so adamant about wanting to be my savior and a part of my life, it makes me wonder if everything I've always assumed is incorrect.

Why does he have to be so confusing?

Tony takes a step forward, stopping just inches away from me. His cologne hits me, inebriating my senses and making me slightly dizzy. He towers over me, and I can't bring myself to look up. If I do, I'm sure I'll regret it. He's so close, I'm afraid to look him in the eyes and lose my bearings.

"You could never be considered a mistake, Chloe," he murmurs, his voice husky. My legs turn into jelly, and I bite my lower lip so as not to say anything. I don't trust my own voice at this moment. "You sure as hell weren't one to me."

I snap my head up to look at him, and before I know it, his lips are on mine, devouring me with desperation and passion. I moan involuntarily when he wraps one arm around my waist, pulling me flush against him, and the other reaches the back of my thigh, hoisting me up from the floor. His warm hand on my ass is enough to set me aflame.

I can't think about what we're doing, and to be honest, I don't want to. I've missed him so much that I can't find a single reason in me as to why this is wrong.

Tony walks us blindly backward to the couch, and I wrap my arms around his neck to steady myself. My legs are locked behind his back, securing me in his arms, even though I know there's no way he'll let me fall.

My core is on fire, and I hope he doesn't stop what he's doing. His tongue explores every inch of my mouth, and I can't find it in me to feel embarrassed about the moans escaping my throat. Clearly, he's aroused, so I let each whimper resound uninhibited.

Both of his hands are on my ass now, squeezing my flesh and enticing me even more. His legs suddenly bump into the couch, and I fall on my back, his body hovering over me. But he doesn't stop kissing me. In fact, Tony lowers his kiss from my jaw, to under my ear, and down to my neck.

I arch my back slightly, searching for some friction, anything that will help me satiate my desires. At this rate, Tony will undo me before he even takes off my clothes.

"Fuck, I missed you so much," he whispers against my skin, his mouth dangerously close to my cleavage. I'm glad I chose this dress after the shower. It's loose, the fabric soft and thin enough for it to feel like he's touching my skin directly. Tony's hand cups my breast and massaging it through my dress, and I feel everything.

"Oh, God," I hiss, arching my back again, granting him more space to touch me.

Tony chuckles while his mouth is still on my neck, and as if my frustration is the encouragement he needs, he lowers the kiss even more, kissing my nipples through the fabric.

I tug at his curly hair, trying to convey how much I love what he's doing. I'd love it even more if he would just get rid of this dress completely. I'm glad he can't hear my thoughts because I don't sound like myself. I've never been a prude, but I'm usually not this needy.

"Tony, please." I don't know exactly what I'm begging for—or maybe I do—but Tony will probably be able to interpret my few words. When he pulls away from me, his eyes darkened with lust and need, I wonder what he's about to do.

If he walks away from me, I might melt into a puddle on this couch.

"What are you doing?" I whine, my voice weak and barely audible.

"Are you sure about this?" he asks with uncertainty in his tone.

I widen my eyes at him. "Is that even a real question?"

Tony chuckles , his eyes lowering to my almost exposed breasts. My nipples are hard and visible through my dress, and I see the way his Adam's apple bobs up and down as he takes me in.

"If that isn't confirmation enough for you… " I say, boldly grabbing his hand and guiding it between my thighs, his fingertips edging my already soaked panties. My skin burns as I pull my underwear to the side with his finger, and I brace myself for what I'm sure is to come. "Maybe this will be."

26

AT LAST

Chloe

WHEN TONY'S FINGERS BRUSH AGAINST MY SENSITIVE, SWOLLEN CLIT, I whine, squirming under him. He hisses immediately, feeling my wetness soaking his fingertips, and his other hand, which is still on my breast, squeezes it hard.

"Shit, you're so wet, Chloe," he murmurs, lowering himself on me once more.

Then his hand pulls the top of my dress down, finally releasing my breasts. My mind threatens to explode when Tony takes one nipple in his mouth, licking and sucking it while his other hand plays with my slick heat. I'm overwhelmed with sensations, unsure of what to do with myself.

"Tony," I cry again.

I want him to send me over the edge, but I also want him to take as long as possible. He makes me feel so good, and we have barely even started. The one and only time we slept together, we were both drunk. And even though I still dream about that moment to this day, it isn't as clear to me as I wish it was.

I can't believe I'm getting to experience this again.

He doesn't seem to be concerned about my pleading because he's too focused on making me come undone with his fingers and mouth. His tongue savors my breasts, gently biting at my aroused nipples, while his fingers circle my clit, making me bounce my hips up and down, riding his fingers, desperate for some more friction.

"What do you say we take this dress off? It's getting in the way," he suggests with a grin, pulling away from me.

"I definitely agree," I reply between pants, already sitting up to help him remove it.

He pulls it over my head, and as soon as I'm free of the extra layer, I watch Tony taking me in hungrily in only my panties. His eyes stay on my breasts long enough until I motion at his torso, my eyebrows raised.

"Aren't you the one who is overdressed now?" I tease, smirking at him.

His shirt is on the floor before I can even finish my sentence. Then he lowers me back on the couch, his hands guiding my knees up and spreading my legs as he reaches for the hem of my underwear.

"What are you doing?" I ask, biting my lower lip provocatively.

I know damn well what he's about to do, and I can't wait for it.

"Making sure you regret ever lying to me," he tells me in a warning, but also sensual, tone.

My jaw drops with his audacity, but when he slides my panties down my legs and tosses them away, lowering his head between my thighs, I have to bite my lip as hard as I can so I don't wake Ellie up.

Tony laps at me as if I'm the most delicious delicacy in the world. He drinks me in, sucking and licking at my most sensitive spot, and my eyes roll to the back of my head as I try to control myself.

"Tony, I'm about to…" I trail off, unable to finish my sentence before that familiar wave of electrical shock courses through my entire being. "Shit!"

He doesn't stop working his magic while I ride my orgasm, my core spasming with pleasure.

Then he straightens up, pulling back to look down at me. I'm panting and sweating, my legs shaking and my core still tightened.

"That wasn't fair," I tell him, not sounding the slightest mad at him for making me come so quickly. However, I do hope he continues. I'm not ready to go to bed yet. Not until he claims me completely.

"I told you I'd make you regret it," he jokes, his lips curling up in a smirk.

I look him up and down, noticing the bulge in his pants. Good, he doesn't seem ready to stop, and I hope he doesn't mean he's making me pay by keeping me wanting more. If making me regret it means he will leave me hanging, desperate for more of him, I'm doomed.

"Are these staying on?" I ask, gesturing to his pants. I lick my lower lip, hoping that will be enough for him to grant me my wish.

"I don't know. You tell me," he says, not moving an inch.

I reach for his belt, unbuckling it while looking at him, not daring to break eye contact. My hand brushes over his erection, and that's when he winces, forcing a smile out of me. I pull his pants down and stroke him through his boxers, causing him to squirm under my touch. I massage him, and his hand darts to my hair, yanking my head back, forcing me to look up.

"I hope you know what you're doing. I won't be able to stop," he warns me, struggling to restrain himself. But then I pull his boxers down, setting him free, and I don't need to say anything else before he pushes me back on the couch.

Tony steps out of his pants and boxers and returns to his initial position between my legs. He studies me once more, watching me as if I'm the rarest, most beautiful jewel in the world.

"I can't believe I get to have you again," he murmurs, mesmerized. It makes me feel so beautiful, desired, like all women should feel when they are about to give themselves completely to someone they care about.

I want to say I've always been his, but I don't. I'm not ready for that next step. I don't want to overthink this moment, so I shove those thoughts away, focusing on here and now.

"What are you waiting for then?" I ask instead, encouraging him to take me. "I'm yours for the taking."

I spread my legs slightly, giving him more space. The tip of his cock brushes against my entrance, and I swallow hard. *God, this man will be the death of me. I'm sure of it.*

The fire in his eyes is so intense that I force myself to hold his gaze. Then, without warning, he plunges himself inside me all the way, making me choke on a groan. I'd forgotten how thick his cock is. But he fits me perfectly, like no one else ever has. It's like we were made for each other.

Tony hisses again, closing his eyes and burying his face on the nape of my neck while he thrusts into me slowly. "Fuck, you're so perfect," he murmurs against my skin, causing shivers to run down my spine, all the way to my core.

We move in sync, my hips meeting his as he speeds up. I hold onto his shoulders, grasping for some control, but it's pointless. Especially when I'm about to have another orgasm any moment now.

"You're so beautiful, Chloe," he whispers, and I close my eyes, only feeling the sensations he is causing me.

This is purely sexual, passionate longing, but my heart seems about to explode with the countless emotions he evokes in me. I never thought this would happen again. But now, here I am, sharing the most intimate experience possible with Tony. And even though I'm not supposed to overthink it, I can't shake the feeling that it seems to be much more than just sex—for both of us.

I don't want to give myself false hopes, but when Tony stares into my eyes as we both come together, there is no way I'm imagining the way his eyes sparkle with a different intensity.

It's something I can't explain; I can only feel it.

I might be wrong, but right now, I don't care. I choose to believe it's true. Because I don't think I have ever felt happier and more fulfilled in my life before. For a brief moment, it feels like I can finally have all I ever wanted—Tony and Ellie.

For a brief moment, it feels like Tony actually loves me.

After we finish, Tony doesn't move away from me. We are both panting heavily, composing ourselves, and I remain quiet, not wanting to break this dreamy moment. I don't want to go back to being angry with each other. I don't want to go back to being his fake wife.

Then he stares into my eyes again, his fingers gently caressing my cheek, observing me with a slight frown on his face.

"What?" I ask softly.

He shakes his head almost imperceptibly. "Nothing. I was just wondering if you wanted to sleep in my bed tonight. I'm not ready to let you go yet."

My heart starts beating rapidly again with his offer.

I'm glad he said that because it's exactly what I wanted to hear.

"You don't have to if you don't want to," he adds, misinterpreting my hesitation.

"No, I want to," I tell him firmly, holding his gaze. "I'd love to, actually."

2 7

THE NEXT MORNING

Chloe

After Tony and I make love in the living room, my senses start to return to me slowly, and I suddenly feel embarrassed for my behavior. It occurred to me that I acted like a desperate, horny teenager. Not having sex in a while did that to me, but even so, I wish I had controlled myself better.

However, when he asked me to sleep with him afterward, in his bed, I didn't hesitate in agreeing. I grasped the opportunity like I'd fallen into the ocean, and it was a lifesaver. I didn't know what to expect from the next morning, so if I could have a little more time with Tony, I'd take it.

We didn't have sex again, even though I desperately wanted to, but having his arms around me while I drifted off to sleep made me feel safer than ever before. His scent calmed me immensely, and his slow breathing, close to my ear, sounded like a lullaby.

The first rays of sunshine beam through the half-closed curtains of his bedroom early in the morning, and I stretch lazily, turning on my back. A heavy weight on my stomach makes me realize Tony's arm is still wrapped around me. I turn to look at him and his peaceful features, his eyelashes beautifully curved over his shut eyelids. He seems almost ethereal when he doesn't have the weight of the entire world on his shoulders.

A faded whining echoes through the closed door, and I sit up in a jolt. Thankfully, this doesn't wake Tony. It only makes him grunt and turn to the other side. When I hear Ellie's cries getting louder, I hurry out of Tony's room, grabbing his shirt from the floor on the way out to cover myself, and getting to Ellie's room in less than ten seconds. She's standing in her crib, holding the bars with her little hands, her face stained with tears.

"Oh, no need to cry. Mommy is here now," I say softly as I walk toward her and pick her up. "Good morning, baby." I give her a kiss on the cheek, taking in her scent, so sweet and soft it makes me melt instantly.

She cries for another minute until I manage to calm her down with shushes and murmured songs.

"All right, so, Mommy is going to get you dressed, and then we're heading downstairs for breakfast, okay? What do you want to eat today?" I ask, putting her back in the crib and walking to her closet. I choose a yellow dress with little white dots that my mom bought for her. "Bananas? Or maybe some scrambled eggs?" I suggest.

"Nana," she mumbles as an answer, a cute smile plastered on her face.

"Oh, you're saying 'nana' now?" I muse, surprised, my eyes widening at her. "That's a new word!" I squeak, excited.

I quickly change her diaper and get her dressed before carrying her to my room to get dressed myself. Even though I'd love to wear Tony's shirt for the rest of the day, I need to look somewhat presentable in case someone from the Saints drops by. I put on a T-shirt and leggings then head to the kitchen, sitting Ellie in her high chair and getting her a plate of sliced bananas.

When I start preparing pancakes for Tony and me, the doorbell rings. Before I have the chance to get to answer, I hear the password being typed in, and a second later, my mom yells from the doorway. "Can I come in?"

"Haven't you already?" I mumble to myself before answering her. "We're in the kitchen, Mom!"

As soon as she walks in, I narrow my eyes at her. "This isn't your house. You shouldn't barge in like that," I scold her, although gently.

It's not like Tony would be walking around the house naked or anything, not with me and Ellie living here, but images from last night flood back to my mind, and I fight the blush creeping up my cheeks. If my mother walked in on us like that... I'd die of embarrassment.

I have no idea if having sex again with Tony is even a possibility, but my mom needs to have some boundaries.

She tosses her arms up in surrender, widening her eyes at me and looking anything but regretful. "Sorry. Bad habit, I know. I was just worried about you." Then she scans me up and down, setting her hands on her hips. "You look well," she points out in a disapproving tone. "You didn't pretend to be sick just so I couldn't throw my party, did you?"

"Wasn't it supposed to be *my* party? And no, Mother, I did not. I wasn't feeling well yesterday," I answer, rolling my eyes and turning my attention back to my pancakes, which almost burned because of her.

She clears her throat, walking toward Ellie and swiping her thumb over her chin to clean off some banana. She's just sitting down in the chair beside Ellie when Tony strolls into the kitchen, fully dressed for the day in his black suit with his phone pressed to his ear. His face is stoic, but there's a slight crease between his eyebrows that sets me on edge.

He's listening to whoever is talking on the other end while stooping to give Ellie a kiss on the forehead, before coming over to peck my cheek. The touch is brief, yet it leaves my skin tingling and asking for more. Tony nods at my mother, quickly addressing her, and then he's off to whatever he has to do today. Or whatever problem he is dealing with on the phone.

The door closing behind him leaves a trail of silence, my mother's shocked expression evaluating me.

"What the hell was that about?" she finally asks after a whole minute in utter silence, her eyebrows raised so high they almost disappear under her bangs.

"What?" I play dumb. I don't want to tell her what happened between Tony and me, but knowing her, she already realizes something's up.

"Don't take me for an idiot, Chloe. What was that about?" she insists, not taking her eyes off me, gesturing to the door Tony just walked out of.

I sigh, turning off the heat and leaning back on the kitchen sink.

"Tony knows," I tell her bluntly.

She pales. "What do you mean *he knows?*"

"He knows about Ellie," I clarify.

"I thought we were going to keep it a secret, even after the wedding," she argues, her voice weak. I don't blame her. I felt the same fear yesterday when he told me he'd figured it all out.

"Well, apparently he found this picture of his mom when she was Ellie's age, and they look exactly the same," I explain calmly. "I couldn't deny the obvious."

"Shit," Mom hisses under her breath. Thankfully, Ellie is too entertained making a mess with her food that I'm not as bothered as I'd be if she was paying attention to us, and my mom cursed in front of her. "Okay, well… you clearly have things to work out, so I'll take Ellie to spend the day with me."

"Tony just left," I tell her, even though she saw it herself. "I have no idea if he'll be back before midnight."

She shrugs, getting to her feet. "I'm sure he will. I'll get her bag while she finishes eating. And you go and get yourself more presentable. You're the queen of the Saints now. Please…"

Mom is out of the kitchen before I can think of a retort. She wouldn't be herself if she didn't chastise my appearance. I'm at home, for goodness sake. I don't need to be uncomfortable in a Chanel suit like she always is when there is no one around to see it.

Half an hour later, I'm kissing Ellie goodbye and preparing to officially start my day. The house is as neat as it can be, and I don't see much to do other than put some of Ellie's clothes in the washing machine and take care of the breakfast dishes. After I'm done with those, I grab a book I'm taking longer than I'd like to admit to finish and spread myself on the couch.

Tony is not home yet, and like I told Mom, I don't think he'll be back any time soon. To be honest, I'm dreading the moment he returns. Sure, he gave me a kiss before leaving, but we didn't get to really talk about how he feels now that he knows he's Ellie's father.

And now, we have another subject to add to our conversation–the sex last night. What is he going to say about it? Is he going to say anything at all? What if he thinks that was a mistake? He made sure to let me know last night that I was never considered a mistake to him before, but still… everything between us is so confusing that I don't know what to think.

A knock on the front door pulls me from my reverie. I frown, wondering why someone would knock instead of ringing the doorbell. I scolded my mom about barging into the house, but I don't think she learned that quickly. She would also ring the doorbell like she did the first time, not knock when there's a bell right there.

What if this is another one of Tony's mistresses? A voice in my head questions.

I'm definitely not in the mood to face another bitch this morning. One time was more than enough for me. I'm not the type to get physical most of the time–in fact, I'm usually the opposite–but that woman got on my nerves in a way no one has ever managed to do.

If there's another woman like her outside, I don't know what I'll do.

When the knocking gets insistent, I stand and slowly, cautiously open the door, afraid to find out who is on the other side.

My jaw drops to the floor as I stare at the last person I expected to see on my doorstep this morning.

"Hello, Chloe."

2 8

FROM BOSS TO BOSS

Tony

CHLOE'S SCENT ON MY SHEETS WOKE ME UP, BUT NOT FINDING HER beside me left a sour taste in my mouth. For a moment, I wished she was there with me so we could spend some time together, even if it was just talking. I wouldn't mind doing more if she wanted, though. Judging from the way she groaned and squirmed under me last night, I can only assume she liked it.

Now, I can finally remember what she looks like when she's under me. I can finally remember her moans when I pleased her. I can still feel her soft skin on my fingers.... God, she is so damn perfect it hurts.

I wish I could've stop time and just had her to myself for an entire day, not having to worry about anything other than making her happy and satisfied. That'd be a fucking dream.

But when I stepped out of the shower and saw an incoming call from Dante, I stiffened on the spot. He doesn't normally call me, so I picked it up immediately. When I heard he was in town, I stormed out

171

of the room, quickly kissing Ellie and Chloe goodbye before heading out of the house.

It didn't go unnoticed that Nicky was already there, probably prying to see if I was lying about Chloe's condition yesterday, but I didn't have time to indulge her. I rushed to my car, and that's why, right now, I'm parking outside the stately home Dante and Eleni still own here in the city.

Since Dante told me over the phone to just come inside whenever I arrived, I show myself in. As soon as I cross the foyer, two-year-old Alexander runs toward the kitchen, his five-year-old sister Tasia chasing him, drawing giggles from him while he flees from her grasp. They don't seem to notice my presence, so I follow after them carefully so as not to scare them.

"Come on, guys! Your breakfast is ready," Dante calls from the kitchen. "Can we sit down and have a proper meal? No playing until you've finished your pancakes."

"I'm here!" I announce to no one in particular, hoping Dante hears me from the hallway. I get to the doorway just in time to see him set the kids' plates in front of them on the table. He snaps his head up as soon as I'm in sight.

"Hey there, man!" he greets me, gesturing for me to come inside. "Say hello to Uncle Tony, guys."

"Hi, Uncle Tony," both kids say in unison.

"Hello, everyone. That looks like a very good breakfast, huh?" I note, staring at their plates filled with fruit cut into animal shapes, pancakes with smiley faces, and toast with a bit of grape jelly. I raise my eyebrows at Dante, who simply shrugs at me.

"The things you learn to do when you're a father," he explains, turning to the counter and pouring two mugs of black coffee.

I'm thankful when he hands me one. Missing Chloe's breakfast almost killed me. Her pancakes smelled delicious when I left, and I almost told Dante he'd have to wait to see me.

But I was too curious to know why he showed up unannounced with his entire family, so I came rushing over as soon as I heard from him. I look around, missing one person.

"Where is Eleni?" I ask.

"She's on her way to your house, actually," he tells me with a grin. I'm sure he heard about Chloe and I, but I'm not looking forward to talking to him about it.

"Care to tell me why you're here?" I add instead, changing the subject abruptly.

"I had to close a deal with an exporter for my restaurant... and underground olive oil smuggling," he answers nonchalantly, as if this is just another day at the office for him. Which, honestly, it kind of is. I guess you can take the man out of the mafia, but you can never take the mafia out of the man.

"Smuggling, huh?" I tease, lowering my voice so the kids don't hear us.

Dante shrugs again, sipping his coffee. I do the same, welcoming the hot liquid into my system. It tastes surprisingly good. "Never took you for a house-husband," I add in a joking tone.

"Like I said, the things you need to learn..." he chuckles, gesturing with his head to the open door that leads to the backyard.

I follow him, leaning against the door and folding my arms over my chest.

"So, back to the subject of why Eleni is on the way to your house.... A little bird told me about you and Chloe being a thing now. I'm a bit reluctant to offer you my congratulations," Dante tells me honestly.

I nod, clenching my jaw. I can't blame him. I wouldn't offer my congratulations, either. When he decided to get married and start his new life with Eleni, I couldn't understand why.

"What the hell were you thinking, man?" he continues, but his tone is playful, almost teasing. I look at him with a frown. "Chloe is way too good for you," he notes.

A snort escapes my lips. I was not expecting him to say that at all. "I couldn't agree more," I concede. "She definitely is."

Dante glances behind him to make sure the kids are behaving then turns his attention back to me.

"Did anyone tell you what actually happened?" I have no idea who he heard the news from, but as far as I'm concerned, other than Nicky and Armando, no one knows the truth behind my marriage to Chloe.

"Hmm, not really. But from what I know about you, I'm sure you wouldn't rush into something like this if it weren't for a good reason," Dante points out. "Is it bad?"

I nod, the picture of Chloe's bruises flashing before my eyes. That fucking image has haunted me every single night since I saw them. I had to look away while we had sex last night so I didn't get distracted by the faded scars I spotted on her arms and back. Otherwise I would've had to stop and hunt the motherfucker down right then and make him pay.

'She's in a tough spot," I answer, choosing to leave the details out. I don't want to share Chloe's secrets, even if it's to someone I trust completely. "The De La Cruz cartel is after her."

Dante's eyes widen with surprise. "Fuck…" he whispers.

"Yeah, precisely," I murmur.

"You know I'm not getting myself involved in any of that anymore, man," he says apologetically. "I trust you'll do the right thing, though. I really hope you get this sorted out sooner rather than later."

I nod, hoping to convey my gratitude even though he can't do anything to help me. He chose to step away from this life, and I gladly accepted his former position, so I can't ask him for help. We didn't always see eye to eye, but I trust him. And I guess I could use his experience as a married man to try and understand my situation with Chloe.

I have no idea what to expect from her, from us, after last night. I don't want to scare her. I'm not even sure if I want to *be* with her—completely—knowing how risky that can be for her and Ellie.

I'm lost, and more than ever, I have no idea what to do when it comes to her.

Dante could help me understand my confusing feelings, but before I have the chance to think of a way to word it without sounding like a loser, my phone buzzes in my pocket with a text message from Cal.

'Need to meet ASAP.'

I feel Dante's eyes on me while I reply to Cal saying that I'm on my way.

"Still enjoying running New York?" he asks smugly.

I look up to see him grinning at me, amusement in his eyes.

"Wouldn't have it any other way," I tell him bitterly. "Having a wife does complicate things though," I admit, shoving my phone back in my pocket.

"Reschedule?" Dante offers, gesturing between us with his mug. "Maybe with a glass of bourbon next time?"

"Just text me the time and place," I agree, patting him on the shoulder and going back into the kitchen, placing my cup on the counter and turning to the kids. "I have to go now. It was great to see you. You're growing so fast I'm afraid you'll be bigger than me next time we see each other."

They both giggle, and I wave goodbye to them before seeing myself out.

I just hope whatever Cal has to tell me gets us closer to ending this fucking nightmare with the Miami cartel.

2 9

GIRL TALK

Chloe

"ELENI?" I BLURT OUT IN SHOCK.

My old friend smiles at me from the doorway, her newborn cradled in her arms. He is so cute, his round cheeks reddened by the chilly breeze outside.

"Oh, my God! Come inside!" I rush her, urging her to get out of the cold weather with her baby. "Are you crazy? What are you doing here? Didn't you just give birth?" My mouth is agape as I take them both in.

Eleni chuckles, rocking the baby, who looks like he's almost asleep, his little eyes blinking heavily. "This is Ilias," she tells me with amusement in her voice. "And yes, I did. But that's one of the perks of having a private jet. I get to travel more comfortably. How have you been? I missed you a lot." She manages to give me a hug while still holding Ilias, and I welcome it, having missed her as well.

"I missed you, too. And I don't even know where to start," I admit, guiding her toward the living room. "I can't believe you're here. Come on, I'll make some coffee. Do you want decaf?" I think back on Ellie's newborn days and my mom's insistence that Ellie wouldn't sleep if I

177

started drinking coffee again since I was breastfeeding her, but Eleni gives me a knowing smile.

"Do you have tea?"

"Yeah, of course." I motion for her to sit and move into the kitchen, pouring myself another cup of coffee and starting on her tea. "So, what brings you back to the US so suddenly?" I ask when I return to the living room and set the cup in front of her on the table.

"Dante had some business to handle, and I wanted to bring the kids to get to know the city. And well, I also missed my friends," Eleni explains. "We thought it'd be okay to come now, after staying out of the country for such a long time. Life has just been... easier, you know?"

I nod, understanding her completely.

"I am so happy for you," I tell her, grabbing her hand and squeezing it lightly. "You deserve everything you have today."

"Thank you, Chloe." She smiles at me. "I don't have to ask you to know there's something going on in your life. I'm here if you want to talk. I don't mean to brag, but I think if anyone can understand the hard life of being the mafia boss's wife, that would be me."

We both chuckle, and I take a deep breath. Eleni is right. My situation is so delicate that I can't talk to anyone about it. My mother is biased, and even though I love her, she doesn't think the same way I do. We barely agree on things, and Eleni has experienced so many situations already that I just know she will be able to help me figure this one out. Or at least help me get through this in a less painful and confusing way.

"Like I said, I don't even know where to start..." I murmur, sipping from my coffee. "You remember I told you about Mateo, right?"

"Briefly, yes," she answers with a nod. I kept in touch with Eleni during the years after she moved away from the city, but with her pregnancies and everything that happened to me, it wasn't easy to share so much over the phone. She knows about my "*marriage*" to Tony, and about Ellie, of course, but other than that, I don't recall telling her much more.

"He is a very possessive and toxic person. By the time I realized who he was, I couldn't get away," I begin, my voice low. "He threatened me and my family over and over again. And he made sure to prove his point whenever I confronted him."

Eleni's eyes fall to my arms, and since I'm not wearing a long sleeve shirt this morning, it's obvious she can see my scars and make the connection herself. She swallows hard, her eyes finding mine with an unspoken compassion. I hold back my tears and carry on, not wanting to shed anymore tears over what Mateo did to me.

"When my father died, I knew I couldn't stay there anymore. I had to run away before it was too late," I continue. "That's when I decided to come to Tony for help. I knew he wouldn't turn his back on me. And if anyone could protect me and Ellie, that someone would be him."

"That's true," she agrees firmly. "How did he react when he found out about Mateo? I assume he knows who the man is, right?"

"He does, yes. And he sort of freaked out," I reply. "I don't think he understood how bad the situation was until he learned Mateo was from the De La Cruz cartel. Then he came up with this idea of a fake marriage, and well, here we are."

Eleni takes a deep breath, leaning back on the couch more comfortably, now that Ilias has fallen asleep. "I'm so sorry you had to go through all of this, Chloe. But you were right, Tony will do everything he can to protect you. He always had a crush on you."

I smile, memories from the moment we shared last night still vivid in my mind. "You know, it took me a while, but I finally admitted to myself that I feel the same about him. I guess I always did."

"Of course you did," she teases.

"But I might have messed things up big time by hiding Ellie from him," I say, bringing to the table my biggest concern after yesterday. I know we had sex after he found out the truth, but since we still haven't addressed the elephant in the room, I'm still not sure he has forgiven me.

"What do you mean 'hiding Ellie from him'?" Eleni asks with a frown.

Of course she doesn't know. No one is supposed to.

I clear my throat, shifting in my seat as I prepare myself to tell her the truth. Since Tony knows about it now, and she is a good friend, I don't think it's a problem to share it with her.

"Well, Ellie is Tony's daughter. He didn't know until last night, so… I don't know where we stand right now."

She blinks at me a couple of times, her mouth open in shock.

"He wasn't supposed to know until we dealt with Mateo and everything else. I guess… I didn't know how to tell him. I was too scared, El. What if he hated me for keeping it from him, you know?" I confess. "He probably hates me right now, but I couldn't come back to him when she was born. Mateo threatened my parents and said he'd take Ellie from me if I ever tried to run away from him…."

A sob escapes my throat, and I feel tears running down my cheeks even though I promised myself I wouldn't cry anymore. But the fear of missing Tony and all the ghosts lurking around from my past are still too much to handle sometimes.

"Oh, Chlo, I am so sorry," she comforts me, patting me on the shoulder since she can't hug me. "I can't imagine what you must have gone through. But you're not alone anymore."

I sniff, wiping my tears with the back of my hands.

"I'm sure you'll both figure it out. Tony really likes you, and I can't imagine he would turn his back on you or Ellie. Just give him some time," she suggests with a soft smile.

"Thank you, Eleni. I have missed having you around with your wise advice," I chuckle. "How long are you staying in town?" I ask, hoping to change the subject.

"Honestly, I think we're leaving in a day or two. It depends on how Dante's business goes," she answers simply.

"So quickly?" I widen my eyes. "You don't show your face here for years and when you do, you spend less than two days? That's not fair."

"Yeah, I know. But Dante doesn't think it's a good idea to spend too much time here yet, and I don't blame him. Our life in Greece is so peaceful, we don't want to risk it, you know?"

"Yeah, I do. Maybe when all this nightmare is over, I'll make a trip to visit you. I could use some time in Greece to just relax." I laugh.

"I'd love to have you there. I miss having a friend. Sure, the kids keep me occupied twenty-four-seven, but still… a woman needs some time off, right?" Eleni rolls her eyes. She still looks as beautiful as ever, but I notice, from the bags under her eyes, that she isn't getting much sleep. I can't imagine going on a long flight right after giving birth, with a newborn in my arms and two other kids to take care of. I'm sure Dante is a great husband and father, but still, there are things only a mother can do.

"I promise I'll stay in touch better. We can video call sometimes, whenever you feel like you could use some woman talk." I give her a reassuring smile.

"I'd love that."

"So, do you have to go now or do you think you can stay for lunch? I can cook us something," I offer, hoping she doesn't have to leave so soon since this is probably the last time I'll see her before she has to return to Greece.

"I can stay until late in the afternoon. I wanted to see Ellie, but I don't think she's at home right now, is she?" She looks around as if Ellie might pop out of nowhere.

I shake my head, getting to my feet to start preparing our lunch. "She's with my mom for the day. I don't know what time she'll be back, but you might bump into her before you leave."

After that, I go to the kitchen and tell Eleni to put Ilias in Ellie's play pen so we can enjoy a nice, comfortable lunch together. The afternoon is incredible. We share how our lives have been lately and everything we've been through since we both got married and had kids. Eleni is such great company, and by the time she leaves, I feel my heart bursting. I wasn't expecting her to show up in my doorway this morning, but now that she has, it feels bittersweet to have to say goodbye so fast.

She does manage to see my mother and Ellie, though, and she plays with my daughter for a few minutes before her driver comes to pick her up.

"She looks fine as hell for someone who just gave birth, doesn't she?" my mother notes as soon as Eleni leaves with Ilias.

"Yeah, she does," I agree. My mother is not very subtle about it, but she isn't wrong.

Ellie is in my arms, her head on my shoulder. Her breathing is calm, so I assume she has fallen asleep, so I excuse myself and take her to her room.

When I return to the living room, my mother is seated on the couch, her phone in hand while she swipes through the Chanel website. I roll my eyes, sitting beside her.

"How was your day? Did Ellie behave?" I ask, trying to make conversation.

"We went to the park, and then I visited Val. Ellie played with Lorenna a little bit, and then we went to the grocery store so I could buy some stuff for my house. The fridge has been empty ever since you left," she informs me.

"What? What have you been eating all this time?"

She shrugs. "This and that. Restaurants or at the girls' houses. They all fight to invite me now that I'm back in town," she gushes, proudly flipping her hair over her shoulder.

"Right, of course." I laugh.

"You know, we should think about Ellie becoming a model. She's such an attention grabber. There was this guy at the store who didn't stop saying how beautiful she was, fawning over her and saying that she would be very popular with model agents. He seemed to know a lot about the business...." She trails off, letting me digest the suggestion.

However, something doesn't sit well with me. I haven't seen the guy or anything, but something about the way he seemed to have approached my mother and Ellie makes me feel uneasy, on the edge of my seat.

"What was this guy like, Mom?" I ask instead, my tone worried and dry.

She creases her brows immediately, looking at me with narrowed eyes. "What? Do you think he was one of Mateo's men or something like that?" Her voice is soft and cautious this time, as if the thought only occurred to her now. I didn't say that is what I'm thinking, but my mother knows me better than anyone. She knows what I'm thinking without me having to say it most of the time.

"I don't know, but we have to be careful. Mateo has been very quiet lately, and I don't know if that's a good thing or a bad one," I answer, feeling the blood run through my body like ice.

30

———

SCARE

Tony

I get to Cal's casino bar in record time. I hate when he is enigmatic in text messages, but since our businesses have to be kept in the dark, I can't blame him for not telling me right away what the problem is. The urgency in his words made my skin crawl, and I have no idea what to expect when I walk into his bar.

His guys gesture for me over by the basement, a place I have been only twice since I met him. Both times weren't for nice businesses. That's where he deals with dirty shit in every sense of the word. My stomach twists as my footsteps echo through the empty, sultry hallways. I bump into a few other men who seem to be guarding the place, and that only makes me anticipate even more what I'm about to find.

When I reach the last door to my left, I encounter a scene that isn't at all unfamiliar to me. A young man who looks to be in his early thirties is tied to a metal chair, his arms and legs wrapped with tight ropes. The room is dark, but I can see his face is swollen and bloody, his sweaty hair falling over his eyes. His clothes are torn, and his

185

breathing is heavy. Clearly, he's been beaten up recently. I clench my jaw as I take in the scene, feeling uneasy for not recognizing the man. I can only imagine he might be one of Mateo's men. Otherwise, Cal wouldn't have called me here.

There are two of Cal's bodyguards watching the guy in the chair, but only when I get inside the room does Cal walk through another door to my left, cleaning his bloody knuckles on a rag. He looks up at me and nods, his eyes dark with malice.

"Hey, lad. Sorry I couldn't wait for ya. I was kinda bored," he tells me with a smirk.

Then he turns to the young man, kicking the chair hard and making it move a few inches backward. The guy groans in pain, probably from a broken rib or something. He looks pretty beaten, but who knows how bad the internal damage might be.

"Care to repeat to me boy over here what ya told me?" Cal taunts. His accent is thicker than normal, and I assume he must be trying to use it to intimidate the guy.

But apparently it's not working. The young man spits on the floor, too close to Cal's feet. *Bad move.*

Cal sneers and, in a swift movement, punches the guy in the gut. He contorts and bends forward, grunting in pain. I don't tear my eyes away from the scene, even though I still have no clue what the guy has done to deserve such punishment. I can only trust Cal and assume he's doing the right thing. If this man is responsible for scaring Chloe, or feeding information about her to Mateo, he'll feel much worse when I take the lead.

"Just spill it," Cal snarls, preparing for another punch. But I grab his fist in the air, pulling him away from the man who seems about to faint. I have no time for this shit show. I just need to know what the hell is going on.

"It's all right, man. Just tell me yourself what he told you," I press, the taste of blood strong on my tongue.

Cal darts a deadly glance to the guy before turning to face me. "He said a few lads are in New York searchin' for the baby," he begins.

"The fuckin' bastard put a target on your woman and said she can be killed on the spot. But he wants the little lass."

I clench my fists this time, struggling to keep myself at bay. I swear to God I'll kill this motherfucker before he has the chance to give me more information. It terrifies me to know this is Mateo's plan. I never thought he wouldn't want Chloe and would want Ellie instead—not to use her as bait to lure Chloe, but to just *keep* her? It makes no sense.

This freaks me out even more. I can't imagine an innocent baby like Ellie in the hands of a devil like Mateo. It scared the shit out of me to imagine Chloe being in his claws, but Ellie….

A low growl escapes my throat, and I turn to the man who looks horrified as he stares at me with wide, swollen eyes.

"What else did he order you to do?" I ask in a low snarl. My vision reddens, and blood is all I can think about. I know this guy isn't directly responsible for the nightmare Chloe is living in—or me, for that matter—but he *is* doing what his boss told him to, and if he had any qualms or principles, he'd know women and children are off limits.

And because he doesn't, I grab the gun from Cal's belt and aim at the guy in the chair, not waiting for Cal to have the chance to stop me. I pull the trigger, the loud noise deafening me momentarily. The blood in his dirty gray shirt starts spreading as his wound starts to bleed out, but he is gone already. I made sure to aim for his heart, not giving him a chance to regret his actions.

I hope Mateo gets the message. I'm not to be messed with. And if he thinks he can touch Chloe or Ellie, he has another thing coming.

I will make sure to send him back to Hell, from where he should have never left.

"Ah, lad, you ruined my fun," Cal complains from beside me.

I turn to him and hand him back the gun. He takes it with a smirk on his face, holstering it back to his belt. Then I reach for my pocket and take a pile of cash neatly arranged and give it to him.

"Thank you for your help. And please keep an eye open for anything that might help us get to Mateo. The motherfucker is too close to home."

Cal nods, taking the money and handing it to one of his men.

"I don't want any trouble with the fuckin' De La Cruz family, but I don't want them sniffin' around my business either."

"Them coming here is bad for everyone, not just the Saints," I tell him firmly. "I don't fucking mind if he wants war, but he's not coming anywhere near my wife and kid. I'll kill every single one of them myself if I have to. And whoever is not on my side is against me," I warn.

Cal is a longtime friend, not to mention my ally, but if he's second guessing his choices, I just made sure he thinks it through before he decides to act against me.

"Don't worry, lad. I'd never turn my back on ya," he affirms.

I give him another nod before heading out of his basement. This place makes me claustrophobic as fuck. Or maybe I'm just too worked up. My hands tremble slightly as I head for my car. My mind tries to force images of Chloe and Ellie being murdered at home into my thoughts. What if Mateo sent the guy I just killed as bait so he could have the house clear of me to get to Chloe and Ellie? I have soldiers there to protect them, but they are not immortal. If Mateo ambushes them, I don't even want to imagine what could happen.

I step on the gas as I drive back to Staten Island, not slowing along the way. I need to get home as soon as possible. Thankfully, every cop in this town knows not to stop me.

The idea of finding Chloe's body on my floor and Ellie missing has me sweating and feeling like I'm about to vomit. My knuckles are white from gripping the steering wheel too hard, and my throat is dry. I don't want to think about these fucking things, but I can't help myself either.

The tires screech as I pull into my driveway half an hour later, barely parking the vehicle before jumping out and heading for the house.

"Chloe!" I yell from the porch as I struggle to punch the password in for the door. I spot a few soldiers from my peripheral vision, and they seem well enough, but my brain can't seem to comprehend that. I need to see her with my own eyes. "Chloe!" I repeat, finally walking inside and slamming the door behind me.

I head for the kitchen, noticing the lights are on. My heart almost falls out of my mouth when I get to the door and find Chloe by the stove, cooking up something for dinner. She looks at me with widened eyes, her cheeks pink and her smooth hair cascading down her back. She has a short, blue dress on, her thighs on full display, looking as sweet and hot as ever.

"*Fuck…* thank God!" I murmur, my voice barely above a whisper.

"Tony? Is everything okay? What happened? You seem like you've just seen a ghost," she points out with her soft voice. It sounds like an angel singing. My entire body feels light as I force my legs to move forward, in her direction.

Before any other word spills out of her mouth, I wrap one hand around her waist, pulling her toward me, and claiming her lips with mine, desperate to feel her.

31

POWERLESS

Chloe

After my mom left, I took a shower and decided to prepare dinner for when Tony arrived. Ellie only woke up to have dinner and then went back to sleep, and I was glad, because I'd have time to cook something nice without having to watch her. Mom must've worn her out today. I hope she's not getting sick.

I wasn't sure Tony would come back for dinner. I hadn't heard from him since he left that morning, but when I hear his voice frantically calling me from the front door, I don't know what to think.

He sounds worried, disturbed even, and when he shows up in the kitchen, I notice how pale he looks.

I ask him if he's okay, my voice full of concern.

But he doesn't say anything. He simply strides toward me, wraps one arm around my waist, and pulls me flush against him. Then he kisses me so desperately that it catches me off guard, almost stealing my breath away.

I don't know what's gotten into him, and even though I'm dying to ask him, I don't want to break our kiss. All of my concerns melt away as he holds me firm in his arms, like I might disappear in the blink of an eye if he lets go of me.

Blindly, I reach for the control knob on the stove and turn it off, hoping I can save the meal I'm cooking and not let it burn.

Tony moans against my mouth, his arms tightening around me as he walks us backward until my back hits the kitchen counter. His hands roam over my body until they get to my hips. I can't deny I like what he's doing, especially how he seems to have missed me, but the look on his face when he got here still worries me.

I know Tony, and I'm positive something happened for him to come home so worked up the way he did.

"Tony?" I ask breathlessly, pulling away from him just an inch. His eyes are dark with need, but his brows are creased with concern. "What happened?"

He doesn't answer me. At least not the way I expected him to.

"I just missed you," he tells me, finding the soft spot on my neck and kissing it, enticing me and making me forget about my worries completely.

I grip his shoulders, steadying myself while his hands find the back of my thighs and hoist me from the floor, setting me on the counter. The marble is cold against my hot skin, but I don't mind. In fact, it causes shivers to run up my spine, making my core tighten with need.

Tony adjusts himself between my legs, the bulge in his pants brushing against my bare thigh and making me gasp. His hands dart to my legs, his fingertips torturing me as he slides them up my skin, raising the hem of my dress as they go.

I'm so glad I chose this dress after my shower. I admit I had certain intentions in my mind when I picked it from my closet, but I never thought it would work so well in my favor. Or so fast. It was supposed to be used as my weapon for after dinner, not before.

"I thought you'd regret what we did last night," I say, cursing myself inwardly.

Why would I say such a thing? I don't want to start an argument right now or make him lose interest in me by bringing the topic of our relationship up.

There's a time and place for everything, Chloe. Just enjoy the moment and shut up.

I shake my head, pushing away the intrusive thoughts, and focus on Tony's hands and lips on me. My entire body is in flames, and I groan when his fingers slide under my dress to find my panties.

He pulls away from me, his eyes shining with malice and desire.

"How could I ever regret that?" His voice is hoarse and low, and I feel my need for him pooling in my panties. "In fact, I don't think I'll ever be able to get enough of you," he adds while slowly removing my thong and sliding it down my thighs.

It's so sexy, provocative, and torturing.

Without thinking, I reach for his belt, unbuckling it and pulling his pants down along with his boxers. If he's in a rush, I don't mind granting him what he wants. I am desperate to feel him inside me, too, so I might as well just speed up the process.

Tony groans as I set him free, his lips finding mine again. His tongue dances with mine, hungrily and possessively. I don't remember seeing Tony act like this before, but I like it.

I'm so wet for him already that no foreplay is needed. I cross my ankles behind his back and pull him forward, boldly connecting our bodies. His tip brushes against my entrance, and I brace myself to feel him claim me completely.

He doesn't wait for another confirmation from me. He doesn't hesitate, and he doesn't ask me if I'm sure like he did last night. He simply thrusts himself inside me, slamming into me so deep I can't breathe, holding me close to him like I might slip from his fingers at any moment.

"Fuck, you're so perfect," he hisses against my skin, his face hidden in my neck. He reaches for my breast, squeezing it through the thin fabric of my dress, making my eyes roll to the back of my head.

It's mesmerizing how he knows exactly what I like, how to make me come undone with the simplest of acts. He doesn't need to do much, and I'm putty in his hands.

He speeds up, and I can't form coherent sentences while I feel my walls tightening around him, the spasms in my entire body showing their first signs. My legs are weak, and my vision blurs, and I sink my nails into his shoulders, somehow asking him not to stop.

"Tony..." I trail off, my breathing erratic. "I'm so close," I manage, hoping he understands what I mean. If he deviates an inch, it might break the spell, and I can't have that. Not now that... "*Shit...*" I hiss, my orgasm hitting me so hard that I have to bite my lips so I don't wake Ellie up.

She's upstairs in her room, but even so, this is so good that I might scream loud enough to wake her if I don't control myself.

Tony follows right after me, pumping inside me while he releases himself, his arms tightened around my waist.

We stay silent for what feels like a whole minute, panting while trying to catch our breath.

"That was... something else," I finally say between deep inhales. My entire body is still sensitive, and I don't dare move while he's still inside of me.

Tony chuckles, his chest reverberating beneath my hands. "I hope it was a *good* kind of 'something else.'"

"An *amazing* kind of something else," I admit, still sucking in air when he pulls himself out of me. I miss him immediately, but it allows me to gather my bearings as I straighten my messy hair.

Tony zips up his pants and then holds me by the waist, pulling me off the counter and setting me back on the floor. He kisses my forehead gently and smiles softly at me, his eyes studying my face.

"What?" I ask, noticing he seems to want to say something, but he's hesitating. I hate that he feels like he can't talk to me, but I don't want to push him either.

He shakes his head, pulling me into an embrace. "Nothing. I'm just glad you're here."

My heart feels like it is about to burst, and I smile to myself, leaning my head against his chest. This feels so right, being in his arms....

"I was cooking us some dinner. You must be starving," I note, pushing away from him and turning to see my work on the stove. I managed to turn off the heat before it burned the vegetables I was cooking.

"I *was* starving," he tells me seductively, hugging me from behind and placing his chin on my shoulder. "But you took care of that already."

I laugh, pushing him away playfully. "You need actual food, you know."

"Yeah, that too…" He grins at me, and I clench my legs, turning my attention back to the meal. I can't go another round now. Otherwise, dinner will never be served tonight.

"You're sleeping with me again tonight, aren't you?" he asks, and I can't deny the joy that his question brings me.

"If you want me to," I answer with a shrug, trying not to show him how much I want this. I have no idea what is going on between us, and even though I'd love nothing more than to be with him, I need to tread carefully. More than worrying about my own heart, I have Ellie to consider now. I can't act harshly or make decisions irresponsibly. Especially if she might be directly involved or affected.

Tony makes my concerns invalid as soon as he takes a step forward, wrapping his arms around me once more and pulling my back against his chest. I fight the urge to moan under his touch, my skin still alight.

"I'd love nothing more than to have you by my side every night, Chloe," he tells me softly.

Good Lord, how is he so good with words?

Then he spins me around, making me face him, and kisses me again, this time softer, but equally intense.

How can he make me so powerless?

I never thought I'd be this type of woman, but Tony makes me feel like no one else has ever made me feel before. I feel young, desired, careless, irresponsible sometimes, but more than anything, he makes me feel like he needs me. Like I am part of his life, a part he can't let go of.

And as much as I hate to admit it, I love it.

ENDLESS NIGHTMARE

Chloe

IT TAKES LONGER THAN I PLANNED TO HAVE DINNER SERVED, BUT eventually, I manage to get the food out of the pan and onto our plates. Tony and I eat together, talking about trivial things. I feel the elephant in the room lurking in the shadows, but I don't bring the sensitive topic to the table.

We're both in such a nice place now that I fear if I mention Mateo, the little bubble of happiness we are building might pop, and my life will return to its usual nightmare. I dread the idea of it.

I don't know how to bring up the topic of Ellie being his daughter, either. He's probably still mad at me for keeping it a secret from him, and even though I know we will have to address it eventually, I want to postpone it for as long as I can.

When we finish dinner, I tell Tony to go take a shower while I clean up the kitchen. At first, he insists on staying to help me, but eventually he gives in and does as I suggested. Once I'm done with my chores, I go to my own room and put on a beautiful pink lace nightgown that contrasts nicely with my skin and brush my hair, letting it cascade down my shoulders and back.

I know how Tony loves my hair, and honestly, I hope he wasn't asking me just to *sleep* with him tonight. After he claimed me in the kitchen earlier, he has me hoping that was just a sneak peek of what I might expect tonight.

As soon as I knock on his door, he opens it and pulls me inside, pulling me to his bed in less than a second. We go for another round, and this time we both take our time with each other. By the time we finish, I'm exhausted, my eyes are heavy, and I have to fight sleep while we both catch our breath.

My brain starts overthinking, trying to make sense of everything that's happening with us lately. The truth is, I'm not ready to face my real feelings for Tony. Let alone tell him how much I care for him.

But I also can't deny I'm not ready to be away from him. Whatever's going on between us, I hope it lasts for a long time. We have a lot to discuss—Ellie being the major topic—and it pains me because I don't know what to expect from whatever this is.

"Are you okay?" he asks me in a whisper, turning to face me.

I nod, staring into his beautiful eyes. "Yeah…" I answer.

"What's on your mind?" he insists, his brow creasing with concern.

I take a deep breath, wondering what the best way to share my thoughts without revealing much might be. "I thought this was just business between us," I murmur softly.

His frown deepens. "Do you *want* it to be just business between us?"

"I…"

I can't force the words out of my mouth. I know damn well what I want, but I'm scared. There's so much on the table, so much at stake for the both of us. Being with Tony will only cause more trouble. Everything is moving so fast that I can't make sense of what our lives have become.

Before I manage to say anything else, I hear Ellie crying. I sigh, conveying my apology through my expression and starting to get up from the bed. But Tony gently holds my wrist and pulls me back to mattress.

"I'll go," he offers, placing a gentle kiss on my lips before sliding on his boxers and disappearing from the room.

I'm left to myself with my unwelcome thoughts.

What should I do? Accepting my feelings for Tony will only make me more vulnerable than I already am. I have no idea what Mateo is planning, and we haven't heard from him in a while. I'm officially married to Tony, and to the outside world, we're truly a couple in love. It should make no difference to our enemies if we're really together or not.

So, why can't I simply accept him? What am I so afraid of?

I know the answer to that, but I'm not willing to acknowledge it.

Opening my heart to him would hurt me more than Mateo ever did. I don't even know if Tony sees me the same way I see him. I don't know what goes on in his heart, and I am scared as hell to find out.

If he ever tells me he doesn't feel the same about me, I don't know what I'll do. So, for now, it's better that I just keep my feelings to myself.

Before anything else, I need to make sure he's not still mad at me about Ellie. I'll never be happy if I know he resents me.

It takes Tony a long time to return, and I begin to worry. If Ellie is taking this long to fall asleep again, he might need my help to put her to bed. So, I toss the sheets to the side and go to her room to check on them.

The door is slightly open, and I push it slowly, finding Tony by the window with Ellie asleep in his arms, her head resting on his shoulder. He's looking outside at the dark night sky, focused on whatever is going on in his mind. Even though he's physically here, I don't think his mind is present.

"Is everything all right?" I whisper, not wanting to scare him or wake Ellie.

He looks at me over his shoulder, not daring to move too much. He nods and puts Ellie in her crib, kissing her forehead before pulling the blanket over her.

My heart threatens to burst while I watch how he takes care of her so gently. It's everything I could have ever wished for.

After making sure Ellie hasn't woken up, he gently grabs my hand and guides me out of her room and back to his. The muscles in his back are tense, and he's silent the entire way, which makes me anxious.

"Tony, what's going on?" I ask softly as soon as he closes the door behind us.

He looks at me with knitted eyebrows, his jaw clenched. "I need to tell you something, but you need to listen to me very carefully, okay?" he begins, and of course that doesn't help my anxiety.

I nod, unable to trust my own voice, and I struggle to keep my hands from shaking. Based on his tone and expression, I know something happened. That must be the reason why he showed up so worried earlier.

I sit down on his bed, preparing myself for whatever he has to say. He sits by my side and grabs my hand, squeezing it lightly while looking into my eyes.

"Mateo's men are in the city, looking for Ellie," he tells me with his eyes narrowed.

My blood freezes even though this is something I've been expecting to happen. "You mean he's looking for *us*," I correct him.

But Tony shakes his head firmly, not breaking eye contact with me. "He wants Ellie. And he put a mark on your head."

"What do you mean he put a mark on my head?"

There's no way this means what I think it means. Mateo would never do that. Why would he want Ellie? Why would he *not* want me?

"He wants you dead," Tony clarifies. I appreciate him not lying to me, or keeping the truth from me, but I don't know how to take in this information. In all of my nightmares, Mateo does everything he can to get *me*. Not Ellie. Me. The idea of Ellie being his target now is sickening.

Why would he change his approach? Why would he change his mind all of a sudden?

"That can't be true," I manage, my voice shaking. "This is another one of his evil plans. He probably wants to use Ellie as bait to get to me."

"I don't think that's what he wants," Tony counters. "His men had orders to kill you on the spot, Chloe. You need to be more careful than ever now, hear me? I can't afford to lose you. And I won't let him get anywhere near Ellie. I promise you."

Tony's nervous. He's trying his best not to scare me, but I can tell by the way his eyes roam all over my face, and the strength he's using to squeeze my hand, that he's just as terrified as I am.

Something doesn't feel right to me, though.

It makes no sense that Mateo would suddenly want me dead. Not that I think that highly of myself, or that I harbor any… jealous feelings over his decision to put a mark on my head rather than keeping me alive to torture me, but still, he's not the kind of man to accept defeat. If anything, he'll do whatever he can to prove his point, to show me how he can get whatever he wants and that no one escapes him, especially not me.

This must be a trap, something he's doing to get closer to me, to my family.

Then an idea occurs to me, and I feel a shiver run down my spine as I realize he must be coming for Tony, too. Now, this is no longer about me or Ellie. I have somehow involved Tony deeper than ever in a problem I can't figure out how to fix.

"Listen to me." Tony's voice pulls me back from my thoughts. His hands cup my face, forcing me to look him in the eyes. "I promise you that motherfucker won't put a finger on you or Ellie. I just need you to be careful, that's all I'm asking."

I nod, unsure of what else to say or think. No matter how much I try to comprehend what he just told me, nothing makes sense. And more than ever, I have to accept that Mateo is getting closer and closer to us.

Tony pulls me back to bed, and I lay on his chest, feeling emotionally drained but too utterly uneasy to fall asleep.

When will this nightmare end? Will it ever?

33

CLOSING IN

Tony

Chloe's sweet scent hits my nostrils before I even open my eyes. Having her sleep in my bed again feels like a dream. I stretch my hand to her side, hoping to find her and pull her into my arms, but all I find is emptiness, the sheets already cold from her absence.

I snap my eyes open and sit up straight, looking around the room, looking for her. But she's nowhere in sight. She's not in the bathroom, either.

Fear threatens to consume me before I pull myself together.

There's no way anything happened to her inside our house. I have my men stationed outside, and I'd have woken up if anyone burst in. But it doesn't sit well with me that I can't hear or see her anywhere, so I jump out of bed and head for Ellie's room, hoping to find them there.

But the room is also empty.

My heart beats rapidly against my chest as I move through the house searching for them. I let out a sigh of relief when I find a note written on an orange Post-It saying they went out to meet with Eleni

203

before she has to return to Greece. Chloe wrote that she didn't want to wake me up, so she thought she'd leave a note to assure me everything was fine.

I don't like the fact that she managed to leave the house—my bed, even—without me waking. I must have been really tired that I didn't hear her getting up or leaving with Ellie.

After sending her a text message and making sure Rocco has eyes on Chloe the entire time she's out, I head for the shower. I get ready for the day, receiving updates every five minutes from my men handling several business deals taking place this morning. I have nothing but black coffee and a muffin Chloe baked the other day, and by the time I leave the house, it's almost noon.

I climb into my car and drive toward Lou's Deli, hoping to get some actual work done. I have so much paperwork on my desk that it's been driving me nuts for the past few days. With everything going on lately, I haven't had the time, patience, or frame of mind to focus on papers.

Lou is cleaning the counter when I walk in, and after greeting him with a nod, I go straight downstairs to my office. There's no sign of his staff around the establishment yet, only some of my men hanging around here and there, waiting for orders from me.

Since I haven't been as active as I'd like lately, there isn't much happening, so I can't really blame them for not having shit to do.

I dive into my paperwork right away, instantly getting a headache when the numbers stop making sense to me. Math and finance can be a pain in the ass sometimes. I rub my temples, trying to shove away the pain, and my eyes dart to the bottle of whiskey sitting on the bar in the corner of the room.

But I shake my head. It's barely past lunch time, and I haven't eaten anything but a muffin. I need to stop these shitty habits, especially now that I'm a father.

That reminds me of the conversation I'm postponing with Chloe. Her excuses for not telling me about Ellie before didn't sit well with me, but I wasn't in the right mood or mindset to discuss it with her. I knew I'd say something stupid that would end up hurting her feelings, so I simply left the house to clear my head.

But then everything else happened after that, one thing leading to the next, and I couldn't believe it when I finally had her to myself again. I guess I'm dreading having that conversation with her.

And by the way she's been tense around me lately, I can tell she expects me to drop this bomb on her lap at any time. But at some point, we'll have to address it. There's no way we can let this go and pretend it didn't happen. Sure, we have a lot of shit to deal with right now, but how am I supposed to put it past me that she kept my daughter from me for almost two years?

I don't want to resent her, so she'll have to talk to me about it eventually.

A muffled commotion coming from upstairs catches my attention, pulling my eyes away from the paper in my hand and toward the closed door of my office.

When I hear the sound of glass breaking, I get to my feet, my hand instantly snapping to the gun holstered on my waist.

"Armando? What's going on?" I ask as I carefully approach the door.

If someone barged in, I need to be careful. But when I don't hear an answer, I swiftly open the door and head up, not hearing a single sound down here.

Realizing whatever the issue may be, it's happening upstairs, I dart up the steps, coming across Armando handing a towel to Lou who has a split lip and a black eye. Some glasses are shattered on the floor around them, but other than that, the deli looks exactly the same as it did a few minutes ago.

I look around once more, making sure no one else is in danger or lurking behind a column or something.

"What the fuck happened?" I demand bitterly when I'm certain the place is clear.

"Some motherfucker tried to rob me," Lou tells me, hissing as he touches the wound on his lip with the towel.

I immediately frown, my skin crawling. No one would dare to rob

Lou. Every sane person in the area knows this place is protected by the Saints. The only one who would try something as stupid as this definitely has to be an enemy of mine, not a random stranger hoping for some cash for the ferry.

And I'm pretty damn sure I know who it is.

"What did he look like?" I growl, drawing my gun from my belt, already tasting blood in my mouth.

"He had a Yankees shirt and a black cap on. I didn't see his face clearly, though..." Lou shakes his head and gestures to his left. "He went that way."

I storm out of the deli, heading for the alley where he pointed. I think I spot the man turning the corner, but when I dart after him, two other guys jump from out of nowhere, ambushing me.

Fuck.

I don't recognize any of them, but by the way they're dressed, I can tell they are from Miami.

I don't wait for them to make a move or say anything, I just point my gun at one of them–the one closest to me–and pull the trigger. But my pistol jams, failing me, and I clench my teeth, knowing I'll be fucked up soon. There's no way I can wrestle with these guys without one of them shooting me first. I'm not close enough to fight either of them, so even if I chose one, I would be hit first by the one who's left.

The young man standing furthest from me, and closer to the deli, chuckles, looking at me like I'm a fucking puppy lost from its mother.

"We could just kill him right now. I never thought it could be this easy," he suggests, narrowing eyes at me. "Isn't he the head of the Saints?"

"He wants the woman, not this guy," the other one replies bluntly. He seems to be the more serious and centered amongst them, and I assume he must be the one in charge here.

"We can at least hurt him a little. The woman is clearly not here," the first guy says, pointing his gun at me. I doubt his will fail when he tries to kill me.

I wonder where the guy that punched Lou went, but right now, he's the least of my concerns.

"Just tell your fucking boss he won't get anywhere near her," I snarl, my fists tightening beside me.

The two men laugh, making me see red. A single gunshot deafens me, and I feel a sting on my left arm. I look down, realizing the fucking bastard shot me, missing the muscle by an inch, the bullet having grazed only my skin. It stings like hell, but at least he didn't hit any organs.

Yet.

That's when I hear more gunshots echoing through the alley, and the men lower their heads, protecting them with their arms. I take the opportunity to dodge to my right, hiding behind a metal dumpster.

"What the fuck?" one of them mumbles, already walking backward toward the main street.

I spot Armando coming out of the deli with his gun in hand, but by the time he gets outside, the two bastards are already gone.

Shit, shit, shit!

"Are you all right, Boss?" Armando asks, coming toward me with an angry expression on his face. "Sorry I got here so late." His eyes snap to my arm, noticing the bloodstain growing on my sleeve. "Fuck, man! You were hit?"

"My gun misfired," I grumble, pressing a hand to my wound to slow the bleeding. For a single scratch, it hurts like fuck.

"Damn, man. Let's get you to the family doctor," he says, looking around and making sure no one can surprise us again.

"I'm fine," I say begrudgingly, following him inside the deli. "Call Chloe. Now."

34

———

PUSHING ME AWAY

Chloe

Brunch with Eleni and the other wives is funner and more entertaining than I expected. When she texted me this morning to meet her before she had to return to Greece, I figured she meant just the two of us—and maybe the kids—but it turned out she invited all the other wives, too.

After the night I spent with Tony, I wanted to stay beside him when he woke up, but I didn't want to miss out on the opportunity to see Eleni one last time. Who knows when we will see each other again? With a newborn, I doubt she'll be coming back to the states anytime soon. It's already surprising that she's here just weeks after giving birth. I don't think she'll try this again soon.

That's why I got up, took a quick shower, put on a dress, got Ellie ready, and headed out of the house without talking to Tony. I made sure to leave him a note so he didn't freak out when he didn't see us, but I didn't speak to him.

We still have issues to discuss and resolve, but life seems to be getting in the way a lot lately, and I'm worried that opening that door will burst this happy bubble of delusion we've been living in. I wonder when he'll bring up the topic of Ellie again, but I also think we won't be able to solve this until the whole problem with Mateo is over.

I can't help but dream about when that day will come. I can't stand running or hiding away anymore. I just want to live my life without fear and give Ellie a peaceful one, like she deserves. She's just a child in the middle of this fucked up situation. She shouldn't have to go through any of this at such a young age—or at all, for that matter.

Right in the middle of the meal, my phone buzzes in my purse. Only three people have my new number–Tony, Armando, and my mom–and since my mother is here with me, it's either Tony or his second in command. Whoever it is, it has me on the edge of my seat already since they never call me during the day.

Armando's name flashes on my screen, so I excuse myself from the table, asking Mom to watch Ellie while I head to a quieter corner of the restaurant.

"Hello?"

"Mrs. Bellini? Is everything all right?" Armando asks me bluntly as a way of greeting. His voice sounds dark and concerned, and it has my stomach twisting with fear.

"Yes, I'm all right. Did something happen?" I reply, biting my lips.

"The boss asked me to call you and tell you Rocco is on the way to pick you and Ellie up," he informs me, not answering my question.

"Why? What's going on?" I press, knowing something must have happened if Tony is sending someone to pick me up in the middle of lunch with the wives.

"Just get in the car immediately and come straight to the house. Don't stop anywhere," he warns before the line goes dead.

My hands are shaking while I stare at my phone screen, gathering my thoughts. I take a deep breath, deciding to trust God that Tony is all right, and head back to the table, preparing myself to take Ellie home with me.

I spot Rocco's car already by the entrance, and I barely have time to say goodbye to everyone, coming up with a stupid excuse as to why I have to leave so suddenly.

My mother is looking at me with concern in her eyes, her forehead furrowed as she hands me Ellie. I say goodbye to Eleni, pulling her into an embrace and apologizing for leaving so soon. She shakes her head at me and murmurs a quick, *"Don't worry, I get it,"* before squeezing my hand and telling me to be careful.

In less than five minutes, I'm in the car heading home with Ellie half asleep in her car seat.

"Rocco, do you know what's going on?" I pry, hoping he can be sympathetic and share something with me–anything at all—to keep me from worrying too much.

"Sorry, Mrs. Bellini. I was just told to take you both to the house. I can't say anything else," he answers, glancing at me through the rearview mirror.

I know something is definitely wrong when we arrive at the house. The driveway is filled with cars belonging to Tony's crew, and some of the guys are holding their guns while others are communicating through their earpieces. I rush inside as soon as Rocco parks the car, finding even more men inside. One of them gestures toward the kitchen, so I follow his lead with Ellie in my arms.

Tony's leaning against the kitchen counter, his dark hair tousled, his white dress shirt unbuttoned, one of its sleeves soaked with blood. My legs falter at the sight, but when our eyes meet, I let out a sigh of relief. At least he's alive.

"What the hell happened?" I ask, my voice low and weak. I take a few steps forward, reaching for him, but he raises his hand to stop me. I come to a halt, looking around, trying to understand what I'm missing.

"Can you watch Ellie for a while, Armando?" Tony asks, looking away from me to glance at his second. Armando nods and comes toward me, taking Ellie gently from my arms and giving her his car keys to play with.

I open my mouth to argue with Tony as soon as they're out of sight, but he takes me by the hand instead, leading me toward his office at the end of the hallway. He closes the door and takes a deep breath, clearly exhausted, but also worried. I can tell by the crease between his brows, and the way his jawline is so tense and sharp that it might be able to cut through glass.

The amount of blood on his shirt also scares the hell out of me, especially since I can't see the depth of his wound. I reach to touch it and move the fabric out of the way, but Tony's hand grips my wrist, preventing me from doing what I want.

"Let me see it," I demand, staring into his eyes.

"I'm sending you and Ellie to my safe house in Vermont," he informs me bluntly, completely ignoring my concern for his health.

My mouth snaps open, my jaw almost hitting the floor as I take in his words. "What did you say?"

"You and Ellie will stay in Vermont for now," Tony repeats, holding my gaze.

"No, we're not. I'm not going anywhere. Now, just let me see your wound." I breathe, forcing my arm out of his grip.

"This isn't a question, Chloe. I'm informing you about what will happen," he counters firmly.

"Just let me see your damn wound, Tony!" I snap. "What happened? Did you get shot?"

With a swift movement, he tugs my wrist, pulling me toward him, our faces now inches from each other. "You are my wife, and whatever I say goes. Do you understand?" he retorts through clenched teeth.

His words make me so mad that I pull away from him with more force this time, wrenching myself from his grasp.

"You may be my husband, but you don't own me," I snarl back, hurt by his words. But mostly because *he* got hurt.

I know this is Tony's way of keeping me away from trouble, but I don't need to see the extent of his wound to know this happened because of *me*. Especially since he's pushing me away and sending me to a safe house. I can read between the lines.

"This is my fault," I murmur, more to myself than to him.

"This is not your fault, Chloe," he murmurs. "And even if it were, I knew what I was signing up for when we got married. I just need you to do as I say. I can't protect you if I'm worried about you every fucking second."

"I don't want to go anywhere. I don't want to leave you behind," I argue, my heart shrinking with the idea of staying away from him. Sure, I don't know where we stand right now, but I can't imagine going to a safe house and leaving Tony here, not knowing how he is and what he's up against. "I'm done hiding, Tony," I plead, looking into his eyes and hoping he can change his mind.

But he looks away, breaking eye contact and walking toward the door. "This isn't debatable. You'll leave soon, and your mom will go with you both."

"Why are you doing this? Don't you feel anything for me?" I blurt out. "Anything at all?"

His hand stops on the doorknob, his back turned to me. His muscles are stiff, and even though I can't see his face, it seems like he's considering my question, so I wait for him to answer.

I didn't mean to bring it up, but I freaked out when I felt him pushing me away. I know he's worried about Ellie and me, but I feel the need to hear from his mouth that he's doing all of this because of something else. Something *more*.

His hesitation makes my heart beat faster than normal, anticipation eating me alive. But then Tony opens the door, walking out and slamming it behind him, leaving me alone in his office, my question unanswered.

I'd rather be outright rejected than ignored like this.

It hurts more than anything I have ever experienced. And I've had my fair share of rejection in my life.

"You fucking coward," I whisper to the dark room, my vision blurring from the tears welling in my eyes.

35

VERMONT

Chloe

My eyes are full of tears a few hours later, while I'm on a flight to Vermont on Tony's private jet with both my mother and Ellie beside me. The other seats are occupied with the soldiers Tony assigned to guard us while we're at the hideout. There are five men with us on this plane, but others will be meeting us there.

I have no idea how large the tactical force that Tony has set up to watch over us in Vermont is, but I hope most of the Saints stay in New York–specifically Staten Island–to protect him.

I hate that he made me leave like this. I hate it even more that we didn't get the time to talk through our situation. I didn't want to leave him behind. I didn't want to run away. And even though I understand why he's doing this, I just can't accept it.

I knew Mateo was coming for me all along, but running away again wasn't an option. I have to protect Ellie, and if Tony is sending us to a safe house, he must not have everything under control like I thought he did.

He didn't confirm it, but I know the wound in his arm was caused by a bullet. One that was probably meant for me. I still don't under-stand or accept the idea that Mateo ordered his men to kill me, but even so, Tony wasn't supposed to get hit.

I hate myself for bringing him into this.

The rest of the flight and the ride from the airport to the safe house feels like a blur to me. I barely pay attention to anything outside the tinted window of the bulletproof car. Rocco is driving us while my mom talks to Ellie cheerfully, pointing out trees and build-ings to her outside.

The neighborhood seems nice, peaceful, remote. I spot an older couple walking their dog on the sidewalk, a few children heading home from school, but nothing exciting seems to be happening in this place.

It's a stark contrast to the chaotic life back in Staten Island. I don't know how to feel about it.

A couple of minutes later, we get to a simple, but cozy street. I wonder how much if it is owned by the Saints. We pass by several houses, some inhabited and others that look like they haven't seen a living soul in years.

Tony's safe house is the last one on the right at the end of the street. It isn't as big as the one we were living in back in Staten Island, but the entire property is surrounded by cameras and alarms, a high tech security system to make even famous people envious. Somehow, whoever installed them made it seem like this is just another regular house. It doesn't stand out from the rest of the homes on the street, but I have only seen it from the outside.

As soon as Rocco parks the car, another Saints soldier opens the door for my mom to climb out with Ellie while I open the door on my side, stepping out and heading for the house. I have an entourage following me everywhere anyway, so having the autonomy to open my own door seems slightly normal.

The interior of the house is cozier than I expected it to be. It reminds me of a countryside manor, although with lots of upgrades, like automated systems for the AC and lights.

Rocco tells me the place has already been searched before we got here, so there's nothing to fear, but surprisingly, it doesn't make me feel any better. I want to know about Tony and what's going on with him back in New York. I didn't dare call him after I left. I'm still pissed with him and how he dealt with this without asking for my opinion first. Yet, I'm still worried about him anyway.

"Thanks, Rocco," I say with a soft smile. "I'll get Ellie's room unpacked," I inform him.

"Of course." He nods at me. "Her bags are already upstairs, and I'll be outside if you need anything."

I didn't bring all of Ellie's stuff from New York since I know this will be only temporary, but I also don't know how long we'd be staying here, so I had to fill at least two pieces of luggage with her clothes and toys. I set about organizing her stuff in the closet, peeking out the window every now and then when I hear a car approaching or voices talking to each other.

I notice a black car pulling up a few houses away from ours, and I know whoever's inside must be more of Tony's guys arriving. They'll be stationed outside, undercover, watching us. It's protocol not to call unnecessary attention, and judging by the neighborhood we're in, if the residents knew a New York's mafia boss's wife was living on their street with an entire escort system, they would freak out.

It's already dark outside by the time I finish with Ellie's stuff. I haven't even gotten to my own luggage, but I need to eat before I can continue with this exhausting task. I have nothing else to do to keep myself occupied, so it seems like a good distraction.

I go downstairs, finding Mom by the stove preparing something for dinner. It's an odd sight, but since our luxuries are limited now, we need to make do with what we have available.

"I just finished with Ellie's stuff," I tell her conversationally as I walk into the kitchen and sit down at the table. I lean back in the chair, stretching my arms and back.

"You didn't have to do all of it today," my mother notes, looking at me over her shoulders. Whatever she's preparing smells delicious, and my stomach growls. "You'll have plenty of time to unpack during the next couple of days. There's no need for you to overexert yourself like that."

I shrug, even though she's not looking at me. "I know. I just had to keep my mind busy." I sound sadder and more frustrated than I want to, and that seems to pique my mom's interest.

She turns to look at me, her hands on her hips. "Do you remember when your dad had us go into hiding while you were a kid?" she asks me in a soft voice. "There were more than a couple of times we had to do it, and it wasn't that bad. It was like a vacation. You used to like it."

"I didn't have any concerns back then other than having all my toys with me," I counter bitterly. "All of this is happening *because* of me, because I left Mateo and brought Tony and the Saints into this mess. How can I relax knowing that, Mom?" I whine, feeling my heart shrinking in pain.

She shakes her head at me, coming toward me at the table and grabbing my hand. "None of this is your fault," she assures me firmly, squeezing my hand. She gazes hard at me, her unyielding confidence steadying me. "If anyone is at fault here, it's Mateo. And as for Tony and the Saints are concerned, this comes with the job, sweetheart. He'd do it for any of the other members if he had to. So, you shouldn't feel guilty about it."

I still do. And I hate to admit it, but I don't like the idea of knowing Tony would do all of this for just anyone. Even if they are members of the Saints. A part of me knows I'm being selfish, but after I left things with Tony so inconclusively, it's nagging at me that he doesn't see me the same way I see him.

I've known the entire time that our marriage was fake, but I still allowed myself to fall in love with him. If it's really love. I can't say for sure. My emotions are all over the place, and they're too over-whelming for me to make sense of them clearly.

But one thing I know for sure. His rejection stings more than I'd like to admit.

I hate that he has the power to make me feel like this, especially after I promised myself I'd never allow another man to have the reins of my life, or my heart, for that matter.

"Listen to me." My mom's voice brings me back to reality. "This will be over soon. We need to have faith. Mateo might be cunning and powerful, but this is Tony we're talking about. This is the Saints, the family you've known for your entire life. They will take care of it like they always do."

Her words are encouraging and reassuring, but I know that all of this comes with a price. Risking the soldiers' lives, not to mention Tony's, makes me wonder if all of this is really worth it.

Maybe I should have stayed with Mateo and endured everything he did to me in order to allow others to live peacefully. At least I wouldn't have this much guilt crushing my heart and weighing me down daily.

But then, Ellie's image comes to mind, and I choke on a sob. How could I ever allow her to live in such an unhealthy environment? How could I ever consider raising her with Mateo breathing down our necks twenty-four/seven? What kind of life would she have had if I stayed?

Maybe Mom's right. I need to have faith that Tony will come out as the winner in this war. Maybe happiness is a possibility at last.

3 6

MESSED UP

Tony

It's been a couple of days since I sent Chloe, Ellie, and Nicky to Vermont along with several of my men. I knew she'd be pissed at me the moment I told her the news, but it didn't go the way I'd planned. It was way worse.

I wasn't expecting her to be so concerned about me, wanting to check on my wound, and then blaming herself for what happened. I was really mad at her for doing so, but mostly, I was mad at myself for not having the situation under control.

When I got into this to protect her, I expected Mateo to act faster. His silence lately has been bothering me immensely, and when I got caught off guard at the deli, I was fucking furious for being so stupid and unprepared.

Chloe got to me at such a vulnerable moment, and I wasn't planning on being harsh or even rude to her. But that's how it ended up going.

The look of disappointment and sadness that crossed her face when I told her I was sending her to Vermont will never leave my mind. I hate myself for it, but deep down I know it was for the best. It's the only choice I had.

But then she had to bring up my feelings for her, and I almost lost it. I almost allowed myself to tell her what I really feel. Thankfully, I managed to keep my mouth shut. I have so much shit on my plate right now, I can't think about this—about us—or even allow myself to pay attention to anything other than my duty.

I'm pulled back to reality when I hear my phone buzzing on my desk, Sal's name flashing before my eyes.

"Yes?" I answer, anxious, if not desperate, for some action. That will help me vent some of my pent up frustration.

Ever since the incident with Mateo's men outside of the deli, I made sure my guys increased the search around the territory for any leads that will take me to him, but we've been unsuccessful until now.

"We got two of them, Boss," Sal informs me bluntly. My heartbeat spikes, and I'm on my feet in a second, gathering my car keys from the table and rushing out of the office. "We have them at our bar on West Forty-Ninth."

"I'm coming," I reply, already climbing into my car and starting the ignition.

My veins are pumping with adrenaline by the time I get to the bar and park in the side alley. My guys are already waiting for me at the back door, and I storm inside, itching for a fight. Not having Chloe and Ellie nearby is driving me insane, and my darkest demons are just waiting for a reason and an opportunity to lash out.

I guess tonight's the night I'll vent some of my anger.

"Hey, Boss," Sal greets me as soon as I walk in.

The bar is crowded even though it's a weekday. But then, anymore, it's crowded almost every night. People need a way to forget about their troubles, and my bars provide them with that outlet.

"Where are they?" I ask straightforwardly, not wanting to go through formalities.

Sal gestures with his head toward the back door, and I follow him, cracking my knuckles as we go. This bar is old, built before people got so big. The hallways are narrow, the rooms cramped, and we need to walk in a line so as not to bump into each other.

He takes me to a dark room we use for storage, filled with boxes and unopened bottles. I haven't been in here for a while, so I take a look around. It all looks like legit bar supplies.

Two guys strung up by a rope tied to an iron hook in the ceiling are the only thing my eyes can focus on at this moment. They've been beaten pretty badly, one of them barely conscious, but I stride forward, my footsteps echoing loudly in the packed room.

"I assume you're here because your boss is too fucking scared to come over himself," I note, my tone bitter and barely restrained.

My hands are shaking, and my blood is pumping in my ears, but I need to control myself so I get something out of these bastards. Otherwise, this will be a wasted opportunity to get closer to Mateo and end this shit once and for all.

The man on my right, the one who looks like he's about to faint, chuckles, his shoulders shaking slightly as he tries to look up at me. Both his eyes are swollen, and he is drooling blood, but he seems cocky enough to laugh at me even in such a state.

"You don't think you're in a shitty position to be laughing at me right now?" I ask through clenched teeth.

"This one is fucking daring, Boss," Sal informs me from behind where I'm standing. "It took us a little work to get him. That's why he looks like this."

I get what he's saying. The guy does look like he's been beaten pretty badly, but I can understand my men handling him a certain way for not being... cooperative.

"Should we try a little harder, then?" I suggest with a grin.

The guy to my left winces at my suggestion, and I turn to focus my attention on him.

"Unless *you* want to cooperate with me?" I add, taking a couple of steps forward, my nose inches away from his. The smell of blood is nauseating, but it also has me salivating. "It's your choice. Either you tell me where to find your boss, or we'll start all over again and the only peace you'll find is in death. Although, I don't think Hell has any of that to offer you."

The guy chokes on a sob, and his asshole partner laughs again, straightening up and lifting his chin. I turn swiftly, punching him in the gut before he has the chance to laugh at me anymore. I am so fucking tired of this game and frustrated that I haven't gotten anywhere near Mateo. I have no patience or time to deal with this.

He spits blood on the floor, too close to my shoes, and I swallow, closing my eyes and taking a deep breath. Then, in the blink of an eye, I unholster my gun and aim for his head, pulling the trigger without a second thought.

He wouldn't have given me any information. I know his type.

If I can get anything at all from anyone, it will be his scared partner who is now crying after seeing me kill his friend beside him.

"I'll give you one more chance. Either you give me something, or you'll follow your friend," I warn him in a low snarl.

"I don't know where he is," he manages to choke out. "He doesn't speak to us directly. He gives orders through our superiors," the man tells me, his voice weak and cracking.

Maybe it should make me pity him, but I've lived this life long enough to know better. He's young and could probably have a better life if he had the chance, but sometimes it just isn't possible. It's all about the opportunities we're given, not just the choices we make. Most of us don't even have a choice. Most of us fall into this hellhole and never manage to get out.

It's sad, but it's reality.

I don't want to kill him. I don't doubt what he's telling me is the truth. It will get me nowhere closer to Mateo to end his life.

So, instead, I decide to send a message through him.

"Since your boss loves messengers, I'll send you back to him with a warning, then," I say, leaning forward to whisper the message as close as possible so he'll hear me clearly. "Tell him if he touches a hair on my wife's or her daughter's head, it will be fucking war. And I won't spare anything or anyone again. I will go to the ends of this earth to get to him, and I will make sure he regrets every single thing he ever did to Chloe. Hear me?"

He nods eagerly at me, swallowing hard, but hope glimmers deep in his eyes. I know he's seeing a way out, but I doubt Mateo will give him one after he delivers the message.

People like him don't get to simply walk away.

Without saying another word, I turn on my heel and head out of the room, desperate for a breath of fresh air. The strong, metallic smell of blood turns my stomach. I'm used to it, but it's honestly not my favorite part of the job. I wish I could leave the beatings to someone else, but as the boss, sometimes, I'm the only one who can do it.

As soon as I'm out on the street, I inhale deeply, feeling the cold evening breeze hit me. I run my fingers through my hair in frustration, considering what to do next.

Everything in my being is yelling at me to go and check on Chloe, but that's the least safe thing to do right now. Mateo is likely watching my every move, and I can't give him an opportunity to get to them.

Also, we left things on a sour note. She probably hates my guts right now. And no matter how much I want to see Chloe and hold her in my arms, I can't. It pains me to admit that I've fallen for her. I was stupid enough to let that happen.

What began as infatuation has turned into a fucking tangle of feelings I can't comprehend or control. Things are already hard enough without me having to make it worse by adding my own feelings to the mix.

Continuing to treat this as a business and keep my distance from Chloe is the best thing to do. But it's also fucking hard when my body and heart tell me to go the other way.

Checking on her will only make this more confusing–for me and for her. And even though it pains me to go against every cell in my body, it's not fair for me to lead her on or confuse her any further.

CLOSE BUT DISTANT

Chloe

A FADED COMMOTION DOWNSTAIRS WAKES ME UP, MY MIND TAKING A few seconds to adjust and understand where I am. It's been a few days since we moved to Vermont, but I still haven't gotten used to this place, or this bed, for that matter.

The safe house isn't uncomfortable at all, nor inconvenient, but no matter how hard I try, nothing makes me feel the same way I feel at Tony's house back in Staten Island. My house—it's my house, too.

I ponder going back to sleep, deciding whatever's going on downstairs is probably irrelevant. My mother must be giving orders to Tony's soldiers to go get groceries or something like that. Since she can't go out by herself, she has no choice but to ask them to do the errands for her.

But when I hear a familiar, deep voice, I get to my feet immediately. What is Armando doing here? Tony sent several men to watch us, but his second shouldn't be here, not when they're likely facing a war back in New York.

Tiptoeing out of the room, I get to the top of the stairs, doing the best I can to stay hidden, hoping to eavesdrop on their conversation. Soon enough, I realize Armando's voice is distant and coming through the speaker of my mother's phone instead. Of course, he wouldn't be here. But why is he calling my mom?

"Why does she need to go? Tony sent us here for a reason. It makes no sense he wants her to return now all of a sudden." She's arguing with him, not doing a good job at keeping her voice down—if hiding this from me is even her goal, which I assume it must be. She's usually trying to keep me in the dark, and I bet she knows more about what's going on than me.

"We need her help with something, Mrs. Bertolucci. And you don't need to worry. The guys will accompany her the entire time. It's safe, I can assure you," Armando tells her over the phone.

My mother sighs, and even though I can't see her face from up here, I can picture her rolling her eyes at her inability to do anything to stop this. She hates not having control, and I know she hates the fact that Tony sent her here as well.

"Fine," she concedes. "I want reports about her by the hour, though. I won't stay here with the baby without knowing what's going on with my daughter," she argues, making sure her demand is heeded.

"I can guarantee you that," Armando agrees. "Rocco will take her to the airport where she will meet two guys who will fly with her."

"Okay, I'll get her to leave the house in thirty minutes," my mom informs him.

It bothers me immensely that I'm not involved in any of this at all. It's *my* life they're discussing, *my* steps they're deciding, and not once did they ask about my opinion. I'm just informed of things as if I can't make decisions of my own or think by myself.

I'm also bitter because I haven't heard from Tony since I left New York, and I'm bored as hell inside this house, not being able to step one foot outside without being surrounded by guards.

I can't be selfish and complain about the precautions being taken to protect me and my family, but still, I can't help but sulk over my current situation.

Before I manage to return to my room, my mother shows up at the bottom of the stairs, looking surprised to find me here. It's obvious she knows I was listening. Otherwise, she wouldn't look so guilty.

"Chloe, I didn't know you were up," she says, trying to sound casual.

I clench my teeth before answering her. "Thank you for letting me decide this for myself," I retort sarcastically.

She has the decency to appear remorseful. "I'm sorry, sweetheart. It's just for a few hours, and you have to leave in thirty minutes, so please hurry up. I'm sure Tony must have a good reason. We just need to trust him."

"Of course," I manage to grumble.

I don't even have the strength to be mad at him for doing things his way. Why can't he just call me and ask me if I'm okay with whatever he's planning? Why can't he talk to me instead of ordering his second to call my mother to discuss the plans they have for me?

I turn on my heel, too pissed off to carry on with this conversation. Since I have no authority or will of my own, it's better that I just do what I'm told. Arguing will get me nowhere.

I go back to my room, take a quick shower, and put on jeans, a white T-shirt, and a brown blazer. I pick white sneakers, deciding I don't want to risk wearing heels since I have no idea what I'll be up to during the day, and I don't want to be uncomfortable during the flight either.

Once I'm ready, I head over to the living room, finding Mom feeding Ellie while she puts on some cartoons to distract her. I'm still bitter by the time I say goodbye and head out of the house, finding Rocco already waiting for me in the car.

I greet him with a bitterness in voice, hoping I don't sound rude. I know he's only following orders, and I don't want to be unfair by aiming my anger at him.

Something deep within me is anxious and hopeful that I will at least get to see Tony today, but I push that emotion down, back to the well it just crawled up from. He doesn't deserve my eagerness to see him. I'm supposed to be mad at him. I'm grateful, yes. He's taking care of us in his own way, but I can't help but wish he had dealt with this differently.

I wish he could have taken my opinion into consideration. That's what hurts me the most.

This and the fact that he all but rejected me. But I have no time for that right now.

The flight to New York ends up being more stressful than I anticipated. The hours seemed to be stuck, time frozen as we fly through the clouds. By the time we arrive and leave the airport, we are caught in a heavy downpour, the road ahead barely visible.

Since Rocco stayed back in Vermont, Tony assigned another driver to pick me up, one I've never met before. He takes a different road than what I'm used to, and I begin to realize Tony must have planned to have this meeting in less risky territory. When I ask him where he's taking me, he simply ignores my question, his eyes focused on the world outside of this vehicle.

I lean back in my seat, crossing my arms and staring at the rain hitting the windows. I love rainy days, the sound and smell of it, but right now, I can't even pay attention to it.

When the car stops in front of an old, shabby hotel in a remote neighborhood close to Brooklyn, I narrow my eyes, my nails sinking into my palms as my driver guides me toward the entrance.

This looks like the last place on earth I'd walk into if I cared for my life. But I guess this is part of Tony's plans, and since I heard Armando talking to my mom about it, I feel a bit more reassured.

A bit, but not enough to step inside the place without feeling like my heart is about to burst out of my chest. Why did Tony have to pick such a scary place to meet me?

"Room eight-oh-two. Knock twice and go inside without waiting for an answer," the driver whispers to me before turning back to the car and leaving me by myself.

There's not even a receptionist by the front desk to greet me and show me the way. It feels like a freaking horror movie to walk through the hallways and take the elevator alone. I feel goosebumps shooting up my spine every time the wooden floor creaks beneath my feet or the wind blows through a broken window.

I make a mental note to scold Tony about his choice of places. If he wanted to scare me, he got it just right.

Once I reach the eighth floor, I do as I was instructed, walking into the room right after the second knock. The room is dingy and dark, and my eyes take a second to adjust to the surroundings. Two men stand on different sides of the room, one to my left and the other to my right.

I immediately recognize Tony, even in the darkness. His silhouette is slightly taller than the second guy, but my body is instantly drawn to him, and that's why I simply know it's him.

"Ah, there she is," the second man says with a thick Irish accent. As soon as he finishes the sentence, he turns on a dim light on the night-stand beside the bed, making it easier for me to see his face.

I've never seen him before. His stately nose and auburn hair are the first things that stand out to me. He has a funny expression on his face, his eyes darting between me and Tony while his lips curl up with amusement.

"Can't believe I'm finally meetin' the lass," he adds, picking a cigarette from his pocket and lighting it up. I want to remind him we're in a closed space and that I hate the smell of cigarettes, but since I just met him, and I have no idea how helpful he might be in our cause, I remain silent, opting to just grimace when he blows smoke into the room.

"Chloe, this is Cal," Tony introduces us, speaking to me for the first time.

It's dark, but I can tell he isn't looking at me while speaking to me. I don't need to say how this annoys me immensely.

"He's the boss of the Irish Kings here in New York City," he continues, leaning against the wall, still not looking at me. He has his arms folded across his chest, and his downcast eyes tell me he's not happy to be here.

Or maybe that *I* am here.

I've heard about the Irish Kings before and how they turned from enemies to allies, and even friends. I'm relieved to know Tony has people outside of the Saints helping him chase Mateo. Or at least, that's what I assume Cal is doing here.

"It's a pleasure to meet you, Cal," I say, nodding at him and offering a soft smile.

"The pleasure's mine, love. Now I see what me lad here saw in ya." He seems to be having fun, and I'm positive I'm missing an inside joke here, but I don't mind. For a first impression, I kind of like him already. There's a nice aura about him, almost as if he enjoys seeing Tony pissed off.

Which is exactly what seems to be happening right now.

Tony clears his throat, shooting a deadly look at Cal.

"What did you bring me here for?" I ask Tony, staring at him and hoping he can look at me so I can read his expression and make sure he's okay. "Can I finally come home?"

I know the answer to that, but it doesn't hurt to ask it anyway.

"You and Ellie need to stay in Vermont for a little longer," Tony informs me darkly. "I just need some information from you."

"Couldn't you have asked me over the phone?" I blurt bitterly, unable to keep my anger from boiling up.

Cal snorts, shrugging as Tony glances at him once more.

"No, I couldn't," Tony replies seriously. "This is classified information, and I can't risk any of this leaking."

I sigh, already feeling where this is going. "What do you need to know?"

"I need you to tell me everything you know about business and safe houses that Mateo has in Miami," Tony demands.

His eyes roam over the room, even behind me, but not once does he look me in the eyes. It makes me want to cry. I'd rather he tell me he hates me than ignore me like this.

"I don't know much about it. He didn't share those things with me," I tell him.

"You might have heard something through the years," Tony suggests. "Just think about it carefully."

Cal nods in agreement but remains silent, smoking his cigarette quietly.

I rack my brain for anything that might be useful. I meant it when I said Mateo didn't share business information with me. Even though he was obsessed with me, he never trusted me to let me know about his dealings.

Some names of bars and people I heard being dropped here and there in meetings and hushed conversations between him and his men pop into my mind, and I mention them to Tony. I make sure to remind him it might mean nothing, but Cal assures me they need something to start with. He will have his men look into the information I provide cautiously, and Tony says he will do the same with the Saints.

That's when I realize what he's planning. He's going after Mateo. Tony will stop waiting for him to come to us and will go after him first. After Mateo and the De La Cruz Cartel.

He's done waiting.

"Got all you need to start looking?" Tony asks Cal, who seems too comfortable in this shabby room. It makes me wonder what he must have been through in his life. A guy like him must have experienced a lot so as not to be shaken by anything.

"Sure do. We'll get the bastard soon, I promise ya." Cal nods, putting out the cigarette and looking between Tony and me.

They share a glance, an unspoken message being exchanged through their eyes. Then Cal looks at me and bows his head slightly. "I'll be makin' me way now, love. It was a joy to meet the one causin' this lad such a fierce headache lately." He chuckles and passes by me, leaving the room.

The atmosphere instantly gets heavier, the silence around us almost deafening. I hear nothing but the sound of our own breathing and the rain outside, but I don't dare say anything. I simply stare at Tony, waiting to see if he will finally look at me and stop pretending I'm invisible to him.

He clears his throat awkwardly, and his eyes finally meet mine, causing me to shiver from head to toe. "This is only temporary, Chloe," he tells me softly, his voice barely audible.

"Sure," I murmur, still too upset with him to be casual about this. "As if this is not what you want, right? This distance between us..."

38

DROWNING IN SORROW

Tony

I CAN'T FORCE MYSELF TO ANSWER CHLOE. I'VE BEEN STRUGGLING TO keep a stoic facade ever since she arrived here. I knew bringing her back was a mistake from the moment Armando suggested it to me, but he was right when he said I couldn't ask what she knew over the phone. Despite spending hundreds of thousands of dollars every year to keep the inner communication of the Saints untraceable, I still don't trust that someone might not be able to hack into our phones and listen to what Chloe had to say.

In the end, she didn't give me much information, but it seemed enough for Cal and my men to start digging. Anything that will help me get closer to Mateo at this point is already a win.

A part of me also wanted to see her, to make sure she was all right, to make sure she was taking care of herself while being away from me. But the moment she crossed that doorway, the moment her sweet scent hit me, I knew I made a mistake. I couldn't look at her. Otherwise, I wouldn't trust myself enough not to get close to her.

Then Cal made fun of me, and I had to silently tell him to leave if he didn't want me to punch him in the face. I could tell she was mad at me from a mile away. Because of the way we left things, there's no way she doesn't hate me right now.

And at last, I made the biggest mistake of all by looking at her. I had done a great job until then. But when she suggested I want to keep my distance from her, my eyes automatically diverted to her beautiful face, her intoxicating eyes searching for an answer in my eyes.

An answer I can't give her.

Because the truth is, if I tell her how I really feel, I won't let her go ever again. And right now, this is counterproductive. I need her to be safe so I can carry on with my plan to get Mateo once and for all.

The expression of pain and sadness that crosses her face when I don't answer breaks my heart. I have to bite my tongue as strongly as possible so as not to give in under her intense gaze.

Fuck, I miss her. How I miss running my fingers through her hair, her smooth skin, her lips…. It physically hurts to be in the same room as her and not be able to touch her.

Chloe clears her throat, clearly uncomfortable standing here without receiving an answer she so desperately wants.

"Well, I know my opinion doesn't matter to you, but if you allow me to give you advice, don't go after the cartel. I know I've said this before, and I know I'm the one who asked you for your help, but Mateo won't play nice. It's not worth risking your men over this."

I sigh, rubbing my hands down my face in frustration. "I have to, Chloe. You know that. He started this. This needs to end."

"Your men will die because of me, Tony. I can't carry that guilt," she counters, pleading with me with her eyes and soft voice.

I stride across the room, stopping a few inches away from her. Her intoxicating scent inebriates me momentarily, and I need to close my eyes to gather my bearings for a moment. When I open them, Chloe is looking at me with flushed cheeks, breathing erratically. It always drives me to insanity, but I manage to keep myself together. More importantly, I keep my hands to myself.

"None of this is because of you. Mateo should have thought better before coming after my wife," I say to her, my voice barely above a whisper. My body is aching, begging for me to step forward and take her into my arms, claiming her in this dirty, dingy room. It's not what she deserves, but I wouldn't mind doing it if it meant I could feel her one more time.

I clear my head. "Your driver is waiting for you downstairs. Have a great flight, Chloe," I hiss instead, cursing myself inwardly.

She stares at me for a few seconds in utter silence, her eyes blinking so rapidly I wonder if she's about to cry. I know that the moment I see a tear in her beautiful eyes, I will break. That's why I look away, diverting my gaze to the dirty, small window in the corner of the room.

I hear her huffing, then the door opening and closing behind her, and only after she leaves do I take a deep breath. My entire body aches from her absence already, and my head is pounding like hell.

I walk toward the bed, sinking onto the edge, the thin mattress giving under my weight, the structure creaking loudly. I rest my head in my hands, my elbows propped on my knees as I allow myself to sulk.

As much as I hate to admit it, now I understand what Dante must have gone through with Eleni in the past. Maybe I should have been easier on him back then. I couldn't understand what he was feeling, but now, everything is so much clearer to me. I get it now. I get why he went through all of that because of *her*.

I can't think of doing anything differently with Chloe now. Sure, I hate that I have to make her suffer, that I have to push her away to keep her safe. But knowing she is alive gives me the strength I need to fight. To know I have a home to return to, that I have her and Ellie waiting for me, is all I can ask for. All I can grab onto.

I can only hope she'll be there when all of this is over. I pray she can understand my methods and reasons, that constantly hurting her won't push her away from me for good.

I don't know how long I stay like this, but when I finally leave the hotel, I'm in desperate need of a drink. I can't go back to an empty house sober. There's no fucking way.

Chloe's smell is everywhere around the house, even though it's been days since she left. My sheets still smelt like her, and I had to fucking change the bed so I didn't lose my mind completely. I just need to drown myself in alcohol tonight so I can go home and collapse in my bed without thinking about her.

Aphrodite's Lounge is the only place that comes to mind, so I get in my car and drive there, finding my usual booth empty, inviting, and waiting for me. A glass of whiskey is in my hand before I sit down. I gulp it down immediately, receiving a curious look from the waitress. But she tells me she'll get me another as quickly as possible, and I nod absently at her, leaning back in my seat and focusing on another faceless dancer twisting around the pole.

I don't recognize her, nor do I try to. None of this does anything for me anymore. All I can think of is Chloe's face, and I curse myself for being here while I should be in her arms instead. I just want to be at home, putting Ellie to sleep and then going to bed with Chloe, talking about trivial things and spending time with her.

That is exactly the kind of life I promised myself I'd never have, but right now, it's the only life I can think of having. It's the only one that makes sense in my head.

After four drams, I order the waitress to just leave the bottle on my table to save her the trouble of coming and serving me every five minutes. By that time, I'm already dizzy as hell and pondering the stupidest things in my head.

My hands are itching to call Chloe and apologize for being an asshole. The pained look on her face is still imprinted in my brain as if I'm seeing her in front of me still. I hate myself for being the reason she is so upset.

But I can't call her.

I can't be that weak.

I grab my phone from my pocket, struggling to unlock the screen. Good God, I must look pathetic right now. I can't fucking hold my phone in my hand after drinking... what, half a bottle of whiskey?

What is wrong with me?

My finger hovers over Chloe's name. She might still be on the flight. I doubt her phone is on, but even if it is, I have to convince myself I can't call her.

So, instead, I decide to call Armando and hope he can save me from embarrassing myself any further.

"Yes, Boss?" he answers on the first ring.

"Can you come and pick me up?" I ask, my voice dragging. "My car is parked outside. There's just no fucking way I can drive right now."

I think I hear a chuckle on the other side, or maybe he just cursed me, but Armando answers me right after, not giving me time to think about it. "Sure thing, Boss. Same place as usual?"

"You know it," I reply, leaning my head back and closing my eyes. I feel exhausted. "Just don't make a fuss about it."

This time he really laughs. In fact, he cackles so loud that I grimace.

"Yeah, right…. I'll be right there, Boss. Don't do anything stupid."

I already did, I want to tell him.

I fell in love. And I might also have lost her before I ever even had her.

39

A DIFFERENT MORNING

Chloe

It's been one week since I last saw Tony, and I'm losing it. That's the only way I know how to put it. My days are all the same; nothing happens, and having no news from Tony or his men back in New York is leaving me awake at night, too anxious to relax.

Only God knows how many times I pondered calling him, checking in on him, or anything at all to ease my mind, but nothing I do seems to work. Whenever I ask Rocco or any of the guys outside to let me know what's going on, they always tell me the same thing—they're not allowed to give me any information.

And what annoys me the most is the fact that even with all of this happening, I can't find it in me to hate Tony. I simply can't. All I care about is knowing he's all right.

I have no idea what he and Cal did with the little information I gave them about Mateo. Judging by how calm his men seem to be, though, I can only assume that nothing major has happened yet.

My mornings look all the same. Mom and I do our best to keep ourselves entertained while taking shifts watching Ellie and taking care of the house. Not being able to go out has also taken its toll on Ellie, who seems to be more irritated than usual.

But today, when I go downstairs for breakfast, something feels different. I can't tell what it is at first. Nothing out of the ordinary seems to have happened while I was in my room getting ready for the day. Mom is feeding Ellie her breakfast in the kitchen while the soldiers are cheerfully talking to each other outside.

"Good morning, Mom. Morning, sweetheart," I greet them, giving my daughter a kiss on the forehead. "Is everything okay?" I ask my mom. It's become a habitual question of mine, an attempt to get anything she might know out of her. But her answer is always the same.

"Yes, everything's great," she replies. "Did you sleep well?"

I nod, even though she's not looking at me. I plop on the couch, too depressed to pour myself a cup of coffee. The weather outside is cold this morning. That's why I decided to wear a comfortable pair of sweatpants and a hoodie. It's not like I have anyone to impress here anyway.

"You're not having breakfast? I made waffles," my mother calls from the kitchen, stopping with Ellie's spoon of mashed bananas midair, frowning at me.

"I'm not really hungry," I grumble, lying down on the couch.

She brings Ellie into the living room and sets her on a blanket on the floor with some toys. I feel her eyes studying me, and a few times, she opens and closes her mouth to say something but decides against it. I count to ten, knowing she won't let it go, though.

"Listen, I'll take Ellie to the park today with the guards," she informs me.

I sit up straight, surprised to hear this. "What? Why?"

She shrugs as if this is nothing big. "Honestly, we're all bored in this house, and Dice assured me there was no problem going outside as long as they come with us."

"You don't like going out with the guards," I remind her, my frown deepening.

"I know. But I thought it'd be nice to get out of the house and also give you some time alone." Her voice is softer and kinder this time, and I can see the empathy in her eyes.

Mom knows how much I'm suffering being trapped in this house, away from Tony and not knowing what's going on back home with him and Mateo, so I truly appreciate her doing this for me.

I can definitely use some time to myself, and since Dice guaranteed they would be safe, it sets me more at ease.

"Thank you, Mom," I whisper, looking at my hands. "Are you really okay going out?"

She nods eagerly. "Absolutely. I could use some time at the mall as well, just getting some new stuff for myself... and Ellie. Right, baby? Grandma will buy you something really nice today."

She turns to Ellie, receiving a huge smile and excited claps in return. Ellie tries to say something, but it comes out as an incomprehensible babbling that none of us can interpret.

After breakfast, they leave the house, and I immediately feel like this wasn't as good as I'd originally thought it would be. It's not like I have much to do here by myself, anyway. Books and the TV only keep me entertained for a couple of hours, and after that, I need to be creative and find something else to do.

The house is sparkling, all the clothes are washed and put away, and there are no dishes in the sink. I wouldn't like to spend my free time doing chores, anyway. However, since I didn't have breakfast, my stomach growls when it gets close to noon.

I spend some time in the kitchen preparing a quick meal for myself and also deciding to bake a cake for when Mom is back with Ellie.

It's almost 4:00 P.M. when I start getting uneasy. Mom hasn't reached out since she left, and I had no clue she was planning on spending the entire day out. I call her a couple of times, but she doesn't answer.

I'm immediately nervous.

I ponder calling Dice or one of the guys but opt for calling Mom one last time instead. I almost give up when she picks up the phone.

"Good Lord, Mom! Why didn't you answer the first time I called?

Is everything all right?" I blurt, scolding her even before she has the chance to say 'hello.'

"I was playing with Ellie," she tells me defensively. "You were supposed to be relaxing. I told you we'd be fine. Why are you so worked up?"

I gasp in disbelief. *Is she kidding me right now?*

"Oh, I don't know. Maybe because we're in the middle of a mafia war, and there are literally people out there looking for us and wanting our heads on stakes?" I counter bitterly. "What are you thinking, Mom? It wouldn't hurt to give me some news every once in a while."

"I know, I know. I'm sorry. I thought you'd be... doing something fun," she points out, a note of something in her voice that I can't interpret.

That's when the alarm in the house goes off, almost deafening me.

"Fuck," someone hisses from the front door, and my body is instantly on alert.

Who the hell is here? Did any of the guards try to come inside and forgot to type the password? They wouldn't make such a stupid mistake, would they?

It takes less than thirty seconds for the alarm to be turned off.

"Damnit to hell, why does it have to be so loud?" the same familiar voice grumbles.

Frowning and confused, I slowly walk toward the entrance, aware that if this was someone trying to kill me, they wouldn't be announcing their presence so easily and like such an amateur.

But what I find, or better yet, *who* I find staring back at me when I get to the foyer is the last person I was expecting to see today.

"I'll call you later, Mom," I whisper into the phone, not bothering to wait for an answer before hanging up.

Tony is looking at me from across the room. His ice blue gaze holds mine, his eyes so intense I almost lose my balance.

"What are you doing here?" I manage to ask.

He looks somewhat out of breath, almost as if he had to run to get here.

"I just had to fucking see you," he tells me, striding across the room toward me.

In a blink of an eye, his arms wrap around my waist, pulling me hard against his chest. His intoxicating cologne envelops me, and I instantly melt in his arms. I'm thankful that he's holding me so tight, because I don't trust my legs to keep me steady right now.

I might be dreaming. That's the only explanation for Tony to be here, in this house, holding me in his arms.

"Did something happen?" I ask in a whisper, searching his face for any sign of trouble, or worse, a wound.

But he just shakes his head at me, reassuring me nothing bad has happened. Then he leans forward, sealing our lips together, devouring me like only he knows how.

REUNITED

Chloe

MY ARMS VOLUNTARILY LOOK FOR SUPPORT AROUND HIS NECK. HIS hands on my waist tighten their grip, my skin burning up with the contact. Our tongues move together in a hungry dance, exploring each other's mouths as if this is the first time we've ever kissed.

I missed him so much; I can't even put into words what I'm feeling as he guides me backward toward the living room. This is not how I imagined, or even wanted, to reunite with him, but pulling away from him right now might break the spell he's under and make him regret coming here in the first place.

That's why I follow his lead, making sure to hold him and never let go.

Once we get close to the couch, instead of tossing me on my back and climbing over me, Tony turns us and sits down, pulling me onto his lap. I straddle him, immediately feeling his hard cock against my thigh, which ignites something within me that feels primatial and animalistic.

My entire body is sensitive right now–any small contact of our skin entices me from head to toe. My core throbs as I scoot forward, desperately looking for some friction to release the built up energy.

Tony groans against my mouth, pulling backward just an inch to look me in the eye. The intensity in his gaze is so much that I have to force myself not to look away.

"Are you okay?" he whispers, his breath fanning against my lips, causing me to shiver.

I shake my head, choking on a sob. I'm so relieved to see him here. I am so happy that he came here to check on me. "Not really. I missed you," I confess in a whisper.

His eyes dart to my lips and back up. They're filled with so many emotions I can't interpret what's going on inside his mind. I know he's going through a lot right now. That's why I don't want to push him into sharing anything with me, but I can't stand seeing him like this.

Tony seems to be suffering just as much as I am from staying away from me, from our family. This might just be wishful thinking on my part, but I don't think there's any way I'm misinterpreting this. Even if he won't admit it.

"I fucking missed you, too," he replies, cupping my face and bringing our lips close again.

As soon as we're back to kissing, my heavy outfit starts annoying me. I regret picking it today, even though I seemed to have a plausible reason for it earlier. I wasn't expecting Tony to show up today, that's for sure. And it is really cold outside. But right now, with my entire body bursting into flames, it's hard to be reasonable and understand my thought process from the past.

Tony removes my hoodie, yanking it over my head, and shoving it aside, leaving me completely topless. I didn't wear a bra this morning since I'd planned to stay home, and I'd rather be as comfortable as possible. Because of the cold weather, and my current arousal, my nipples are hard, and at the sight of them, Tony swallows hard, devouring me with his gaze.

I arch my back with pleasure as soon as his lips are on my breast, licking, sucking, and making me see stars. I relish the feeling he evokes, rocking back and forth on his lap, desperate to feel more of him.

My hands roam over his hard chest, and I blindly remove his jacket and button-up shirt. It's only fair we're equally undressed. I assume the bulge in his pants might be bothering him since he shifts uncomfortably under me. So, not wanting him to stop doing what he is doing, I reach for his cock, grabbing it through the fabric and squeezing, drawing a moan from his throat.

His grip on me tightens, and when he pulls away from my breasts, clearly ready for the next step, I slide from his lap, getting rid of the last layers of clothes preventing me from feeling his skin against mine.

Tony does the same with his pants and boxers, and soon I'm back to straddling him, sliding down on him, and taking him in completely. I bite down on my lip, preventing a moan from escaping. Right now, I can't even think about the possibility of my mom coming back with Ellie and making us stop. I can only hope she knew Tony was coming, and that's why she offered to take Ellie out for the day.

His hand finds my hair, twisting and tugging it, making my head fall backward, and leaving my neck free for him to ravage. When his lips find the sensitive spot under my ear, I finally let out a moan, speeding up as I ride him.

It's incredible how no man on this planet ever made me feel as happy, satiated, and desired as Tony does. Whenever we're together like this, the way he looks at me, the way he touches and pleases me… it's like he worships the ground I walk on.

And I can't pretend I don't like it. Having suffered my entire life at the hands of men that are good for nothing, this feels like a breath of fresh air. Like I'm finally seen as someone worthy of being loved and adored.

And that's exactly how Tony makes me feel, even if he doesn't say it out loud. His actions speak volumes.

I feel the pent up energy within me reach a new level, and I dig my nails onto his shoulders, supporting myself as the first wave hits me, leaving me momentarily numb with pleasure.

Tony speeds up, getting close, too. "You're so perfect," he murmurs, looking me in the eye as his orgasm hits him.

He leans his head back against the couch while I continue to ride him, making sure he's just as satiated as I am. It's only right that I return the favor, after all.

As we gather ourselves, steadying our erratic breathing, we stay in the same position, staring at each other, sweat dripping from our bodies.

Tony's cheeks and lips are flushed pink from exertion and it only makes him look hotter than ever. He finds a strand of hair falling over my face and gently pushes it out of the way, sweeping it behind my ear.

It's such a soft, yet romantic, gesture that it makes my heart beat even faster than before.

For a moment, we simply remain like this, looking into each other's eyes, no words spoken. But it's almost like we can read each other's minds.

"Are you okay?" I finally ask, softly, aware that my question might scare him away.

But he doesn't move or signal that he wants to leave. Tony nods slightly, his eyes never leaving my face. "I'm okay," he assures me, caressing my arms. "How have you guys been?"

"Bored out of our minds," I admit, rolling my eyes and causing him to chuckle.

"I know. I'm sorry you've had to go through this. Is Ellie doing all right?" he asks, genuinely curious.

"Yes. She doesn't really know what's going on, so it's us who need to be creative and keep her entertained most of the time," I explain, offering him a soft, but not as positive, smile. "She gets irritated sometimes, so Mom decided to take her out today for a change."

Tony nods, but he probably already knew that. I doubt anything happens here without his knowledge and consent. I'm sure his men report to him every hour or so.

"I miss her," he confesses with a sigh. "I feel like I'm missing so much."

I gulp, guilt washing over me. I know I'm partially responsible for him sending us away, and mostly, I'm responsible for keeping Ellie away from him for almost two years. I don't think I'll ever fully forgive myself for it.

I take a deep breath, fighting back the tears threatening to make an appearance.

"Can't we come home? Can't we figure out another way to deal with this—together? It's excruciating staying here without knowing how you are. I can't do this anymore, Tony," I plead, my tone filled with sorrow.

Tony's features darken, and he clenches his jaw, his entire body stiffening.

The moment for this conversation has arrived. There is no way I can keep this inside me any longer.

CORNERED

Chloe

"WHAT DO YOU MEAN?" HE ASKS WITH A FROWN. "YOU CAN'T DO *WHAT* anymore?"

"I can't do this push and pull anymore. I...." I choke on my words, feeling uncomfortable all of a sudden.

So, with pain in my chest, I get up from his lap and start gathering my clothes from the floor, putting them back on. I feel his eyes on me the entire time, but he doesn't say anything. He probably realizes there is no way we can escape this conversation any longer.

Tony silently picks his boxers and pants up from the floor and puts them on, and for a whole minute, we're both mute, neither of us daring to continue the conversation.

Once we're dressed, I look at him, finding him staring at me from the same spot on the couch.

"I am tired of not knowing what *this* is," I finally clarify, gesturing between us. When Tony doesn't answer, I add, "Maybe you shouldn't have come here after all."

I don't mean it, but I'm mad at him for always being quiet when I need him to say something, anything at all, to ease my mind and heart.

It's frustrating not knowing what to expect from him, from us, from our *fake* relationship that doesn't feel so fake anymore.

"What is it that you want from me, Chloe?" he finally asks, sounding tired.

And that's what makes me snap at him.

How come he can't see what I want?

"Isn't it obvious?" I yell, disappointed.

He sighs, propping his elbows on his knees and holding his head in his hands. "Chloe, you know we can't do this…. *I* can't do this. I can't give you the life you deserve. You'll have a target on your back for the rest of your entire life," Tony tells me.

I sneer, frustrated. "Are you kidding me right now? Come on, Tony. You can come up with a better excuse than this. I'm already your wife. And, in case you've forgotten, I was born into this life," I counter bitterly. "I'm the daughter of a Capo! The fact that you think that will change because of you is ridiculous. There's nothing about this life that is new to me. Except maybe my feelings for you," I confess, my voice lowering slightly at the end of the sentence.

My eyes meet his again, and with courage I can't locate the source of, I take a deep breath and lay out my heart to him—something I promised myself I wouldn't do.

"I love you, Tony," I say softly, holding his gaze. "I think I might always have loved you."

He stares at me, completely dumbstruck, as if I just hit him with a car or something. I know I caught him off guard, but the fact that he's not saying anything, or at least slightly happy that I shared my feelings, breaks my heart.

A scoff escapes my lips when I realize he's really not going to say anything. "Great. I never took you for a coward, but I guess there's always room for disappointment in life."

Without waiting another second, I turn on my heel and head down the hallway toward the office. It's a room neither my mom or I ever use, but right now, I just need a moment to myself.

I close the door behind me and lock it, sliding down against the wood and sitting on the floor like a little girl who has just been sent to her room. I wrap my arms around my legs, pulling them tight against my chest and sinking my head onto my knees.

I can't face Tony right now. I feel rejected, ignored, and disappointed, not to mention heartbroken. I was always aware that my marriage to him was fake, that I shouldn't nourish feelings for him. This was *my* mistake. This is on me.

However, it's not like I can control my heart or my feelings. It's not like I can tell myself not to love someone. Because, if that was possible, I would have done it in a heartbeat. Because I've always known Tony has this barrier against feelings and emotions. He's scared of getting involved, of being vulnerable. Anyone who looks at him–really looks–can see that.

And I don't blame him for it. The life we lead–the life *he* leads–it's not easy. It takes great courage to let someone else in. And I understand the fear he has to get me more involved, to put Ellie in danger....

But, like I said, it's not *because* of him that our lives are at risk. I was born into this. And to make things worse, I got involved with Mateo. Even if Tony wasn't here, I would still be in trouble. Right now, if anything, he's my guardian angel. He is the only person I can count on to take care of me and Ellie.

Why can't he see that?

Memories of moments we shared together invade my mind, and for a moment, I allow myself to relish them, to relive them.

I don't know how long it's been when a soft knock on the door pulls me out of my reverie.

"Chloe?" Tony calls from the other side, his voice muffled by the thick wood. There's a pause where I imagine he might be taking a deep breath and thinking about what to say, and I simply wait, not giving him any sign that I am listening. I also don't trust my voice right now, not with tears welling up in my eyes.

"Listen, I'm leaving for Miami tomorrow." He pauses again, giving me a second to take in what he's saying.

He's going after Mateo after all.

I don't know what to do with this information. My heart feels so small right now, and I can barely breathe, the possible outcomes of his trip to Miami invading my brain for a moment.

"I'm really sorry," Tony adds. Then I hear his footsteps fading away.

The front door slams. He's gone. I finally let out a sob. In fact, it's like I opened a dam, the tears I've been holding back rolling down my cheeks nonstop.

It takes me a long time to compose myself, but I force myself to be strong. I can't appear to be upset when my mother returns home with Ellie. She might be here any second, now that Tony has left.

I pull myself from the floor and head upstairs to take a shower. I still have Tony's scent all over me, and even though it pains me to wash it away, it hurts even more to smell him and not be able to be near him.

The hot water makes me feel slightly better, but I don't take as long as I'd like in the shower. I get out and dry off after his scent has faded down the drain.

The mirror is still fogged up by the steam, so I don't have to look at myself, thank God. I pull my robe off a hook on the door and walk out of the bathroom just in time to hear the alarm go off again.

In my heart, there's a small seed of hope that it might be Tony coming back. The alarm is shut off almost immediately, and I remember how he struggled with the alarm the first time he came in.

I come to a halt, immediately frowning.

Maybe it's Mom, I think, but I shove the thought away. I don't think she'd make this mistake with the alarm after living here for a while now.

Slowly, I head out of the bedroom and down the stairs, fastening the belt around me and tying it in a knot. My heart beats fast at the prospect of seeing Tony again. Maybe he regretted not giving me an answer. Maybe he gave it a second thought and considered the idea of us being together. Maybe I proved my point after telling him there was nothing in this life I'm not already used to.

But when I get to the foyer, I see the one person I hoped I'd never have to see again.

Mateo stands by the door, holding a gun in his hand, a stupid grin plastered across his face. I feel a cold shiver run down my spine, and I have to force my knees to stay steady so they don't buckle under me.

"Hello, love," he greets me in a cold, dark voice, taking a step forward, toward me. "I guess you have some explaining to do."

Then, with a swift movement, he points the gun at the camera in the corner of the room and shoots it. The bang of the gun deafens me for a moment.

He's coming at me now, his steps slow and precise, almost like a wolf hunting, stalking its prey. My back hits the wood handrail of the stairs, and I realize I am cornered.

This is it....

The moment I've been postponing ever since my dad died.

All those nightmares are finally coming true—and there's absolutely nothing in the world I can do about it.

42

FAILED PROMISE

Tony

COMING HERE WAS A FUCKING MISTAKE.

Seeing Chloe did everything to me that I was trying to avoid. It just left me even more confused than before. We haven't spent more than an hour together, and I still managed to screw it up.

Being with her felt natural as if this was the only place I could be. Whenever I'm with her, holding her in my arms and feeling her close to me, everything just seems to go away. Every concern, every fear, every bad thought I ever had... I finally feel at peace.

That's the sort of effect she has on me.

But I was not expecting her confession. Hearing her say she loves me and not being able to say it back shattered my heart in ways I can't explain. The look on her face will haunt me forever. It seems to have become a pattern lately. I can't seem to be able to stop hurting and disappointing her. I know what she expects from me, but unfortunately, I can't give it to her.

It's clear to me that I have fallen for her, harder than I could ever have expected. It's a fucking nuisance–but also frightening. I don't

259

know how to manage it. I don't know what to do with it. Everything is so new to me.

Leaving her behind was one of the hardest things I ever had to do. My entire body ached as I walked out the door and away from her.

But even if it makes her hate me, I can't put her in any more danger.

Or maybe this is indeed an excuse I've been using to convince myself to not be with her. Because the truth is... this feeling scares the shit out of me. Being this vulnerable, this dependent on someone... I am not used to it. And I'm not sure I'll ever be.

But as I drive back to the airport, something within me is urging me to go back. I can't explain or even understand what it is, but it's like my instincts are telling me that I'm doing something wrong.

Which I know I am. But I don't want to confuse Chloe any longer. And until I have things figured out with Mateo–and myself– it's unfair to put her through more pain and suffering. I need to understand my feelings first before I can commit to something more.

That's when a distinct but familiar *beep* on my phone pulls my attention. Initially, I didn't even look at it since it goes off every time someone walks into the safe house. It's something I had installed on my phone so, even though I have my men watching over them twenty-four-seven, I can still know what's going on in there while I'm away.

Originally, it felt like a silly way to be in control of the situation from afar. But sometimes, it eases my heart when I go to bed at night, and I can check on them and make sure they are safe. It came in handy whenever I missed them dearly and needed to just look at them having dinner together or watching TV in the living room.

It gave me this peace I so desperately craved.

I grab my phone and open the app, checking the cameras at the house and notice something is off. The outside video surveillance and the front door camera are blank.

Pitch black.

My stomach churns as I realize something is wrong.

My fingers fly over the screen as I speed dial Armando. He answers on the first ring.

"Did you guys turn off the cameras after I left?" I ask straightforwardly before he has the chance to say anything, my fingers tightening around the steering wheel.

"Boss," Armando answers in a deep voice, although sounding breathless. "I was just about to call you. After you left, two of our soldiers guarding the house got shot. Sal is taking them to the hospital in Vermont right now. One of them is badly injured," he informs me, the sounds of honks blasting behind him.

"Where are you?" I press, feeling my entire body stiffening. I swallow down the feeling of sickness washing over me.

"I'm heading to get Nicky and Ellie. I tried calling to check on them, but no one answered, so I thought it'd be better to just get there since I was close," Armando explains to me.

Fuck!

I can barely hear what he's saying, the blood pumping in my ears is so loud. I pull the car around, making a sharp U-turn in the middle of the highway, getting some curses and yells in return from the drivers I miss by an inch.

But I can't find it in me to care right now. I need to get back to the safe house. I need to make sure Chloe is okay.

If the guards watching her were shot....

I can't force myself to think of what might have happened. If Mateo really meant it when he ordered his guys to kill Chloe on the spot, I can't even imagine what he'd do if he got to her himself and found her alone.

Regret and guilt washes over me so strongly that I can't see straight. I'm driving on autopilot, barely registering what I'm doing as I speed down the highway.

"Boss?" Armando's voice echoes inside the car, and I shake my head, trying to focus on the road ahead.

"I'm on my way to the safe house," I inform him, doing the best I cannot to show my voice shaking with fear. "Just make sure Ellie and Nicky are safe. I'll go get Chloe since I'm still near the house. Where are the other guards?" I press through clenched teeth. Two of my men got shot, but I had an entire fucking task force come to Vermont to protect them.

"I can't get a hold of them," Armando replies, cursing back at someone yelling at him. "Some of them were on patrol, and our inner communication seems to have been cut off, too. We have no idea what's going on in the house."

I frown, biting the inside of my cheeks to keep myself from cursing loudly. How the fuck did Mateo manage to get past my security like this?

Guilt gnaws at me as I realize this is partially my fault. I told everyone to leave the house to myself so I could talk to Chloe alone. A few of them went with Nicky and Ellie, but since no one seems to be able to reach them, it's better that Armando is going after them to make sure they are all safe.

But Chloe was supposed to be with me. If I hadn't left the way I did, at the moment I did, Mateo wouldn't have gotten to her. I would be there to protect her like I promised I would. I gave her my word that he wouldn't get anywhere near her or Ellie, yet I failed.

I fucking failed the only promise that I made to her.

A couple of minutes later, when I spot the house in the horizon, my heart threatens to burst out of my chest, it's beating so fast. I jump out of the vehicle before I even pull it into park, noticing the front door is open.

I storm inside, looking frantically around, trying to find any sign of Chloe or Mateo. But the sight that greets me is the foyer floor covered in blood.

"Chloe!" I yell, heading for the living room, then the kitchen, and finally, upstairs, realizing with terror that she isn't here.

Neither is Mateo.

Images of what might have happened pop into my head uninvited. I fight the urge to vomit all over the carpet.

Did he take her alive? Did he kill her and take her body to prove something to me? Or maybe she managed to escape?

However, blood all over the floor tells me otherwise.

I'm spiraling into a fucking show of terror inside my head as I consider what to do next. I need to think quickly, but nothing I come up with seems to make sense.

I can't stay here. I need to do something, to go after Mateo and make sure he pays for this.

But most importantly, I need to find Chloe and make sure she is okay.

I can't accept any other outcome.

I can't even consider it.

4 3

FIGHTING FOR MY LIFE

Chloe

I SHOULD BE DEAD.

I was certain I'd be killed the moment I saw Mateo by the front door.

I don't think I've ever seen him look as mad as he looked a couple of minutes ago.

Somehow, by the grace of God perhaps, when I saw him approaching me with that gun pointed at my face, I managed to take it from his hand after sparring with him and shot him in the shoulder. *I think.*

I didn't stay there to confirm. I didn't wait to see if he was injured or not.

I simply ran out of the house, not daring to look back, not even once.

It's been a few minutes, and I'm still blindly running through the neighborhood, trying to think of what to do or where to go.

There's no one on the street that I can ask for help, and even if

265

there were, I'd be so afraid that Mateo would kill them for helping me that I don't think I would ask for help anyway.

It's cold outside, and I'm still only wearing my shower robe, and even though I don't dare to look back, too afraid of what I'll see, I know I'm being followed.

Either by Mateo or his men. It doesn't really matter who it is. It's just essential that I don't stop running until I know I'm safe and out of their reach.

I can hear car tires squealing behind me. I look around frantically, searching for an escape route that will get me out of the main street.

A short fence by my left catches my attention, and before I can consider it, I jump over it, ending up in someone's backyard. I pray that no dogs are out here. Unsure if someone saw me invading private property, I run to a shed on the other side of the yard and hide behind it, trying to catch my breath.

My heart is beating so fast against my rib cage that it's giving me a sharp pain in my abdomen. I bend over, taking deep breaths, inhaling and exhaling as slowly as possible given the situation I'm in. Sweat drips off my forehead, dripping into my eyes, making it even more difficult to see what's happening on the dark street I just escaped from.

Police sirens echo in the distance, but they're still far away. Whoever's after me is still out here–somewhere.

I silently thank whoever called the police, though. They must have heard the shot I fired at Mateo. I don't think the neighbors are so stupid as to not have noticed something was wrong with an entire task force being around the house day and night.

A black car speeds off in the distance, the tires squealing even louder than before.

I allow myself to close my eyes for a moment and sigh. It seems like I might have managed to throw them off.

That's when I realize I'm still holding Mateo's gun. My hand is sweaty around it, and for a brief second, I consider simply dropping it into the yard and walking away from it. But I can't leave evidence like this in someone else's yard.

I don't want to incriminate an innocent person, and I also don't want anyone to find it and deliver it to the police with my fingerprints all over it.

I look around, considering what to do.

My options are limited here. If not nonexistent.

I can't return to the same street. Behind me, there's a wall separating this yard from another. Another dead end, most likely. I can only go to the right, although I can't see where it leads.

I squat on the ground and start crawling in that direction, making sure the gun's safety is on. The last thing I need right now is to fire it by mistake. By the time I get to the other side of the yard, I realize what I couldn't see before seems to be a greenbelt.

I need to get rid of this gun. But what if I need it? What if Mateo managed to survive the bullet? Or, what if his men get to me? This gun is the only thing protecting me right now.

However, I don't feel comfortable holding it. And I don't want to have evidence *against myself* if the police find me, a deranged woman in a bathrobe, first.

So, with a confused mind, I decide to wipe the prints off the gun and throw it over the fence. I realize the only thing I can do next is try to get somewhere a little warmer. I can't go to the cops. I know better than that. I'm on my own. I need to find a phone. I need to call Tony. I need to make sure my daughter is okay.

I crawl back through the dark backyard, and slowly, cautiously, jump back onto the street. Hiding behind the parked cars along the sidewalk, I storm toward the main street.

A black car flies down the street, being followed by a police cruiser rolling with its lights on. There is no siren on though, and I assume they were trying to ambush Mateo's men. Somehow they managed to get on their tail, although, apparently, without the success of actually catching them.

I hide behind an SUV, trying to catch my breath. What the hell can I do? I don't know where to go. I have no phone with me. And there seems to be no one on the street at this hour.

I sprint in another direction, taking a detour through one of the alleys ahead of me. I invade another yard to escape another suspicious car, and I'm immediately drenched by the sprinklers going off.

"Shit!" I hiss, feeling the thick cotton of the robe getting heavier as it's soaked.

I'm wet, barefoot, and cold, but I can't stop.

I ponder going back to the house. By now, everyone has to know the safe house was attacked. I still don't know how Mateo passed through security, but after all this time, I can only assume the Saints might have established a new combat plan.

Right?

I can feel tears welling up in my eyes, but I can't give up. I need to make sure Ellie and my mom are all right.

Is it possible that Tony was notified before he got onto the plane to return to New York? He left the house not too long before Mateo arrived. So, it is possible that he didn't get to the airport before learning about the attack.

My brain is doing everything it can to prevent me from spiraling and freaking out. I can feel panic creeping up in me, my legs threatening to buckle under me.

I bite on my lower lip, preventing myself from crying.

"Please, God…" I pray quietly, my voice trembling with fear and cold, "just get me out of this."

Stepping out of the yard, my entire body shivering, I turn onto a corner, immediately spotting a silhouette of a man in the distance. I stop abruptly, paralyzed by the sight.

Is that Mateo? Or one of his men?

But as the figure approaches me, lightened up by a dim light coming from the other side of the street, familiar features make my breath catch in my throat.

Those ice blue eyes I love so much are staring back at me, his mouth drawn in a deep frown.

"Tony?" I whisper, my voice cracking.

He gasps, realization and relief crossing his face. Tony sprints toward me, but it's like he's moving in slow motion. My knees finally buckle beneath me, but before they can reach the concrete, strong arms wrap around me, pulling me up and into the warmest and safest embrace.

"It's okay," Tony whispers against my hair, tightening his arms around me. "It's okay. I'm here. I'm here. You're safe."

His voice sounds like a dream. Like an angel singing. Like I've gone to Heaven and have finally found peace.

I sob, my cries finally bursting through the dam I put up to keep myself strong.

"Come on, baby. Let's get you into the car and out of the street," Tony suggests, picking me up from the ground and into his arms.

I don't see where he takes me, I simply allow myself to sink into the safety of his embrace, hiding my face in the crook of his neck and taking in his soothing scent.

The cold leather seat against my cold, soaked skin is what brings me back to reality. Tony rushes to circle his car and get into the driver's seat before he speeds off.

"Fasten your seatbelt," he reminds me kindly, his eyes focused on the road ahead.

I have no strength to argue, ask him where he is taking me, or even what is happening. Right now, all I can do is breathe and gather my bearings.

I do as he tells me, completely silent.

"Are you okay?" Tony finally asks, glancing at me.

I nod, but I don't want him to think that I'm lying or keeping things from him, so I reiterate, "I'm okay."

44

OUT OF HARM'S WAY

Chloe

"Listen," Tony continues, still focused on the road. The police sirens get more and more distant as we drive away from the city, but I still don't ask him where he is taking me. "I know you don't want to think about it now, but I need to know what happened," he requests in a gentle voice. I hear a hint of pain in it as well, but mostly, I can hear the guilt behind his words.

I want to tell him none of this is his fault, but we'll have time for that later. Right now, we just need to make sure no one else gets hurt, or worse, killed.

I inhale sharply, steadying myself enough to share the recent events with him. *I am strong, and I can do this,* I tell myself. I've always told Tony I could handle it all, and even though I was scared as hell back there, I still managed to save myself.

I can do this.

"After you left, I spent a few more minutes in the office before I headed up to take a shower. I don't think I was in there too long, but as soon as I stepped out, I heard the alarm go off again," I begin as calm as possible. "I thought it could be you or my mom, although I knew she wouldn't let the alarm go off like that. So, it occurred to me that it could only be you again."

A dark shadow crosses his face, and his jaw clenches, but I carry on.

"By the time I reached the bottom of the stairs, Mateo was there, holding a gun and looking smug as always once he saw me."

I shiver at the memory. I don't think I'll ever forget the look of satisfaction on his face as he found me alone.

Tony's knuckles turn white as he tightens his grip on the steering wheel, but he doesn't interrupt me.

"He shot the camera in the corner and told me I had some explaining to do. After that, he walked toward me, calling me… names." I clear my throat, not wanting to repeat the monstrosity of curses he threw at me. "He asked me how stupid I could be to think I could hide from him behind a sham marriage." I swallow hard, my eyes darting to my hands on my lap. I fidget with my fingers while recalling the moment in my head.

"I thought I'd be killed on the spot. I don't think he would have spared me even if I obeyed him. But when he started flipping the gun around, too worked up as he cursed at me, I saw a chance to escape him. My only chance. So, I jumped on him and snatched the gun from his hand. We struggled a little, but I managed to grab it from the floor and shoot him in the shoulder. At least that's where I think it hit him. I didn't look back," I confess.

Tony remains silent the entire time, only driving and listening to me. He doesn't do a good job of hiding his reaction, though. I fear he might break his teeth at any moment if he doesn't stop clenching them so hard.

I can tell he's doing his best to remain calm. I don't want to add fuel to the fire, so I decide to shut up for now, waiting for him to put his mind in the right place and tell me what the plan is.

However, I reach for his free hand, squeezing it in a reassuring gesture, wanting him to know I am grateful for him saving me.

I still want to tell him this is not his fault, but I remind myself I can do it later, in a proper moment.

We fall into silence again, and twenty minutes later, Tony parks at a highway motel far away from the city. It looks as shabby as it can get, but I don't complain. Living in the underworld my entire life, I've seen my fair share of shabby hotels. Honestly, as long as I can take another shower, hopefully a warm one, I'll be more than grateful.

"Stay here," Tony orders, preparing to open the door.

But I immediately hold his arm, preventing him from stepping out.

"I don't want to be here alone," I tell him, my eyes wide with fear.

Tony gives me a soft smile and shakes his head. "It will only take a minute. It's okay. We weren't followed. I promise I'll be right back."

Gulping, I nod at him and release his arm. My heart beats fast until he returns a minute later. He pulls the car to the back of the motel, away from the highway, and parks it in front of our room.

He opens the car door for me and helps me inside the room, making sure to lock it behind us. The room is not as bad as I thought it'd be. It has a queen bed, a small TV, and a bathroom. It's simple, but warm, and right now that's all I need.

"Go wash up. Wash the blood off, and leave the robe on the bed," he orders, suddenly serious as he looks at my hands.

Only because he mentions it do I realize I have blood on me. All over me. There are stains on the robe and on my hands, but I have no idea how I got it. I shot Mateo, but not close enough for the blood to have sprayed. Or, maybe I was closer than I realized.

"Are you hurt?" Tony asks the question that hadn't crossed my mind until now.

I search my body, pulling the sleeves up and opening the robe slightly to check my stomach and legs. But there is nothing. Only a few scratches I probably got from running away through bushes and trees. "I don't think so," I reply, confused. The blood must really all be from Mateo. It makes me instantly repulsed.

I throw the robe on the bed and don't wait for Tony to order me again before rushing to the bathroom. I get into the shower, not even letting the water warm up. It takes a couple of minutes for it to start getting hotter, and I can almost cry with gratitude.

At some point, I think I hear the door closing, but I convince myself I'm paranoid. Things are still very fresh, so I might be imagining things.

When I step out of the shower and return to the bedroom, wrapped in a towel, I find a Walmart bag on the bed where I left the robe.

"I thought you might need something to wear," Tony tells me from the corner of the room. He's leaning against the wall, one hand in his pocket and the other holding his phone. "Get dressed while I make some calls."

"Thank you," I whisper. "I..." I hesitate, knowing he's busy and has a lot on his plate. But I simply can't postpone it anymore, no matter how frightened I am to hear the truth. "Are Ellie and my mom okay?"

He looks at me, his frown softening a little. "They're okay. Armando has them in a safe place," he assures me.

A sigh of relief escapes my lips, and I collapse on the bed. I cover my face with my hands, allowing the tears to fall down once more. I feel the mattress sinking beside me with Tony's weight as he comes to me and pulls me sideways to his chest.

"I need to tell you something, and I need you to listen carefully," he whispers in a low voice. I wipe my eyes, looking up at him. "Cal is sending some of the Irish Kings to come and pick you up. He'll take you to their hideout in the city."

I frown. "Why? Why the Irish Kings?"

"The Saints' men are all on a mission now. Some of them were injured, so we're down a few," he explains to me.

Tony doesn't have to say it for me to know what he means. I know what mission that is.

They are after Mateo.

However, the idea of being with what used to be a rival mob doesn't make me comfortable. I've met Cal before, though, and I could tell he was loyal to Tony. And to be fair, I don't think Tony would send me with Cal if he didn't trust him entirely.

"I don't want to be away from you again," I cry.

"I know. But I have things to do, Chloe. And I need to make sure this mistake doesn't happen again."

The look in his eyes tells me he's suffering from leaving me once more, but the resolution behind it also tells me he will never let this go until he sees that Mateo gets what he deserves.

"You're going after him, aren't you?" I ask softly.

Tony's jaw tenses, and his shoulders stiffen.

"Hell yeah, I am. I will make sure he pays for what he did to you."

4 5

───────

SCORCHING THE EARTH

Tony

I warned Chloe not to even try and convince me of doing anything else other than going after Mateo and his men. I'd been doing my best to act cautiously, to consider every single possible outcome from this war, but after he ambushed Chloe at the safe house, making her fight for her life, it left me blind with rage.

My guilt didn't help, either.

I was so relieved when I found her on that dark street, wearing nothing but a robe covered in blood, that I could have cried when I held her in my arms. She felt so small, so vulnerable within my embrace that the monster dormant inside me snapped to life, and I simply couldn't put this aside any longer.

Even if I die, even if I don't get to see her one last time, I will make sure to take Mateo down with me, so he never has the chance to lay a hand on my wife again. Or my daughter, for that matter.

"Do I really have to go with Cal?" Chloe's sweet voice asks from the bed, making me take my eyes off the phone and look at her.

I promised her I'd wait for Cal's men to arrive before I left so she didn't have to sit here by herself, especially after going through something so traumatic a few hours ago. It was the only thing I could do. I could never leave her alone in this motel room, either. I have to see with my own eyes that she is inside Cal's car before I leave and move on with my plan.

My priority is to make sure she's safe.

"We already talked about it, Chloe," I reply with a sigh. "It's the best thing for everyone now. Ellie and your mom are already on their way to the city. Don't you want to be with them?"

"Yes!" she answers, her tone a bit worked up with frustration. "But I also want to be with you!"

Her words cause something within me to stir, but I push it back. I don't have time for this right now. I want to mention our conversation back at the house, apologize for leaving the way I did, for being a fucking coward and not telling her that I feel the same way…

But when I open my mouth to retort, my phone buzzes in my pocket with a message from Cal.

'The lads just got there. Black Mercedes Sprinter, New York City plate.'

I look up at Chloe. "Come on. They're here," I inform her instead, receiving a huff from her in response.

I ignore it, hating myself for having to do it like this. If anything, I'm the one dreading the idea of separating from her again. But like I told her, at this moment, this is the best option we have.

We open the door, and after peeking outside and making sure the way is clear, I guide her toward the vehicle. We're greeted by Cal's second, who I instantly recognize from my meetings at his bar.

He slides the door open for Chloe, and she climbs in, glancing at me with a look of pain and sorrow in her eyes that threatens to break my heart. Again.

So, I look away, not wanting to see that look turn into hatred as I send her away.

"Send me reports, constantly," I request from the guys seated on each side of Chloe. They nod at me, and I close the door, not daring to throw her a last glance.

After I send them off, I rush to my car and drive out of the motel parking lot and toward the hospital. I need to check on my injured men and get an update on the situation first.

As soon as I step into the hospital a few minutes later, and get to the secluded area where my men are being treated, I bump into Sal, who's not even trying to hide the concern from his face.

"Boss," he greets me with a sharp nod as he approaches me, his hands in his pockets.

"Any news?" I ask right away.

"Dice is under observation, but he's still expected to be released tonight. Max is in surgery right now. His situation isn't good," he says darkly.

I clench my teeth, my hands balling into fists beside me. "Do we know what the fuck actually happened? How did they get past us like that?" I press, still not understanding how they managed to cut our internal communication and get into the house so easily.

Sal shrugs slightly, looking guilty and sorry at the same time. "Dice said they were snuck up on right after you left, almost as if they were waiting for you to be out of the way. They must have followed you or hacked into our intel system. There's no way they could have known Chloe was by herself at the house if they weren't watching our every move."

"Is it possible that we have a mole?" I urge, looking him in the eye.

But he shakes his head eagerly. "I don't think so, Boss."

Having a mole would be the easiest explanation for what occurred. Deep down, I wanted it to be that, so I wouldn't have myself and my poor security system to blame. In all truth, the reality is that I hate to admit that I failed.

As a mafia leader, as a man, and especially, as a husband.

It's gnawing at me how greatly I fucked up this time.

"I only want my capos to know the whole plan moving forward. The others only get the essential information from now on, at least until we get Mateo in our hands," I demand, lowering my voice even though the hallway is empty.

"Yes, Boss," Sal agrees with another sharp nod. "We already got a few on the ground, looking for the car spotted chasing Chloe."

I take a deep breath, taking in all the information and storing it in my brain. I look around, seeing a nurse coming out of a room at the end of the hallway, her gaze diverting to the other side almost immediately after our eyes meet.

"What about the hospital staff?" I turn back to stare at Sal.

"The doctor and the nurses taking care of them were easily persuaded to look the other way," he explains confidently.

"Not a chance of the police jump scaring you while you're here?" I ask.

"Not a chance," he assures me.

"Good. But if they do, get the fuck out. We'll find a way to free Dice and Max afterward," I order. "Let me know when he is out of surgery."

"Sure thing, Boss."

I dart from the hospital and head back to my car, dialing Cal on the way.

I feel trapped in a fucking dilemma, wanting to be with Chloe and make sure she and Ellie are okay, but also wanting to have Mateo's body six feet below ground.

If only I could be in two places at the same time....

"Give me some good news," I request as soon as I hear the call has been picked up.

"Blondie's on the plane already, and the baby and angry Italian mama are already at my bar," Cal tells me, the usual hint of amusement in his voice gone.

A sigh of relief escapes my lips. I've never felt more grateful to Cal than right now. To imagine he was considered an enemy in the past, and now, to have my entire world in his hands.

"Please let me know when she arrives," I ask quietly, not having the strength in me anymore to pretend I'm strong. All I wanted was to have a fucking day without a problem to solve.

"Don't worry, lad."

I hang up, resting my head on the headrest of the driver's seat and closing my eyes for a minute.

For me to be able to fight Mateo, I need to have my head in the right place. I can't be distracted. I can't be thinking about Chloe and the long list of regrets I have where she is concerned.

It's a list that only keeps growing and growing. I now have a new regret to add to it–the regret of not telling her the truth about how I feel.

About how I fucking fell in love with her. About how my crush on her turned into this gigantic, frightening, painful, and undeniable feeling that I can't control or shake off, no matter how hard I try. About how it makes me want to go to the ends of the earth to make sure she is well and happy. About how it makes me want to protect her at all costs, doing everything in my power just to see that pretty smile of hers.

About how, for the first time in my entire life, it makes me reconsider my life choices.

My job.

My position as the head of the family….

My phone buzzes, and I open my eyes, finding Armando's name flashing back at me.

"Yes?" I answer.

"We have a location for Mateo's car, Boss."

4 6

***

INTO THE ENEMY'S DEN

Tony

MY VISION TURNS RED, AND I CLENCH MY PHONE IN MY HAND SO HARD that I hear it crack.

"Send it to me. I'll be on my way," I inform him.

Armando clears his throat, and I know he's about to contradict me. "Shouldn't we have a plan first, Boss? We have no idea what he's been up to," he wisely reminds me.

I'm glad I have someone to make me see clearly now because all I can think of is putting a bullet hole through Mateo's forehead and making sure he doesn't take another breath in this world. "What do we know?" I ask, already starting the car.

"They are in an abandoned warehouse outside the city. It's not our territory, but that shouldn't be a problem. No one really rules that part of town," he explains firmly and professionally. "I have all men on hold, waiting for instructions on how we can best approach without being noticed."

"Do you think the cartel is waiting for us?"

I have no fucking clue what Mateo was thinking when he invaded

283

the safe house to go after Chloe like that. It was a precise, but dumb, move. He ended up with nothing, and now he has all of us chasing him.

Was this his plan all along? To lure me to his den so he could get me out of his way to get to Chloe and Ellie?

I frown, trying to find a good explanation for what he's done.

"It's hard to say, Boss."

"What do you suggest we do?" I insist, my patience running thin since this is taking so much time.

"I say we go all in," Armando suggests darkly. "Approach cautiously, study the surroundings, and just barge in. He isn't playing fair. We know that much."

I nod, even though he can't see me. A smirk forms on my lips, enjoying this idea immensely.

"You must have read my mind," I reply. "I'm on my way and I'll meet you there. Tell everyone how we're handling this. I want no fucking mistakes this time. We're not leaving that place until I've fucking killed Mateo myself."

"Roger that, Boss. I guess I'll see you in a bit." Armando hangs up, and I head out of the parking lot, driving toward the location he texts to me.

I don't know a lot about this part of town, and since it's not my territory, I need to tread carefully. However, Armando assured me it shouldn't be much of a problem, so I try not to worry about it for now. I have bigger things to worry about now.

Thirty minutes later, I spot the warehouse in the distance, surrounded by what looks like an entire forest full of thick trees and overgrown and untrimmed bushes. It's a fucking horror movie location, and it gives me the creeps when I turn off the lights of the car, driving slowly so I don't call unwanted attention from whomever might be inside.

It's utterly quiet here, and as I get my in-ear monitor set up so I can communicate with my men, I see the car we've been looking for, the one that was chasing Chloe, parked a few yards away with all the doors open. There's a man's leg hanging out of one of the doors, and I don't even need to get close to know he's dead.

I just don't know if this was the work of my men or if Mateo got pissed with his guys for some reason. Maybe he was just venting his frustration on failing to capture Chloe.

"Was the dead guy inside the car our job?" I ask through the monitor, taking the opportunity to test it.

"Yeah, Boss. He saw me approaching, so I silently put him down. His partner too." Kian's voice echoes in my ear.

That's when I notice the driver perched forward over the wheel, blood staining his dead face.

"Good job," I tell him. "All right, guys. That's it. We wanted some action, so there you have it. I want this entire fucking cartel out of our city. We'll approach slowly, and on my command, you know what to do."

"Roger that." Voices reply to me in unison.

I cock my gun and step out of the car, creeping toward the building. I see a bunch of my soldiers walking out of their hiding places—from behind trees, bushes, cars, and even from behind the warehouse's walls.

As we approach the potential den of the De La Cruz cartel, I hear muffled voices yelling at each other from inside.

"–The fuck did you think I was doing?" a guy is screaming.

"I thought you said we were supposed to kill her. How come you were face to face with her and didn't kill her?" someone else replies.

Rustling noises follow, and then the first guy hisses, his voice a snarl. "What do you think happened, huh? Question me again, and I'll fucking kill you myself," he threatens.

I don't need to see his face to know who it is.

Mateo.

It's a good thing he and his men aren't seeing eye to eye. It means they're distracted and not as united as they should be. It's too bad, this isn't even going to be a fair fight.

However, this might be the only chance I have to put an end to all of this.

Mateo is slippery as fucking soap. I can't risk having him out there after Chloe and Ellie again.

So, with renewed determination, I straighten my shoulders and hold my gun firmly in front of me.

"Light it up, guys," I order my men.

Gunshots deafen me as we all open fire at the windows of the building. Some of the guys from the cartel manage to get out of the warehouse, storming out of the place like cockroaches escaping, scurrying back into darkness when the lights come on.

"I'll get inside and find Mateo," I inform the Saints when I realize the De La Cruz boss hasn't come out with his men.

"Do you need cover?" Armando yells in my ear, sounding breathless and somewhat distracted.

"No, I've got this."

Finding a gap on the right side of the warehouse, I sneak inside, cautiously looking around so I'm not surprised by a random goon. The whole place looks empty, except for the dead bodies spread on the floor.

Although it's fucking dark in here, I recognize Mateo's second hand, Eduardo, lying a few feet away from me, several bullet holes splattered across his chest. No one else is moving, so I assume everyone else is dead.

But a grunt perks my ears, and I swivel my head to the other side, spotting someone crawling their way out toward the opposite doorway I came in from.

My instincts yell at me, and I rush forward in the direction of the man trying to escape, knowing who it is. As soon as I approach him, I crouch, holding a gun to his forehead, using my knee to trap him on the floor.

Mateo's shocked face stares back at me, and even though I can tell he is fucking scared, he still manages to smirk at me. That only makes my blood boil hotter.

"Don't you fucking think I'll let you leave this place alive," I growl, pressing the gun firmly against his forehead.

The asshole dares to sneer at me. "You can kill me, but at this point, I doubt it will make any difference. My men are already on the way to the city. That's where my girls are hiding, isn't it?" he asks in a teasing tone.

My entire body stiffens, my heart beating faster than a fucking hummingbird wing.

But I won't allow myself to fall for his dirty tricks. Not again.

"They are not *your* girls. They never were. Chloe is my wife. And Ellie, well, I doubt you know, but she is mine, too. Did Chloe not tell you that?" I retort through clenched teeth.

A look of doubt crosses his features, and I grin at him, feeling momentarily proud of myself for being able to deal him one more blow before I kill him.

"I hope you rot in hell for all you did to them." I pull the gun toward his stomach and shoot, making Mateo contort with pain. "This is for killing Chloe's father. That was you, wasn't it?"

This is information my men gathered, and I've been keeping it a secret for some time now. I never had the opportunity to talk to Chloe about it, and truth be told, that was the least of her problems. We will have time to discuss everything once I finish all of this.

"And this," I add, pulling the gun back toward his neck, "this is for my wife," I conclude, pulling the trigger and making sure he'll bleed out in this abandoned shithole by himself. "This is what you get for playing with the Saints. And this is what you get from touching what's mine."

I watch him try and gurgle some sort of retort. But whatever he's saying is unclear to me.

I ponder staying here to watch him die. To make sure he closes his eyes to never open them again. I can't risk having him resurrect from the dead or some shit like that. But I also don't want his death to be quick.

"Boss, is everything okay?" Armando's voice echoes in my ear, cutting my thoughts short.

"Yes," I reply through the monitor. "Just making sure they never come after us again."

It takes Mateo an excruciating ten minutes, and finally, I see his eyes blinking slowly, heavy with the weight of death coming to take him.

I might be following him to hell one day for all the shit I've pulled in this life, but it's not my time. Not yet.

Right now, I have to make up for lost time with Chloe and my daughter, giving them the best life, the life they deserve.

And maybe, just maybe, God will forgive me for my sins.

47

EMPTY HOUSE

Chloe

REUNITING WITH ELLIE AND MY MOM FELT OVERWHELMING, ALTHOUGH bittersweet. Even though I was beyond relieved and grateful to hold my daughter in my arms once more, my heart was shrinking by the minute, not knowing what Tony was up to.

The Irish King's bar I was brought to is surprisingly comfortable and welcoming. I was even more surprised when I found Cal playing with Ellie. The way she laughed at his exaggerated movements and jokes, I don't think I've ever seen her this enchanted with another man before.

After I settled down from the flight and kissed and hugged my family, Cal asked one of his employees from the bar to bring me something to eat. Mom and Ellie already had dinner since they arrived here earlier, and when the waitress returns with a tray filled with burgers, fries, and a chocolate milkshake, I almost let out a moan of pleasure.

Only now have I realized how starving I am. I can't even

remember the last time I ate. So much has happened in the past twenty-four hours that it's hard to keep track of everything.

I didn't feel like eating anything on the plane, though, I was too stressed out and worried to consider putting something in my stomach. I surely would have thrown it all up.

Even now, as I take a bite from the most delicious burger I've ever tasted in my life, my stomach feels like it's tied in a knot.

No one is saying anything, and even when I try to ask Cal about Tony and the Saints, he only shakes his head and ignores me, turning his attention back to Ellie. It's annoying, to say the least. I hate the fact they all keep hiding things from me, even when I should be one of the first ones to know what the hell is going on with my husband.

I am, after all, the queen of the Saints... aren't I? Isn't that what they keep calling me? So, why the hell can't I know anything?

"Cal told me what happened to you," my mom says, coming to sit beside me on the couch in Cal's office. I keep my attention on my food tray, but I nod at her so she knows I'm listening. "Are you okay?" Her voice is low, hesitant, and I'd even say, scared. I finally look up at her, seeing a darkness cross her face and eyes. It feels like she has finally understood the gravity of the situation we're in. I mean, she always knew, but I don't think she really had a good perspective on what we're fighting against.

"I'm fine, Mom. I'm just worried about Tony and his men," I tell her, my voice equally quiet. "I don't think I've ever seen Mateo that mad before. He seemed..." I clear my throat, pushing away the image of Mateo's evil face from my brain. "He looked insane."

"Oh, sweetheart," she muses, pulling me into a tight embrace, almost suffocating me. But I don't push her away. My mom might look tough on the outside most of the time, and even though she *is* one of the strongest women I know, if not the strongest, I also know she has a kind heart.

She doesn't always show it, but I bet she felt terrified when she heard about what happened to me back in Vermont.

"I just want this all to be over," I murmur against her hair, wrapping my arms around her and reciprocating her hug.

"I know, I know…. It will be soon," she assures me, her hand smoothing my hair. "I'm sure Tony will be here soon."

God, I really hope she's right.

Hours pass, and Ellie falls asleep after playing with Cal for most of the evening. Nothing else happens in the meantime, and my anxiety has reached a new peak. I can barely stand still, pacing from side to side in the office, trying to eavesdrop on any conversations the Irish Kings are having. But they sure know how to talk in secret.

The sun is almost rising when Armando finally shows up. Alone.

I mean, not completely alone. Some of the Saints are with him, but Tony is nowhere in sight. Armando looks exhausted, so do his men, but they never lose their professional posture as they walk into the room.

"Where's Tony?" I blurt before greeting them.

"We're going home," Armando informs me instead, not even hiding the fact he is outright ignoring my question.

"Where is Tony? What happened?" I insist, the pleading evident in my voice.

"He's still in Vermont," he finally answers.

"Is he all right?"

He nods at me, gesturing at the door, and urging me to move. Mom picks Ellie up from the couch, and we head outside where a car is waiting for us.

"Armando, can you please drop me at Val's? I have some things to discuss with the wives," she requests, leaning back in her seat.

I look at her, my brows creased in confusion. "What are you going to discuss with them? Why am I not included?"

"It's nothing important, honey. And you surely need some rest. You can call me if you need anything, though. But I suggest you take the day off and get some sleep. These last few days have been traumatic. Ellie can stay with me, if you want."

Her tone is kind, and I don't believe she's hiding anything from me. I think she just needs a distraction from all of this. I don't blame her. I wish I could have something to take my mind off things for a couple of hours too. I am exhausted.

But I don't think I will be able to rest until I am certain Tony is fine and out of danger. Until then, my eyes will be wide open.

"It's okay. Let her stay with me. She also needs to sleep in her own bed," I reply.

Armando drops my mom at Val's and drives us to the mansion in Staten Island. It feels strange to be back here. This is my home now, but it doesn't feel like it, knowing Tony isn't around. Funny how we get used to something so quickly.

I go upstairs to put Ellie in bed, and when I return downstairs, Armando is standing in the middle of the living room, his arms crossed across his chest while he paces anxiously.

"Do you want me to prepare something for you and the guys to eat? You must be starving," I offer.

He shakes his head at me. "No need. We'll have another group take the first shift so we can all rest. We'll take the night shift. I'll be in the house next door though, so anything you need, just call me."

"Thanks, Armando." I take a deep breath, studying his stoic expression. "Are you really telling me the truth about Tony being okay? You wouldn't lie to me about that, right?"

"He's fine, Mrs. Bellini. I promise you," he assures me with a soft smile, probably the first I have ever seen on his face.

I stare into his eyes and decide to believe him. Even if he isn't allowed to tell me anything, I still don't think he would lie to me. Maybe partially omit the truth or ignore me, but I don't think for a second that he would look me in the eye and lie straight to my face.

"Thank you," I say again. He nods and excuses himself, closing the door behind him.

The silence that follows is overwhelming. I ponder what to do. My entire body aches, and I am exhausted, but I'm not going to be able to sleep for a bit. I'm more anxious than ever. But maybe I should try and get some sleep. If Tony returns home, or if we have to move again, I need to be in my best shape.

Ellie might wake up soon as well, so I need to be at least rested so I can watch her.

I go to my room, and despite my expectations, I do end up falling asleep sooner than I'd thought I would. In fact, I black out for hours, only waking up when the sun has already set outside. Darkness envelops my bedroom completely when I open my eyes.

I force myself out of bed and rush to Ellie's bedroom, afraid she might have woken up while I was asleep. But she is still sleeping so heavily that I need to get close enough to make sure she's breathing.

A loud noise of what sounds like plates crashing to the ground catches my attention, and I instantly freeze. Is someone invading our home again? My trauma catches up to me, but I force it out of the way. I need to trust the Saints. I need to believe they won't make the same mistake again protecting this house.

Maybe Mom is back home and preparing something for dinner, I try to convince myself.

Walking out of Ellie's room, I silently close her door and head downstairs. Whoever is in the kitchen is making a whole lot of mess, not managing to do it quietly at all.

There is a delicious smell of food invading the house though, so I am certain it's not an enemy before even getting to the kitchen.

And when I arrive, my jaw drops as my eyes fall on Tony, his back turned to me as he tries to set the food he clearly brought home from some restaurant onto trays and ceramic plates.

"Tony?" I call, my voice barely above a whisper.

He turns to me in a rush and the softest smile spreads across his lips. My heart feels like it's about to explode.

I can barely contain my happiness as I dart toward him, throwing myself into his arms, my legs wrapping around his waist. I press a kiss to his lips, taking in his scent and tightening my arms around him, trying to convey all of my feelings through this simple act.

There aren't enough words in my vocabulary to express how grateful and happy I am to see him here–whole and alive.

48

CONFESSION

Chloe

AFTER I WELCOME TONY HOME, I MAKE SURE TO WAKE ELLIE UP SO SHE can have dinner with us. She needs to eat something since she has been sleeping the whole afternoon, and she also needs to wake up now so she can get some sleep later. I'm not looking forward to staying up all night because she slept too much during the day.

The three of us have dinner together as a family for the first time, and it just feels… right. Like how it's always supposed to have been, all this time.

Neither one of us brings up the elephant in the room. I'm sure we'll have time to talk about it, but right now, I just want to enjoy this moment while I can. Watching Tony feed our daughter, playing with her, and getting her to laugh is just so adorable that my heart can barely take it.

It's a dream coming true right in front of my eyes.

"Come on, baby. Let's show Mommy how you're a good girl who eats all her dinner," he muses, making airplane sounds as he flies the spoon toward her gaping mouth.

Ellie chuckles and opens wide. I laugh to myself, propping my chin on my hand as I watch the scene unfold. I even forget about my own food for a minute.

Once dinner is over, I ask Tony if he wants to help me give Ellie a bath. He promptly accepts, but he mostly just observes while I do it, still nervous and unsure how to do it himself. I ask him to help me from time to time, though. He pours some shampoo in his hand and lathers up her hair. I help guide him as he cleans her little ears and in between her fingers with a washcloth.

This is an entirely different side of the cold, stoic man he is when he's leading the Saints. The stark contrast is welcomed, though. I love seeing how caring and thoughtful he is with Ellie even though he hasn't known her that long.

It also makes the guilt I feel for keeping him out of her life lessen slightly. He doesn't seem to be holding a grudge against me, and if he still is bitter somewhere deep down, he's not allowing it to project into his relationship with Ellie.

I let him put her to bed by himself. It's not the first time he's watched over her or put her to bed, and I take that time to relax myself. I go to our suite and into our bathroom, filling up the bathtub again.

The water's warm, and my body instantly relaxes as I sink myself into it, leaning my head back against the tiles and closing my eyes. I don't know how much time passes while I'm in there, and I even think I might have fallen asleep for a couple of minutes.

Once I get out and wrap myself in a robe, I leave the bathroom. I find Tony lying on his bed, his hair slightly wet against the pillow, which makes me think he must've used a shower in another bathroom. He's wearing a plain black T-shirt and gray sweatpants, and even though I know he hasn't even tried, he looks sexier than ever.

His arms are behind his head, and he takes me in with a smirk playing on his lips. I swallow down, tightening the belt of the robe around me.

"Oh, hi. I, uh, was just using the tub," I tell him, justifying the reason why I'm in his suite and not mine. Unfortunately, even though this is a huge mansion, his bathroom is the only one with a bathtub.

"You're free to use it whenever you want. This is your house," he answers me with a shrug.

I nod and head toward the door, telling him, "I'm going to get dressed."

"Can you come back once you're done? I want to talk to you," Tony requests before I leave the room.

"Sure, it will only take me a minute."

I rush to my room and get my pajama set. It's a long-sleeved shirt and pants with printed strawberries in a light pink. They're cute, but before I put them on, I hesitate, considering picking something else. I know he really meant 'talking' to me instead of doing anything else, but maybe I have other intentions for after the conversation is over.

Hopefully, it will end well, considering he's here and not anywhere else in the world tonight. I might take the opportunity to spend some more intimate time with him while I have the chance.

So, instead, I pull a dark blue silk nightgown out of my wardrobe and put it on, feeling the cold fabric slide against my body.

Then, with renewed determination, I head back to his room.

The moment his eyes take me in, I regret not wearing a robe over the nightgown. It will be hard to focus on whatever he has to say if he keeps looking at me like this the entire time.

Tony clears his throat, sitting up on the bed, his eyes diverting from me. "Well, that was a low blow. How the fuck am I supposed to talk seriously with you when you're dressed like that?"

I chuckle, closing the door behind me. "I guess we'll both have to test our self-control," I joke back, sitting beside him on the bed.

He takes a deep breath and looks at me, grabbing my hand and squeezing it.

"Okay, well, there are a couple of things I want to mention, so bear with me for a minute, all right?" he begins.

"Sure," I say with a sharp nod.

Tony inhales again, and when his eyes find mine once more, I can almost feel the palpable intensity irradiating from them. "Mateo is dead," he blurts out.

I blink at him, assimilating what he has just told me. My mouth opens and closes a couple of times, but no sound comes out of it.

"Dice and Max are going to be okay, and no one else got hurt, so there were no casualties for us," he continues, knowing I'm not able to respond at the moment.

So much is going through my head at this instant, everything that Mateo put me through in the past, all he did to Tony and the guys, and how scared he left me and my family. I thought I'd never be able to get away from him, to truly escape him.

And now, Tony is telling me that all of that is over.

"So, you're saying…." I trail off, putting my thoughts together so I can form a coherent sentence. "This is over? He won't be coming after us ever again?"

Tony holds my gaze, and his hand tightens around mine. "This is all over. You're free. Your family is free."

A combination of a sob and a chuckle comes out of my mouth, and I shake my head, not believing it.

But as I reconsider Tony's words, something snaps inside of me, and my mood shifts drastically, my smile disappearing immediately.

Free.

He said I am free.

Which makes me wonder, does he mean something more than just being free of Mateo? Our sham marriage only happened because he needed to protect me and my family. Now that the threat is out of the way, does he mean….

I can't bring myself to finish the thought.

I can't stand the idea of being separated from him.

I can't consider a world where Tony isn't mine anymore. Not after having him to myself for a moment.

But… did I ever really have him? At all?

Tony seems to pick up on my mood swing, and he moves forward on the mattress, pulling himself closer to me.

"Listen, there's something else I want to tell you," he continues, his voice low and deep.

"I'm listening," I manage to say.

"I-I know I've been a dick lately, not dealing with our relationship the way I'm supposed to," Tony carries on, and I urge myself not to jump to conclusions. "You told me how you felt, and I was too much of a coward to say it back or even address what this," he gestures between us, "means."

I lick my lips, suddenly feeling my mouth and throat become dry like a desert.

"But the truth is, Chloe, I've been pining for you for years. I've always desired you, and maybe even would have pursued you, if it weren't for your father. I might have made a move on you ages ago if it weren't for him."

This comes as a shock to me. Not the fact that my father didn't like Tony. I guess it wasn't personal; he just wanted to pull me out of this world. I can't blame him for not wanting me to make a living in the underworld like he did, to have my daughter raised in such an environment, but it makes me feel bitter that he didn't give me the option to choose my destiny and who I wanted to spend the rest of my life with.

Because the truth is, if Tony had made a move on me years ago, I might not have ended up with Mateo at all. Because I always had a crush on Tony.

"Maybe you should have made a move on me," I tell him softly. "We could have avoided a lot of trouble." I laugh.

Tony chuckles, too. The sound is like music to my ears. "Yeah, I deserve the prize for biggest asshole on the planet. Letting you leave me after I had you to myself that night was my biggest mistake. I should have gone after you, but I guess I was just too fucking scared of the consequences it could bring to my life, to *our* lives. I don't know how to do this, Chloe. I really don't," he admits shamefully, his head hanging.

"Hey!" I cup his cheek, forcing him to look up at me. "We'll figure it all out together. I can't say I know how to do it either. My past relationship was as toxic as one can get. But I believe in us. I believe in our family."

His hand meets mine, and he squeezes it, not moving it away from his cheek. His intoxicating blue eyes bore a hole through mine, but I don't care. I love the way it makes me feel seen.

Desired.

Wanted.

Loved?

"I love you," Tony finally blurts out, and I gasp, my breath caught in my throat. "I fucking love you, and I can't imagine not having you or Ellie in my life anymore. I'd rather die than have to live a life where you're not in it," he confesses, reaching for my face and pulling me closer to him.

Our noses touch, and our lips are inches away from one another, but all I can do is stare into Tony's eyes and repeat his words in my head over and over.

He said he loved me.

I've imagined this moment so many times before, but now that it's happening, it's a thousand times better.

I feel my eyes welling up with tears, and Tony chuckles sweetly when he realizes I'm crying about his confession. His thumbs brush my cheeks softly, wiping the tears away, and then he pulls me forward again, our lips meeting in the warmest, softest, and most loving kiss we've ever shared.

4 9

IMPERFECTLY PERFECT

Chloe

OUR WARM KISS TURNS INTO SOMETHING MORE PASSIONATE AS OUR hands begin to roam each other's bodies. There are so many emotions bottled up inside us that it is hard to express them with words. Tony's hands explore my body while he devours my mouth in a heated kiss, suffocating my moans. My head is still spinning from his confession that he loves me, and I can barely focus on what he's doing.

My distraction seems to catch his attention because he pulls away from me, his eyes studying my face carefully. "Is everything okay? We don't need to do this if you don't want to. I–"

My lips are on his before he even finishes his sentence. Like hell I'd let him stop right now. I urge myself to be present, storing his confession for later, when I have time to dwell on it over and over without being interrupted. I wish I could've recorded it so I could listen to it whenever I need reassurance about how he feels about me.

But this is Tony. I know he will shower me with affection and love whenever he can. And whenever I need it.

"Don't you dare stop," I murmur against his mouth, drawing a laugh from him, his hard chest reverberating under my hands.

I push him backward on the bed, straddling him. His hands immediately find my hips, pinning me against him. I can feel his need for me, and it causes something primal within my core to explode.

My lips lower to his jaw and up to his ear where I bite on his earlobe, causing him to hiss beneath me.

"Careful or I'll make you regret teasing me like that, Mrs. Bellini," he warns in a husky voice. But that only makes me more excited for what he has to offer.

"How do you plan on doing that?" I ask against his ear, and I feel the flesh on his bare arm beneath my hand prickle into gooseflesh.

His grip on my hips lowers to my thighs, and he pulls me downward against his hardness. I'm already feeling an ache between my legs, and him putting pressure on my most sensitive spot only makes me squirm more.

"Is that it?" I hiss, pretending to be strong. Truth is, if he really decides just to tease me, I am doomed.

A grin spreads his lips, and he pushes himself up to a seated position. His eyes divert to my mouth, and I bite my lower lip, wondering what he will do next.

"Do you really want me to make you pay?" he asks, his hands sliding up my thighs and approaching where I need him the most.

When his fingers reach my lacy panties, brushing against my slit, I nod eagerly, cursing myself inwardly for giving him so much power over me.

"All right then. Your wish is my command," Tony whispers, pulling the fabric aside and touching me.

His touch on my skin makes me gasp, and when he starts rubbing and circling my clit , my nails dig into his shoulders as I find something to steady myself.

My hips rock back and forth involuntarily, riding his fingers like my life depends on it.

"Shit, Tony," I whisper, my eyes rolling to the back of my head.

"I'm just getting started, baby," he says, his voice heavy with lust. "You're so fucking wet already, I can't wait to be inside you."

"Yeah? What's taking you so long then?" I grumble back, already losing control of myself when he adds some extra pressure with his thumb.

"I still have some things I need to do first," he explains, and in a swift movement, he tosses me on my back on the mattress.

I don't even have time to understand what he's doing when his hands slide my panties down my legs, leaving me exposed to him. Then, he is out of the bed and kneeling on the floor in front of me, and with a hard tug, he pulls me toward him and centers his head between my legs.

When his tongue touches me for the first time, I clench my fingers on the sheets beneath me, biting down hard on my lip so I don't scream and wake Ellie.

"Fuck! Tony..." I hiss, unable to control myself anymore. It's like my entire body is going through a short circuit.

He works his magic with his tongue, drinking me in like his life depends on it, and a wave of pleasure courses through me, leaving me momentarily blind and numb. My legs are still trembling by the time he pulls away and stares back at me, his eyes dark.

"Are you good to continue, or do you need a break?" he asks. He has a smirk on his face as he wipes my juices from his chin. All I can do is lie here and pant since I do need a minute to compose myself. "I'll give you a few seconds," he replies when I don't say anything.

"Why don't you use that minute to remove your clothes?" I ask breathlessly when I can manage.

He smirks at me but does as I asked. I watch as he removes his shirt over his head, revealing his toned abs and chiseled chest. Then he moves to remove his pants and boxers, and I prepare myself for what's to come next.

Tony doesn't wait long after he's undressed. He comes back to the bed, hovering over me, teasing me with his tip against my swollen lips.

"Ready?" He lowers himself down so that he's hovering over me.

I nod slowly, in a daze from how sexy he is. Love pours over me through his eyes.

"I forgot to ask you one thing," Tony adds, gently brushing aside a strand of hair from my sweaty forehead.

"Does it have to be now?" I groan.

"Yes, I'm afraid it does," he replies. He pecks my lips real quickly then pulls back to look at me again. "Will you marry me? Again? And for real this time?"

I stare blankly at him, unsure I heard him right.

"Are you serious?" I manage.

"Never been more serious in my life."

Overwhelmed, I wrap my arms around his neck and pull him down, kissing him and murmuring, "Yes," repeatedly against his mouth.

We kiss and laugh together, and by the time he claims me completely, I'm glad to say I've never felt more loved and happy in my life.

I have all I need right here, in this house. A beautiful daughter, a husband who loves me and worships the ground I walk on, and a mother who supports me, no matter what.

Life has been hard so far, but seeing where it took me, it's impossible not to be grateful. It's funny how some people need to go through hard times to get what they want or what they think they deserve.

But this journey shaped us to become the people we are today. And I wouldn't have it any other way. Sure, it could have been easier. But if it had been, I might not be in Tony's arms tonight. I might not even have met him or found him again.

At this moment, life feels complete. Right. Well-lived.

And I can't wait to see what it will bring us in the future. I can't wait to live a life with Ellie and Tony, to have more children with him, to celebrate birthdays and anniversaries together, to share every aspect of my life with him daily.

"I love you," I whisper against his chest while we lay together afterward, his fingers lazily drawing circles on my naked back.

His arm tightens around me, pulling me even closer to him, and he places a kiss on the top of my head.

"And I love you more," he replies softly. "More than I ever thought was possible. I'm sorry it took me so long to realize that."

I shake my head, tears filling my eyes as I smile up at him. "It's imperfectly perfect. Just like us."

5 0

WEDDING DAY

Chloe

THE FIRST FEW DAYS AFTER I LEARNED THAT MATEO WAS NO LONGER ON this planet were a bit chaotic. Tony and his men had so much to do: cleaning up the mess, assigning the new positions each one of them would take when it came to protecting our family and the house, determining who would go back to dealing with the Saints' businesses, and so on.

In the past couple of weeks, I've managed to create a routine for myself and Ellie. It took me a while to process that I wouldn't have to continue hiding or running away anymore, but eventually things just became... easier.

It's funny how easily and quickly humans get used to things. In the first few days, I was still scared to leave the house by myself, even with a couple of guards accompanying me, or Rocco taking me from place to place inside a bulletproof car.

I would always watch over my shoulder, expecting someone to jump out of a bush or something and kidnap me–or worse–kill me.

But Tony assured me he wouldn't get rid of the security system we had established because we are still part of the mafia, and we never know when the next enemy will strike, and that sort of made me relax a bit.

When I finally started to calm down and enjoy life, my mom came to us, asking if she would be allowed to throw us the wedding reception she wanted so badly. And then, things just became chaotic.

For a good reason now, of course. I'd take this kind of concern every day if it meant I wouldn't have to fight for my life and to protect the ones I love.

Tony and I ended up getting married at the church like my mother always wanted, and to be fair, it'd been a dream of mine ever since I was a little kid, too. I was happy she pushed us to do it, and I was even happier when Tony said he wanted it to happen as well.

The ceremony was beautiful and emotional, albeit quick.

Then we moved to the reception at our mansion on Staten Island. Since it was only for family and friends, and the house's backyard is huge, we thought it'd be okay to throw it here. Safer and cozier.

Tony's arm is around me as we walk around at the party, greeting guests and chatting with old friends we haven't seen in a while. It feels nice to see them and realize nothing has changed even after years without seeing each other.

A slow song starts playing, and Tony turns to me, offering me his hand and the brightest smile I've ever seen on his face. I'm not much of a dancer, much less someone who likes to be the center of attention, but I guess I can't escape dancing with my husband on our wedding day.

It would also be impossible to refuse him when he's looking at me like that.

So, I let him guide me toward the dance floor, feeling the eyes of our guests on us as we stride through the party. But Tony's intense gaze is on me, and that alone makes me forget about everything surrounding us as he places his hand on my waist and slowly pulls me against him, the warmth in his body enveloping me.

I follow his lead, moving from side to side to the rhythm of the song. I lean my head against his chest, closing my eyes and allowing myself to relish this moment.

Never, in my wildest dreams, did I imagine I'd be marrying Tony one day. Sure, I dreamed about it more times than I can count, but not once did I really believe it was something achievable.

I had convinced myself this would always just remain a dream.

But now, here I am, celebrating our official marriage. Not a sham one anymore. But a real one, with all the perks—and cons—that come with it.

"How are you feeling?" His low voice brings me back to reality, his chest reverberating as he speaks.

I look up at him, a huge smile spreading across my face. "Just about how happy I am," I reply with a shrug. "I never thought I'd one day actually get to marry you."

His arms tighten around me, and he brings me even closer to him, dipping his head enough for our noses to touch.

"Me neither. But now that you're mine, don't expect me to ever let you leave me," he warns me in a joking tone, a smirk playing on his lips.

"I don't expect you to," I reply. "I can't wait to start the rest of our lives together."

"Since you brought it up, I have been thinking..." Tony trails off, his eyes entirely focused on me. There's a playfulness behind them, but he looks kind of serious all of a sudden.

"What?" I press, anxiety getting the best of me.

"Do you ever think about having more children one day? Giving Ellie a baby brother or sister?"

His question catches me off guard. I wasn't expecting him to talk about children with me so soon. Sure, we have Ellie, but he is still getting the hang of what it's like to be a father while handling an entire mafia empire. He's doing a phenomenal job, though, and sometimes I wonder how he does it.

But, honestly, I would be lying if I said I never pictured our family growing. I want to have more children with him. Damn, I'd love to have more, to actually allow him to participate in my pregnancy, to be there for me through the good and bad times, to get to live everything we were deprived of when I was pregnant with Ellie.

Just thinking about it makes my eyes fill with tears.

"I would love that actually," I finally say, receiving a passionate kiss in return.

"Good, we can start practicing soon," he murmurs against my lips, his hand sliding down to my ass and squeezing it provocatively.

I lightly slap him on the shoulder, making both of us chuckle.

"I hate to interrupt the happy couple, but there is someone here wanting to be a part of the dance," Mom muses, approaching us with Ellie who is reaching for her daddy with wide open arms.

Tony scoops her up, rocking her to the rhythm of the new song playing.

"Dada," she muses in her sweetest voice.

I smile watching them playing together on the dance floor. The entire song plays, and when it ends, I search for the first waiter I can find so I can grab whatever drink he is serving.

I'm thirsty, slightly sweaty, and already exhausted. I just wish I could get to my honeymoon with Tony. For the next couple of days, we'll finally have some time to ourselves.

But at the exact time I'm thinking about that, as if summoning trouble, someone shows up in our backyard wearing a very dark, serious expression I wasn't expecting to see on any of my guests' faces today.

Cal heads toward Tony, who has spotted him too and is now giving Ellie back to my mom and walking in the direction of his friend. Without even thinking, I follow him, approaching Cal to see what this is about.

He was invited to the wedding, and if it wasn't for his expression, I wouldn't think anything is wrong. But my instincts are yelling at me that something is definitely off.

And I confirm all my fears when I get close to them and hear Cal telling Tony, "We have a problem."

. . .

Thank you for reading! Book 5 will be out soon!

ALSO BY BELLA MOONDRAGON

The Alpha King's Breeder series:

Bought by the Alpha: The Alpha King's Breeder Book 1

Loved by the Alpha: The Alpha King's Breeder Book 2

Lost by the Alpha: The Alpha King's Breeder Book 3

Luna of the Alpha: The Alpha King's Breeder Book 4

Legacy of the Alpha: The Alpha Kings's Breeder Book 5

Daughter of the Alpha: The Alpha King's Breeder Book 6

Descendants of the Alpha: The Alpha King's Breeder Book 7

Shadow of the Alpha: The Alpha King's Breeder Book 8

Son of the Alpha: The Alpha King's Breeder Book 9

Spare of the Alpha: The Alpha King's Breeder Book 10

Claimed by the Alpha: The Alpha King's Breeder Book 11

Atonement for the Alpha King: The Alpha King's Breeder Book 12

Rejected by the Alpha: The Alpha King's Breeder Book 13

Abducted by the Alpha: The Alpha King's Breeder Book 14

Wolf Shifter Fairy Tale Retellings series

Beauty and the Alpha Beast

Sleeping Beasty

Tangling With the Alpha

The Luna's Vampire Prince series:

The Culling

The Kingdom

The Conquered

Pregnant With Four Alphas' Babies

Chosen As the Breeder

Mated to Four Alphas

Threats Against the Breeder

At War for the Breeder

The Stolen Breeder

Four Alphas, Four Babies

Becoming the Luna Queen

Descendants of the Breeder

Desired by the Devil series

Whispers of the Devil

Banter of the Devil

Murmurs of the Devil

The Mafia Kings series

Indebted to the Mafia King

<u>Loved by the Mafia King</u>

Claimed by the Mafia King

Secrets of the Mafia King

Burned by the Mafia King

Kidnapped by the Mafia King (coming soon!)

Dark Stalker Romance series

Tempted by Sin

Fated to Sin

Secret Billionaires series

Finding the Secret Billionaire by Olivia Bhelle Kildare

Falling for My Secret Billionaire by Bella Moondragon

Driven by the Secret Billionaire by ID Johnson

Wolf Shifter Alpha Kings series

Ravens and Ruins

Sundrops and Shadows

Snowflakes and Sabotage

The Vampire King's Feeder series

Claiming the Alpha's Daughter

Loving the Alpha's Daughter

Finding the Alpha's Daughter

Bewitching the Alpha's Son (coming soon!)

Writing as B. Moon

The Boy Who Died

Sign up for Bella's newsletter here.

*Or get a free novella from The Alpha King's Breeder series when you sign up here:
The Beta and the Maid*

Follow Bella on Facebook here.

Follow Bella on Bookbub here.